HOT RAVES F
AND HER NOVELS

SEXAHOLICS

"Raw, gritty, and...shocking...explicit. Pynk dives head first into sex addiction and its players...and she works it."

—BibliophilicBookBlog.com

"Hot and steamy...Pynk's down-to-earth and fast-paced writing style keeps the story moving and entertaining. The sex scenes are plentiful and titillating...Pynk delivers."

—TheBlackUrbanTimes.com

"Intense...unbelievable...raw and real."

—SimplyStacie.net

EROTIC CITY

"Steamy."

—Library Journal

"No-holds-barred...you may want to keep this book under the covers."

—StreetFiction.org

"Sure to enchant the freak in all of you...open the spicy pages...and leave your inhibitions in reality...I really enjoyed every moment in *Erotic City*. It punctures erotica's envelope... And I mean that as a compliment."

—ApoooBooks.com

"Quite a standout for this genre... the dialogue [is] lively and fun, and the plot moves quickly... No matter where you fall in the sexual spectrum, this book is sure to meet you where you'd like [to] get off."

—FeministReview.BlogSpot.com

"Five stars! Excellent... entertaining yet highly erotic ... Fans of both erotica and contemporary literature will enjoy.

—UrbanBookSource.com

"Entertaining... erotic... enough sex between these pages to keep a person hot and bothered, but there is substance there as well."

—ImaniVoices.com

SIXTY-NINE

꧁

PYNK

GⱢC

GRAND CENTRAL
PUBLISHING

NEW YORK   BOSTON

Grand Central Publishing
Hachette Book Group
237 Park Avenue
New York, NY 10017
www.HachetteBookGroup.com

First Edition: March 2011
10 9 8 7 6 5 4 3 2 1

Grand Central Publishing is a division of Hachette Book Group, Inc.
The Grand Central Publishing name and logo is a trademark of Hachette Book Group, Inc.

Library of Congress Cataloging-in-Publication Data

Pynk.
  Sixty-nine / Pynk.
    p. cm.
  ISBN 978-0-446-56333-8
  I. Title. II. Title: 69.
  PS3613.O548S59 2011
  813'.6—dc22

                          2010025834

This third Pynk book is dedicated to all the women of the world twenty-one and over who experience sexual repression, prevented from expressing their sexuality because they were taught or learned to repress or despise healthy sexual desire and bodily sensations. Here's to your successful, long-term healing.

ACKNOWLEDGMENTS

My first thank-you is to you, my cherished readers, who have embraced *Erotic City* and *Sexaholics* so deeply. I graciously appreciate your support. Erotica is a genre that many people desire, and I enjoy writing dramatic erotic stories that bring satisfaction to my readers.

To my family, your love and patience is immeasurable. You are my blood, heart and soul, always and in all ways.

To my KP—feedback, patience, cheering me on and staying positive, believing in me, supporting me, loving me, and just being you. Forever love, no matter what!

I'd like to offer a major thankxxx to HoneyB, Bryan Cleveland, Jean Holloway, Vonda Howard, Cydney Rax, Shani-Greene Dowdell, S. B. Redd, Kendra Norman Bellamy, Denise Bolds, Ella Curry and EDC Creations, TaNisha Webb and the Fall Into Book Literary Conference, Harriet Klausner, Outwrite Bookstore and Coffeehouse, Medu Bookstore, Nubian Books, Tasha Martin and all the chapters of SistahFriend Book Club, Mocha Ochoa and the NAACP, Mashawn

Mickels and SBS Book Club, Novel Vixen's Book Club, APOOO Book Club, OOSA Online Book Club, Book Remarks, Urban Reviews, Michelle Gipson and Written Magazine, the Decatur Book Festival, Angela Jenkins, Heather Covington and Disilgold, Curtis Bunn and the National Book Club Conference, my Cola—for the scene-matching song choices, to all the blog sites that were part of my virtual blog tour for *Sexaholics* (for the features and reviews), and each and every book club who participated in the wild and sexy Pynk's Girls' Night In pajama events across the country.

To my awesome agent, Andrew Stuart—I cherish you, and by that I mean you were hard earned in my career and I value you. You are appreciated for the gem that you are. A big Pynk cheer to you!

Thankxxx to my cherished Grand Central Publishing family: Jamie Raab, executive vice president and publisher, for having me onboard; Karen Thomas, executive editor (this is my fifth book with you), I thank God for your trust, your belief in my work, and for your amazing revision letters—your hard work makes all the difference in the world in my books and your talents have not gone unnoticed; my darling and talented Latoya Smith, as well as Linda Duggins, Samantha Kelly, Anna Balasi, Miriam Parker, Renee Supriano, and others—I am blessed to be a GCP author.

Sexaholics came out at a time last year when sexual addiction was in the headlines so often that the timing could not have been any more perfect. I researched the subject quite extensively, and I've found that some readers referred the title to loved ones who suffered from sex addiction, like the characters from my novel. It's important to show what can happen inside the lives of those afflicted with serious issues, and I'm glad *Sexaholics* was received so well.

The opposite side of the addiction spectrum is the book you're holding in your hands right now, my third Pynk novel, *Sixty-Nine*. It's about sexual repression, a topic that is also very common and extremely serious. Though Magnolia, Rebe, and Darla have different thoughts about sex than those characters in *Sexaholics*, their issues and outcomes are just as dramatic, and as with *Sexaholics*, for them it's a test of will, a test of change, a test of faith, and in the case of *Sixty-Nine*, a test of friendship.

There's more to come in 2012! With all the political scandals involving sexual affairs and coercion, just check out the juicy chapter excerpt from *Politics. Escorts. Blackmail.*, about three call girls and one call guy in New York City, led by madam Money Watts, who get caught up in some kinky and dangerous political wranglings. You'll find the provocative excerpt at the end of *Sixty-Nine*.

Remember, live your sexy dreams, responsibly!

Smooches,
Pynk
xoxo

Please visit me at www.authorpynk.com, where you will find my Facebook link as well as information regarding upcoming titles, and feel free to sign my guestbook. My email address is authorpynk@aol.com.

AUTHOR'S NOTE

⌗

The Undersexed

As I mentioned in my acknowledgments, while my previous title, *Sexaholics*, was about the oversexed, this title, *Sixty-Nine*, is about the undersexed.

Sixty-Nine is not about the literal sexual position, 69; it is about three undersexed women, Magnolia, Rebe, and Darla, who were all born in 1969, and who are about to turn the big 4-0. They are dissatisfied with their lives in general; more specifically, when it comes to sex, they yearn to live their sexy dreams.

I watched *The Oprah Winfrey Show* a while back when she had as a guest a sex therapist named Dr. Laura Berman who talked about sexual problems in women. Some women do not have orgasms and they fake it with their men, who are sometimes none the wiser because often those men tend to get theirs, so that's all he wrote. There are some women who have little, tiny, non-earth-shattering orgasms that don't quite live up to what they see in porno movies, or hear about from their sexual-creature-like friends. Some women get very close to having the big O, but get stuck and hold back because of a thought that creeps into their heads that tells them they're trashy or slutty for feeling so good.

Orgasms are both physical and mental, and though some women really do have medical reasons that affect their libido and their ability to experience an orgasm—usually involving their pelvic floor or blood flow, or as a side effect to certain medications—a lot of women fall into the one basic sex trap that I feel so strongly about dispelling. The thought that we've bought into from the time we were little, *that sex is dirty*.

As some of you may know from reading my first Pynk book, *Erotic City*, that's the main reason why I decided to write erotica, to hopefully educate through fiction.

While I definitely believe that moderation is key, because we must have boundaries and not run off hog wild, so to speak, it is my desire to contribute in some way to the liberation of women and show all sides of sex, good and bad. But in the long run, I hope my books encourage women to love their bodies and feel good about reading scenes that turn them on so tough they can't wait to get home and take care of themselves, and/or pounce on their mates. I hope my writing teaches women about what healthy sex should be. Sometimes you learn that by reading about what healthy sex is not. To read erotica is not sinful, and it is my desire that the guilt so many of us women feel will eventually be shattered to pieces.

We must learn to tell the truth about how we feel about sex and about what we think about sex, and figure out where those bad thoughts came from. Also, as Milan Kennedy, the main character in *Erotic City*, stated, "Women have wet dreams, too." We cannot be afraid to ask for what we want in and out of bed. We women are not second-class citizens. Nor are we sex objects.

All in all, views about sex are sometimes deemed to be issues of morality, and issues of sexism.

I'd like women to learn to be what I call sex-see...seeing sex in a whole new way, mentally, visually, and physically.

After all, we are sensual and sexual beings. We are allowed to experience sexual pleasure. We have to let go of negative messages about sex among consenting adults—negative messages that tell us sex is wrong. I believe we can make a conscious decision to dispel those messages that breed guilt.

I'm talking about safe sex. Yes, there are prices to be paid relating to teen pregnancy and HIV, etc. You are responsible for yourself. Make good decisions based on who you are. And take in the rest as learning tools. When in Rome, don't necessarily do as the Romans do, unless you think it's the best decision for you. Most importantly, love yourself first.

If you are fearful and keep thinking you shouldn't talk in bed or let go and enjoy your orgasm, ask yourself what it is that you're afraid of. We all had messages about sex when we were growing up. Most times, if sex was brought up, we were told it was vulgar and not acceptable, especially when we were young girls. And we were told we shouldn't talk about it. We got dressed up and went to church, and the information we came away with was that sex should only be experienced for purposes of procreation. I know that's how my parents raised me, even though my mother was more liberated than most. Back then, parents who wanted their daughters to remain virgins until marriage surely had good intentions, but the other side of the coin is to encourage safe sex because most of the time, teens are going to do it anyway (I know I did), yet still feel guilty afterward, and that's when, in my opinion, the confusion starts. The more you tell someone they can't do something, the more they want to do it, kind of like the Adam and Eve theory. And from a biblical standpoint, it's all about our own individual interpretations; however, that's a different conversation.

Now back to the orgasm! ☺ The sex therapist on *Oprah* said that when you're about to experience your own orgasm, if you hold yourself back because of the negative voices from your past, you will cheat yourself and disallow the erotic experience of a burst of a beautiful, euphoric, intense pleasure rolling through your body that, from a physiological standpoint, can bond you to your partner just because of the pheromones produced from the rush itself. That is a proven fact. I know there are some women who, even though they may not hear the negative voices from the past, still hold back because the sensation is so strong they get scared and freeze up. I'm there with you. I can *surely* understand that!

If you're one of the many women who have repressed feelings about sex, and you feel you're too frigid and rigid in bed, maybe you need to think about what you can do to begin to let go of the embarrassing and shameful ties that bind. Refuse to carry those old messages and voices in your head that tell you sex is lewd, immoral, and improper. If necessary, think in terms of experiencing romance with your partner, as opposed to quickies, so that you can take the time to really excite yourself and your mate. Take the time to talk about each other's erogenous zones. Make foreplay last longer, starting with a sex text early in the day. Tell yourself you deserve to be pleasured, that it's good and loving, and that you'll still be a nice girl and a respectable lady in the morning. Remember: it's women who ask men, "Will you respect me in the morning?" Why is it men never ask women that?

Anyway, think in terms of nonmissionary, and feel free to masturbate healthily if you so desire. Masturbating in moderation is not slutty either.

Train yourself to replace the outdated messages with new ones. It's called a sexual adjustment. Remember, you are a sensual and sexual woman, and you're allowed to experience a happy and fulfilling sex life as a private, personal choice.

While you turn the pages to get to know the characters in *Sixty-Nine* as they struggle to escape from their undersexed worlds, keep in mind that these three coming-of-age women make conscious decisions to explore erotic sides of themselves they never knew existed. I call it sexploration.

The bottom line is that *Sixty-Nine* is a liberating story about sisterhood and friendship, and about how our past experiences and beliefs can influence our views about life, and about sex. How shame and dysfunction and abuse can keep us repressed. And how guilt can keep us from truly viewing sex as a pleasurable act. *Sixty-Nine* is a novel about going beyond one's self-inflicted boundaries to fully experience true sensuality. But, by taking these risks, one never knows what lies on the other side of our comfort zones. The comfort zone that protected us from our fears of abandonment, negative self-image, broken hearts, being seen as whorish, being rejected and ashamed. Feelings that meant we'd rather be alone than intimate and vulnerable. Though it is true that in some cases, if one is irresponsible, one may find that some things are better left alone.

So, my dear readers, please enjoy my girls, Magnolia, Rebe, and Darla as they find out what it's like to go beyond the missionary, and experience the erotic edge of a real-life sixty-nine.

*There's a place on a woman when you
touch her that will drive her crazy:
her heart!*

CAST OF CHARACTERS

Magnolia Butler—Always the bridesmaid who, once again, picked a freaky serial cheater who just can't seem to recognize a good woman when he sees one, until it's too late.

Rebe Palo-Richardson—Tragically scorned most of her life, she's a former NFL wife who refused to swing from the chandelier when she was married, but now she's swinging from a pole.

Darla Humphrey-Clark—A widow with a dream and a self-proclaimed celibacy vow, whose mind won't let her get past the belief that feeling good now is both a betrayal and a sin.

CAUTION:

Adults at Play
(21 and over)

SIXTY-NINE

Prologue

———————— ❧ ————————

"The Way We Were"

Girlfriends

She really did love her best friends, but less than twenty years ago she slept with one of her best friends' man and got pregnant.

Magnolia Butler, Rebe Palo, and Darla Humphrey were the epitome of BFF's way before the term *BFF* ever came into popularity. In fact, they were so tight and so meant to be, they were all born in 1969, Magnolia and Darla on January 1, and Rebe on February 14.

Magnolia and Darla were juniors at Miami Dade College in Miami, Florida, and Rebe was a sophomore, since she graduated from high school a year late. They no longer lived in dorms. Magnolia and Darla were roommates in a small two-bedroom apartment down the street from campus. Rebe lived less than a mile away in a rented house with her high school sweetheart, Trent. They had a three-year-old girl together named Trinity, yet still managed to maneuver through the rigors of college life, even though their relationship was rocky.

Magnolia and Darla were not only childless, which was just how each of them wanted it to be, but they were still virgins. Magnolia, who was Trinity's godmother, just hadn't made the right connection with any of the guys she'd met so far. Not enough to share her body with anyway. So she decided to wait. Darla made a serious connection and was saving herself for marriage. She was dating a fellow student who was a starting pitcher on the college's baseball team, named Aaron Clark, and Darla and Aaron were set to be married the summer after they graduated. They'd both agreed to wait, postpone consummating their relationship, just to make sure the night was extra special. Aaron had been around the block a few times, but Darla, who was raised with Christian values by conservative parents, witnessed every girl in her family get pregnant by the time they were sixteen. She wanted to be different. Not only did she want it, but her parents required it. "Save yourself for marriage. A man wants a virtuous woman. Sex is not recreational. Sex is between a husband and a wife. No man will want you if you're sullied. Not as a wife anyway. Sex before marriage is a sin." And Darla believed it. It was important to her to honor those puritanical values in the name of her mother, who passed away in a car accident while driving to pick Darla up when Darla was a high school freshman. Darla's father vowed to never remarry. Darla had witnessed a true-love example, up front and in living color. And she wanted the same. But fate, as crazy as it can be, had other plans.

Magnolia was the child of a mistress to a married

man. She never met her father. Her mother had been his chick-on-the-side before getting pregnant. When she broke the news to him, he simply stopped seeing her. One night when Magnolia was a baby, her mother went out to have a final conversation with her married lover, leaving Magnolia alone. She didn't come back. She had suffered a nervous breakdown in a hotel room where they'd met to talk, and when he left, Magnolia's mother flipped out and tried to kill herself by jumping off a fifth-floor balcony. The next morning, when Magnolia's grandparents found out, they rushed to baby Magnolia and took her in, ending up being the only mother and father she'd ever know. Her mother had been a drifter since then. And Magnolia made no bones about telling everyone she could care less about her mom. Nothing else mattered other than making sure she never turned out to be like June Butler.

Born in Maui, Rebe Palo, half-black and half-Hawaiian, and her family moved to Ocala, Florida, when she was four. She grew up in a not-so-nice neighborhood, where her older brother was in and out of what his mother called gangs. Her mom and dad divorced when she was seven. Her dad ran off, being a rolling stone enjoying his newfound freedom, so Rebe and her brother were raised by her black mother who was so overbearing and bossy, she could have turned the tide on Donald Trump and fired him. Rebe dealt with watching her temperamental mother always preaching what she never practiced, so much so that her mother charmed her way into becoming pastor at a small Baptist church by the time Rebe was twelve. Five years later, Rebe got pregnant, but by then, her whole life had changed. By then, Rebe and her brother would be victims, and her life would never be the same.

By Magnolia and Darla's graduation day nearly two years in the future, it would turn out that Rebe and her baby's daddy broke up after she accused him of being an addict, and he spread rumors that she was not only crazy, but so moody he'd almost have to rape her to get her to have sex with him.

Darla and Aaron would end up taking a spring-break cruise to the Bahamas to elope before their senior year just so they could finally have sex.

And Magnolia would date a hot Italian guy her senior year named Gabe Pastore. That is, until she'd catch him cheating on her in the backseat of his car at a drive-in movie. Magnolia had followed him. She always was the snoop.

During that year, one of them would end up pregnant.

And would have an abortion.

Yet her BFF's would never know about it.

Or maybe they would.

And the father was either Rebe's man, Trent, who'd die from a drug overdose four years later; Darla's man, Aaron, who'd have a fatal heart attack in 2004; or Magnolia's ex, Gabe, who ended up marrying a well-known porn actress in Hollywood.

One of them was the father of an innocent baby that never ever had a chance at this thing called life.

A life that has a funny way of paying people back.

Payback that in an instant would flip these best friends' worlds from a six to a nine by the time they were forty, coming to a literal head all in the name of sex.

One

"A Sexier Side of Me"

Girlfriends

INT.—LIV NIGHTCLUB INSIDE THE FONTAINEBLEAU
HOTEL—LATE EVENING
December 31, 2008

It had been the coldest winter in ten years in Miami,
though the temperatures were on a slight upswing
lately. The sharp, beachfront chill that lingered in the
Florida air on the outside was still no match for the
three hot girlfriends who'd checked their coats, sport-
ing their sexy, skimpy evening wear for a celebration
of *out with the old and in with the new*, like no other
year of their lives. It was a recognition of necessary
crossroads.

Divorcée Rebe Palo-Richardson said, with a millisec-
ond smirk on her chocolate face, the face she got from
her mother, "Girl, on my wedding night with Randall, I
started my damn period. That should've been a definite
warning sign that my marriage would not last through
the ebb and flow, so to speak, of holy matrimony." Her
micro-braided head rolled toward the two best friends
she'd known since high school. She tried to speak at

a level just above the blaring celebratory music in the background.

She sat on the contemporary purple leather stool at the fully packed bar with her long, bare legs crossed like a prima ballerina. Her stately gams, formed from her days as a dancer, extended far beyond the hem of her little black dress. A scripted tattoo was etched along her right ankle, one of a few that served as life-messages upon her sexy body. Darla Humphrey, now Darla Clark, sat on the other end, and Magnolia Butler was in the middle.

The trendy hotspot, called LIV, inside the Fontainebleau Hotel on the Miami Beach strip, was deliciously decorated in pale blues and lavender, with dark wood bar tables, draped private VIP rooms, and two mirrored, elongated bars. Oversized plasma TVs graced every wall, showing last-minute countdowns from most major cities.

Magnolia and Darla both lived nearby in Miami Beach. Rebe lived in Coconut Grove.

It was New Year's Eve.

The well-promoted, well-attended bash was wall-to-wall packed.

The sounds of Whitney Houston's "Exhale" serenaded the disco-like, neon-lit room. The soft mixture of pink and blue LED flashing-light designs bounced along the walls and from the ceiling. The glass dance floor was a pastel menagerie of light grids that grooved to the beat of the popular R&B music.

And it was 11:46 p.m.

"What? So after that you didn't have sex because of your monthly visitor?" Extra thick and curvy Darla, a widow, leaned toward her friends with her light brown, precision-cut hair with bangs that covered her high forehead. She wore platinum hoop earrings, and a liquid silver minidress, looking like a lady disco ball. She picked up her fluted champagne glass and took a tiny sip of the yellow label Brut, extending her manicured pinky as she swallowed. And she still wore her princess cut diamond wedding ring on her ring finger.

Rebe scrunched up her nose, and her smoky eyes squinted like a foul wind had blown by. "Ewwww, yes, of course it stopped me," she said, squirming in her seat.

"All I know is he turned out to be a player, just like all the rest." Magnolia knew all too well from the way Randall would always look at her, checking her out whenever Rebe would turn her back. She frowned like she took his infidelities personally, and gulped her vodka and peach schnapps. Her scarlet nails matched her knee-length strapless chiffon dress. Her gold slingbacks were high and sexy.

Darla added, "There are ways to slow down the flow. That's all I'm saying. Even I know that. I mean, it was your honeymoon."

Rebe paused with a hold-up look for them both. "Oh, you, the one who hasn't had sex in what, six years? I can't believe you've got the nerve to be giving me tips on anything." She gave a snarl.

Darla raised her threaded brows. "It's been five years, thank you very much, and I'm proud of it." She gave a long blink. "Anyway, you're the one who started this topic of conversation, not me."

"Yeah, well I wish I hadn't. I was just trying to laugh off why my marriage may have failed, that's all. Feeling a little reflective." Rebe twisted her generous lips and raised her glass, tipping a swallow of Perrier water into her mouth.

Magnolia kept her hands on her cocktail glass. "Hell, at least you had a wedding night. I think my man-picker is broken. It has been as long as I can remember. And it's probably a good guess that I'll never find out what it's like to even have a wedding night. I mean, after all, thirty-nine will be gone in, ah," Magnolia peeked at her diamond watch, "twelve minutes and counting."

Darla, a dental technician, tilted her head toward Magnolia as her lips gave way to her to-die-for bleached teeth. "Me too, girl. I'll be saying good-bye to thirty-nine right along with ya."

Rebe added, "I'm right behind both of you. Remember when we were younger? We thought forty was damn near elderly. I mean, all of our parents were the very age we are now." She thought back for a minute. "Tell me, where in the hell did the time go? My Lord." She shook her head and gave Magnolia a reflective gaze.

Magnolia said, "That's true, huh? Back in the late eighties in college we just swore by now we'd have all the answers. Was that more than two decades ago already?"

Rebe nodded. "Yes, it was." Her eyes shifted to Darla. "And then you and Aaron ran off and eloped. You came back married and I was like, excuse you."

Darla ran her fingertips along the back of her closely tapered neckline. Her full face showed her displeasure. "Oh please. Don't bring him up. Not tonight."

Magnolia spoke right up, "Oh Darla, we love you. I know it's been five years since he passed, but you had a solid marriage and a man who loved you. A faithful man. My relationship with Neal lasted a little more than one damn year before he got with old ghetto girl. Aaron loved you for you, Darla. He told me that himself. And for that, you're blessed."

Darla's shoulders dipped. She leaned her full-figured body back and then forward, and exhaled. "I do miss him. Lord knows I do. But one day, I'm gonna need to move on and get me someone, or should I say, get me some, period." She looked like she was almost joking.

Rebe gave a look of wonder. "But Darla, come on now. I still can't believe you haven't had even one dick in you in all that time. Not a one?" She held up a solo index finger.

"No. And?" Darla waited like she was prepared for battle.

"And, how do you do it?" Rebe asked.

"I mind my own damn business, that's what I do. Just like you don't want us all up in your stuff." She cut her eyes from Rebe to Magnolia. "And we know you get more dick than all the ladies up in this club tonight put together. Fast ass."

Magnolia gave a half-gasp and put her hand to her chest. "Me? Oh please. Talk about minding someone's business. So now I'm the slut? Where'd that come from? All because Rebe shut down the pussy on her wedding night."

Rebe shook her head and managed a snicker.

Darla put her hand up. "I'm just saying. I mean honestly, you've been in more relationships than we have."

"I have. Yeah. You're right. But don't trip just because I can catch, now. That hasn't been the problem, catching. But damn, if I'm so successful in the bedroom, then why did Neal leave my ass? A man who wasn't even that good in bed anyway." Magnolia readjusted her long black ponytail, which hung down the middle of her back. Her scent was her usual gardenia. It was always sprayed over the cherry ladybug tattoo on her neck.

Rebe said, "I did hear on television that it's not only about how much sex you have, but also what kind of sex you have that matters. And I'm not trying to say I'm any expert, because I am surely not." Rebe's eyes were suddenly distracted by nearby testosterone. "They said we women should get off our backs and get on our knees, so to speak. It's about opening our minds and our legs. I mean, I remember they talked about not only having safe sex, but having great sex, too."

Darla stared squarely at Rebe. "Did you hear about that before or after you got stingy on your own honeymoon?"

Rebe kept her sights on the vision of a hunk behind Darla's back, a few barstools away. "Very funny," she said without even a snicker. "I'm just saying, Randall cheated on me just like Neal cheated on you, Magnolia. And when Randall left, he left me and my daughter. Trinity took that hard, especially after not having a father figure since her dad died. So, like I said, I know how you feel." Rebe uncrossed her legs and offered a demure smile, but not to Magnolia.

Darla added, "I know one thing. I don't care what those women out there are doing in this crazy-ass world nowadays. I'm not about to die over a moment of pleasure. I'm sorry but I've just gotta be me."

Rebe batted her eyes and inched her sights back to her buddies. "Yeah, but think about it. Haven't you ever wondered what it would be like to just totally let go and freak out like there's no tomorrow? To have sex with a stranger or have an orgy or buy all the sex toys you can and just screw yourself all night long? Haven't you even been the least bit curious? Come on."

Magnolia said immediately, "Not even."

Rebe sucked her tongue. "Please. Yes you have."

"Orgy. Hell no. Masturbate all night, maybe." Magnolia took a drink, fighting her urge to laugh at herself.

Rebe eyed the view behind Darla again. Her cheeks began to blush. "Well heck, I'll be the first one to break beyond my boundaries. Shit, I might just walk right up to him," she nodded toward the man she'd been eyeing and then looked down toward her water glass, "and ask him to take me home and fuck me like the new freak I need to be. Like he's mad about slavery and shit. I mean do me like it's 1999, instead of 2009. Take me like I'm the last screw of his life and he's about to get hit by a Mack truck in the morning." She shook her brain, and her torso like she had shivers running up and down the slit of her vagina.

Darla gave Rebe a side angle stare and turned around to see a big man, very long, like he could be maybe six-seven if he stood, with a low-cut fade, perfect goatee, and light skin, deep dimple in his chin, eyeing down Rebe like she was the last corner of grandma's secret recipe macaroni and cheese on Thanksgiving Day. "Damn," she said, turning back around to give Rebe a high five with her eyes.

Magnolia glanced behind Darla, too. "Yeah, right.

You do that. And then, and only then, I *will* have an orgy," she said with sarcasm.

"No, you won't," Rebe said as a dare.

Magnolia shrugged her shoulders. "I don't have to worry about a damn orgy because you're not about to say one single solitary thing to that man. Not darling Rebe. And yes, he is a hunk now. I will say that. Oh, yes I will."

Rebe straightened her back. "Yeah, well, I guess you really don't know me like you think you do."

"Please. You don't know yourself." Magnolia looked assured.

Rebe said, "Maybe none of us knows ourselves the way we should." She turned her body all the way toward them and re-crossed her legs. "I'll tell you what. Dare. How about for 2009 we turn up our libidos and make some real resolutions? Some sexual resolutions. Something different. How about if we go into the new year shattering our beliefs about sex? Living our sexy dreams, out loud." She used her hands to assist her words. "I just think we've set these boundaries for ourselves, and maybe they've limited our ability to really experience the sexual side of us. I mean, these comfort zones are getting tired if you ask me. Honestly, I've had enough of this frigid adulthood. I've never been excited about sex much anyway, but for some reason lately, I'll be honest with you, I'm on fire." Eyes agreeing with her words, she circled the rim of her glass with her fingertip, like moonshine was inside versus sparkling water. Darla looked at her like she was on something.

Rebe continued, "I don't know about you two, but

I've been thinking about this a lot. We are not getting any younger. And physically, I can see myself starting to age." She pointed under her eyes. "Right around here. Like little crow's-feet, and dark circles."

"I don't see anything," Magnolia said, squinting her eyes to see.

"Yeah, well I do. First of all, I think I'm peri-menopausal. But in spite of that, I'm about to cross over the erotic line and dive off the edge for real. I'm about to say good-bye to my inhibitions. Hell, it's a new year." She leaned closer toward them. "I say we lighten up like we should've twenty years ago." She sipped her water.

Darla shook her head. "Rebe, girl, please. We're not twenty any more. We can't go back."

"Who says?"

Magnolia reminded her, "We're forty. Hello." Her eyes said *hello*, too. "Our biological clocks are ticking just like yours. I don't even have a kid, you do. Hell, I've never even been married. But I've got the bridesmaid thing down, between you, about two cousins, and one of my old co-workers. Enough."

Rebe smirked and glanced up at the time on the tele-vision screen over the bar. "Hold up now. We're not forty yet. And for the next five minutes, I'm about to dare even myself and open my mind in a way I've never done before. I'm about to take back my sexual freedom, and my first step is—get ready for this—I'm gonna start stripping."

Darla looked amazed. "Stripping. Oh Lord, are you sure that's seltzer water or whatever the heck it is you're drinking? I know you were a dancer years ago and all, but who's gonna hire a forty-year-old stripper?"

"I already have my pole-dancing class set, if you don't mind."

"What?" Magnolia watched Rebe's eyes, which were again focused on the big man to the left.

The crowd started to get louder.

The buzz was more intense.

Folks' glasses were being filled to the rim.

People moved closer together.

Rebe moved her eyes back to Magnolia and Darla. "Anyway ladies, what about you? What is it that you've always wanted to do but never had the nerve to do?"

Magnolia took a long gulp as the bartender walked up. She smiled and pointed toward her and her friends' glasses for fill-ups. The bow-tie-wearing lady nodded and walked away. Magnolia spoke as if she were telling the FBI's most classified secret. "Well, actually, a few months ago I was talking on the phone to this guy, and he told me I sounded like a phone sex operator. I mean he pissed me off a little, but later I actually thought of what it would be like to do that. You know. Turn someone on over the phone while they play with themselves." She dropped her sexy smirk and sat up straight. "Maybe even strange men. Like online."

Darla waved her hand at Magnolia. "See, you trip me out. Your banker look, with your hair always pulled back, wearing suits and carrying briefcases just doesn't match with that madness." She shook her head. "I know you meet guys, but, I can't even picture you doing that."

Magnolia nodded to the bartender as she set down their drinks. She asked Darla, "Well what about you? Like we'd ever be able to picture you doing anything."

"To tell you the truth, I've been thinking about opening a business. I mean, I think maybe it's about time for me to do something with what's left of this life insurance money." She heard her own words and knew it was her overbearing pride that was bigger than her honesty. "And, I was wondering what it would take for me to open an adult store."

"An adult toy store? You?" Magnolia asked, looking baffled. "And you can't picture me online?"

"Well, you know I love lingerie. I was thinking about a lingerie store, and adding in some toys, videos, things like that."

Rebe spoke with energy before Magnolia could say anything else. "That sounds good, Darla. If that's what you wanna do, then I think you should do it." Her eyes flipped between her friends. "I'm shaking off all that 'what we can't picture' crap. So what do you say? Three of us? I mean, it's just sex. It's not gonna kill us. Let's do it."

Magnolia tapped her fingernails along the bar and looked left and then right at her friends. "Shit, might as well."

Rebe smiled, noticing the time. "Then the challenge is on. Grab your glasses, ladies."

Just then, just as the BFF's agreed to their sexploration rules, the boisterous countdown began around them. They all rose to their high-heeled feet, standing side-by-side on the concrete flooring, and raised their glasses high in the air.

"Ten."

"Nine."

"Eight."

"Seven."

"Six."

"Five."

"Four."

"Three."

"Two."

"One."

As everyone began to yell, "Happy New Year," Magnolia said extra-loud, "Here's to girlfriends never being farther away than the arms of our hearts can reach." It was the threesome's sisterhood mantra.

Rebe and Darla nodded and smiled, and all three said together, "Cheers," as they clinked their glasses.

A few of the people along the bar and those who stood behind them offered a touch of their glasses, too, each saying, "Happy New Year," and the ladies saying it in return. Groups of strangers hugged, loud horns blew and noisemakers cranked, and turquoise balloons drifted slowly from the ceiling downward among the many bodies, making a trail to the floor around them.

"Happy Freaking New Year," Rebe said out loud like she started to really get the 2009 feeling, just as she looked over at the big man with the perfect goatee. He stayed seated as people hustled about. His eyes were only for her. Hers met his and stayed. She read his lips: *Happy New Year.*

Rebe heard him loud and clear and mouthed it back with sexy.

She had a new look on her face.

And Magnolia and Darla noticed.

They watched Rebe watch him and then she smiled toward the big man. She spoke with volume. "Freaking New Year is right. And I'm about to start right now."

She took hold of her black clutch from along the bar top and pulled on the hem of her short dress. "Listen. I love you both, but I gotta go."

Magnolia placed her hand on Rebe's wrist. "No you're not."

"Watch me." She placed her glass back down on the bar. "And I might even suck his dick."

Darla's forehead was pissed. She warned, "Rebe. Be careful. You don't even know him."

"That's the whole damn point."

"I'd swear you were on something. Not a drop of alcohol?" Magnolia asked over the loud blare of feel-good voices.

"Nope. Not even a little bit."

Darla spoke close to Rebe's ear, "Look, you text me in ten minutes, and then if you leave, you text me an address. Don't play now."

Rebe acted as though she was deaf. Magnolia and Darla watched her simply sashay away, with her elongated back, and long legs strutting like she was on a runway. She gave a girly fling of her skinny braids and stood before the big man, shook his hand, and brought her lips close to his left lobe. Magnolia and Darla could see Rebe shut her eyes as she spoke.

They could see his chin dimple deepen.

"Celebration" by Kool and the Gang played as folks joined in to sing along, some heading to the dance floor.

In thirty seconds flat, after the big man whispered back to Rebe, he stood tall, proving that he was indeed six-seven, towering over her by a foot. He placed some money on the bar and grabbed Rebe's hand, stepping away with an ear-to-ear smile, while she femininely fol-

lowed, looking back at her buddies, winking and grinning like a teenager.

Fully checking them out, Magnolia said, "Well I'll be
damned," almost giving off a smirk of envy. "The nerve."

Darla's mouth was stuck on open. She swallowed hard
and blinked three times fast, looking at Magnolia as
though prompting her to do something quick, and then
darting her worried eyes back toward Darla's exit. "Oh
my God. She did it. She's leaving. Is she leaving, or are
they headed to that private room? Where are they going? That child cannot be serious." She turned toward
the bar and looked at Magnolia, who was now holding
her BlackBerry Pearl, reading a text message. Darla said,
"I guess I'm the only one worried. You know we've got
to watch that girl. I just wanna know, what happened
to the squeamish girl who just used the word *ewwww* a
minute ago? She has lost her ever-loving mind at the
stroke of midnight." Darla turned back toward Rebe's
departure and lost complete sight of the big man and
Rebe. She stood on her tiptoes. "Heck, where'd his tall
ass take her?"

Magnolia sat down and put her cell back in her purse.
She wore a casual grin. "Rebe's truly taken this forty-
year thing to a whole new height. And I guess that
means our butts need to get serious too, girlie. Like she
said, we just made three sexual resolutions. And I don't
know about you, but I'm in." Magnolia again raised her
glass for a toast. "Happy fortieth birthday, Darla."

Darla cut her eyes away from the crowd and plopped
her body down on the bar stool next to Magnolia.
"Happy fortieth birthday," she said as though weak. She
and Magnolia leaned toward each other for a hug, and

Magnolia patted her on the back. Darla glanced at her tiny barrel purse and opened it, snatching her touch-screen cell, eyeing it with a frown. "That newly freaky girl had better text me. Trying to shake the missionary and get all sixty-nine on us with the Mr. Rick Fox wannabe. Let her hair down, my ass. She ain't forty yet, dammit."

Two

$$\sim\!\!\infty\!\!\sim$$

"Your Body's Callin'"

Rebe

INT.—FONTAINEBLEAU HOTEL—MORNING
New Year's Day 2009

He had her in a sixty-nine position.

Not lying down, but standing up, holding the weight of her body upside down, her head at the point of his strong dick. Her vagina at the point of his talented mouth. He kissed her sweet pussy lips and licked her insides out. Her swaying braids nearly grazing the hotel room's white shag carpet. Her vulnerable pink clit, up close and personal, contracted, dancing to his oral music, happy as hell to meet him.

Head first, she swallowed his cinnamon penis all the way down her throat, her lips down to his hairy base. She used her hand to keep her stroke tight. He fucked her mouth and at the same time held on to her full body weight. He was a superman lover for the ages.

He took a few steps and changed positions.

It had been an on-and-off span of five hours and forty-two minutes, to be exact.

Five hours and forty-two minutes of him devouring her.

The pale green and chocolate fitted duvet had long been kicked onto the carpet in an erotic frenzy.

His brown eyes lavished her body for the hundredth time.

He'd penetrated her tawny vagina for the twentieth time.

Tongue whipped her for the eighth time.

And he was still hungry for more.

He sniffed her sexual scent while he fucked her.

The intoxicating scented oil that she'd dabbed everywhere after her shower.

Belly button, behind the ears, and between her legs.

Her sweet body oil was called Pussy.

And her pussy was what he'd lived in since two in the morning.

They screwed like rabbits in the spacious one-bedroom specialty suite on the thirty-seventh floor of the ritzy hotel, lying on the triple-sheeted platform bed, smack dab in the middle of the expensive pillow-top mattress. The calming sounds of the crystal waters of the Atlantic Ocean, just beyond the balcony, were drowned out by carnal moans and groans, though mainly his.

Her breathing was quiet, yet unsteady, as she took a moment from the sexual pounding she'd asked the universe for, and lifted her head just slightly to view the neon blue digits of the alarm clock. She then rested her braided head back on the feather pillow that had smelled like fresh linen hours ago, but now smelled like their his-and-her body combinations.

She laid missionary, cooperating, receiving, with her

ass cheeks in his massive hands, with her knees back to the padded, white leather headboard, with him deep inside. It was what she wanted, what she'd claimed, what she vowed to experience, but still she said after catching a breath to speak, "DeMarius, baby, I need to get some sleep. It's almost nine in the morning." Rebe's words shocked the morning vixen in her. Even though it was a marathon like she'd never known, it was the old her taking over and being conservative, convincing her that sleep came before sex. But even with her spoken desire to cease, she held on tight through his X-rated conniption fit, sex kitten fingernails in his back. She was as wet as she was when he'd first entered, after eating her to the point of making her come all over his face.

DeMarius begged in a frantic fuck-fury, "Not yet, just wait. Just a minute." The rhythm of his voice was like that of a breathless 10K runner, pushing himself toward the finish line. His penis was at full extension, hiding out at the very back crevices of her cave where his tip secured itself, rubbing against the cherry pink walls of juicy uncharted territory. She felt as if he knew that the word *uncharted* was apropos. As though he knew Rebe had very little experience and hadn't had her pussy explored and roughed up like that, ever. She felt he knew she had low mileage for a woman of forty. She could tell by the way he held her, by the way he was breathing, sweating, whispering in her ear, having her shift positions and lift one leg, lower another, twist, stand, sit, squat, buck, drop it, bounce, and bend.

He kept sliding himself in and out like it would be his first and last time to ever get this close to almost-virginity again, and so, just in case, he hit it hard, all night long, all morning long, making sure to repeatedly poke that soft, rough spot that made him, once again just as he had four times before, come. Hard.

He almost cried. "Ahh, shit. Yeah, damn. Fuck, this tight-ass pussy is good. Ahh, yeah. Uggghhhhh." He gave one last pump and stopped, resting his body weight on her body, and exhaled a long, manly deep exhale. From the back of her pussy she could feel his pleased banana-like penis swell to its maximum, unpeel, and then slowly collapse.

His chest rose and fell quickly on her.

His face was tucked close to her neck.

For all she knew he was sucking his thumb.

Rebe moved her hands from the impassioned grip of his muscular pecan shoulders and wiped the beads of sweat from her forehead, collapsing her arms along each side of her hips. She turned her head to the left, just as her mascara-smudged eyelids began to give way to her exhaustion. The feeling was intoxicating, him inside of her and her still in the receiver position. She felt she could doze off in afterglow sex heaven, and then she remembered.

She was in a hotel room with a man she'd known for only a little more than eight hours.

He was inside of her.

And she didn't even know his last name.

She was butt naked.

He'd gone through nearly a box of condoms.

And she didn't even know his last name.

It was New Year's Day.

Her friends had to be worried sick about her.

She'd never been fucked like that in her entire life.

She'd never desired to be fucked by a man like that in her entire life.

And she didn't even know his last name.

"DeMarius." She spoke his name like maybe he could explain why she was there, because for the moment, she surely couldn't.

"Yes," he answered as though spent, turning his head toward her voice in slow motion.

Her eyes asked him to respect her and make her feel like a good girl, instead of the nymphomaniac tramp that had sucked his dick nine times and let him have his way with her.

"Are you okay?" he asked, looking over at her smooth, angelic dark brown face and almond brown eyes.

She replied after a pause, putting her hand to her mouth, wondering if her breath was on fire, "I need to get up. I need to go to the bathroom."

He first reached down to grab the base of his condom, pulled his now deflated dick from her pussy, and carefully swiveled off just as she lowered her legs and stretched them out. "Ouch," she said in a quiet voice from the feeling of her confined bones and muscles returning to their relaxed positions.

He lay on his back, keeping his hand around his penis, looking over to watch Rebe as she swung her defined legs to the side of the bed and stood. The only light was from the muted local morning news show broadcasting from the plasma TV screen, shining random flashes of grayish highlights upon her fit frame. "You are something else," he said with lust... still. He had a look like he could molest her some more.

"You're the one," she said, grabbing her clutch from the leather chair and heading to the huge marble bathroom. She flicked on the lights, stepped on the cool, large ivory tiles, and left the door open.

He could still see her, and his eyes had a conversation with her ass as she stood at the ebony pedestal sink. He gave a long blink and rolled to a slow stance, again keeping a grip on himself so that the rubber didn't slip off. Nude, he headed to the bathroom, walked past Rebe and tossed his full condom into the ebony toilet as she stood nude, rinsing her mouth out, using every bit of the tiny bottle of Scope.

He actually stood there urinating, as though they'd known each other for decades, not only fuck-hours. He spoke over the sound of his own stream. "Let's hang out today, that is if you don't have anywhere to go."

Rebe acted like she didn't even notice him peeing. "I guess I could. But I just realized I haven't seen my daughter in a few days. She lives with me," she explained, dabbing her lips with a hand towel.

"I see. I thought you wanted to get some more sleep."

"Oh I will, believe me, especially after that workout." She gave his back a smile, eyeing every God-given inch of him from behind, even his round, muscled butt, and wide, protective shoulders. The right shoulder bore her fresh pussycat claw marks. "I'll be falling asleep as soon as I get home."

"Okay." He sounded as though he'd have no choice but to yield. "I understand." He shook himself off, flushed the toilet, and headed to the sink.

Rebe rummaged through the main compartment of her clutch. "How long are you gonna be in town?"

He was at the sink, squeezing sanitizer on his hands, rubbing them together, walking to the bathroom door, and leaning his six-seven body against the frame. "Just until Monday night. I have an interview at Miami Dade on Monday."

"Really?" She watched his face through the reflection of the mirror. She didn't tell him she graduated from there. She wasn't sure why. She just didn't.

"Yeah. Track coach."

"I see. That's where you get all that energy from, huh? A track runner. Or a marathon runner." She smiled, still searching through her clutch.

He grinned. "I'm not normally like that. Believe me. It's you."

"Well, I'm not usually like that either. Never have been. But I'm sure you know that. I'm a little green."

"I think you handled every moment just fine."

"I'd say I had a little trouble trying to negotiate some of those positions you were directing."

"That was an unusual amount of time. You did just fine."

"You should be a porn director. You sure you're not on some of those little blue pills?"

He gave her a handsome grin. "I guarantee you, I'm not."

"Wow. I've never seen, or done, anything like that move you did having me upside down, in that standing sixty-nine. Haven't seen much sex beyond laying on my back, really."

"Why's that?"

"I just haven't. Got pregnant when I was young and even then, it was just so-so to me. I was never that curious about sex."

"Looks like you need to make up for lost time."

"I agree. About to turn forty, getting ready for a new life. It's all unfolding."

He eyed her tip to toe. "Looking at your body, no one could tell. I wouldn't have guessed."

"Thanks." She blushed.

"Were you married to your daughter's father?"

"Not to him, no. I did marry someone about seven years ago, but not for that long." She zipped up her clutch, didn't dare tell who Randall was, and turned toward him and leaned against the sink, crossing her arms over her bare breasts. "But I'll tell you something, our sex life, meaning his and mine, was nothing like that." She pointed to the bedroom. "Maybe that was part of the problem."

He looked like he was fighting to not look at her chest, and instead looked at her face. "It takes two, you know?"

She tried not to look at his penis. It was half awake, and she could have sworn she saw it jump. She squinted and blinked and swallowed. "True. So, what about you? A man like you alone at a club on New Year's Eve. I would think you'd have so many women trying to get with you, and that you'd at least have a date. Surely once they got to know you this way, I mean, they'd be crazy to not want to, you know, want to get close to you."

"I'll be totally honest with you. And I'm saying this because one other time when I wasn't honest, it came back to bite me in the ass. One lie only leads to trouble. See, I made my bed so I'd better be proud to lie in it, so here it goes. I'm here for two reasons. One is my coaching interview, but I came in a few days early because of an assignment. I'm an escort, and I had a job two nights ago when I got here."

"You're kidding me." She placed her hands on the sink behind her.

Her chest was now his full bull's-eye, as if he'd never seen her nipples before now. His glance scooted to her surprise-ridden face. "No, I'm not kidding. But, it was nothing like what we just did. Nothing like you."

"Wow. I see you are really honest, aren't you?" She walked to the wall and took the white terry cloth robe from the hook.

"I try to be."

"So, what's up with that? I mean, you do it for the money?" Rebe put her arms through the sleeves and pulled it on, closing the front.

"Partially. And, it's just easy work."

"For you, I'm sure it is." Her mind was racing. "What else do you get out of it, other than money and other than it being easy? Is the uncommitted sex part of it?"

"Maybe. No strings attached. But having sex like I did with you, if you were a client, would be difficult to walk away from. That's how sex should be."

"Okay. Huh." She shook her head. "Life."

"Yeah. Life."

She reached back for the belt and tightened it around her waist.

"You sure you have to go?"

"I do." She turned back toward the sink.

"Maybe another day."

"Maybe."

"Sounds to me like you doubt it."

"At times I doubt there'll be any day. Nothing's promised, as they say. Not even tomorrow. Really, you just never know."

"True. But I do know one thing. You are amazing,"

"So are you." She meant it, but didn't sound like she did.

He took the few steps that led to her, and took her hair into his hand, lifting her long, thin braids that flowed behind her back, lifting it high enough to find the nape of her ballerina long neck. He bent down to meet her dark brown skin that still smelled of her sexy body oil, moving the collar of her robe.

She sort of raised her shoulder to pull away by an inch or so and gave a nervous, single, small giggle. Her right hand was shut tight.

He leaned down farther, and under the bright fluorescent lighting he placed a kiss on the back of her neck with full lips. His eyes stayed aimed at where he'd kissed, and he asked, "What's that?"

"What?"

"That. On the back of your neck."

"Oh, nothing It's just a scar." She took her hair from his hand and turned toward him, just praying he referred to the tattoo on her shoulder that read, *Maestro*.

"From surgery?"

She cleared her throat, knowing this wasn't about her tattoo. "Just some stitches. It was a long time ago. You know how kids are. I was a tomboy." Her giggle was minor. She again tightened the belt.

"Oh. Okay." He took a step back, eyes still looking curious. He watched her readjust her hair, and then he walked toward the door.

She took a short breath and turned toward him again, speaking to his back. "By the way. What's your last name?"

He barely turned his head to her, facing the door. His reply was delayed and low. "Collins."

She nodded once. "Mine is Palo," she said, giving her maiden name.

He nodded once. "Nice to meet you, Rebe Palo." A gradual smile spread on his face and he walked out, back into the bedroom. Seconds later he collapsed onto his back, on the disheveled bed with his arm over his face, shielding his eyes.

She closed the bathroom door.

Walked back to the sink.

Grabbed the upside-down drinking glass that was on the paper doily and filled it with tap water.

She took a sip, swallowing three pills that had been in her hand. She sipped again, and gulped.

Leaning her hand along the sink, she looked down at her bare feet.

And even though she accomplished her sexual resolution so soon, Rebe Palo-Richardson, quiet as a mouse, cried like a newborn baby.

Three

---❧---

"Grandma's Hands"

Magnolia

INT.—GRANDMA GRACE'S HOME—MIRAMAR,
FLORIDA—EARLY EVENING
New Year's Day 2009

A homemade milk-chocolate cake with a rainbow menagerie of Happy Birthday candles sat on the white-tile kitchen counter in a crystal cake server.

The new morning of the new year had transformed into very early evening. Half past six to be exact, on a Friday. The leftover sun was soon to disappear.

"There are good men out there, now Magnolia. Not every man is going to cheat on you."

Magnolia's seventy-two-year-old grandmother wore wisdom on her oval face like a tattoo. She looked at least thirteen years younger. With her slender frame and straight-from-the-bottle, saucy beige hair color, she was attractive. And her mind was sharp as a tack.

Magnolia called her Gigi, short for Grandma Grace. Widowed, Gigi lived alone in her home in Broward County in a rundown neighborhood that statistically was considered a high crime area, but years ago it was the complete opposite, much more upscale.

Magnolia said to her grandmother, "I hear you say not every man will cheat, but I haven't seen proof of it yet. And honestly, I really don't care anymore." In her cargo pants and eyelet peasant top, Magnolia kicked off her gold flats, getting comfortable. Saying she didn't care was common for her.

The fifteen-hundred-square-foot, two-bedroom house, which at the moment smelled like some serious soul food and homemade cheddar biscuits, was the same home Magnolia grew up in, on Casablanca Drive. The weather-beaten, white house with the taller than tall sweet gum tree in the front, was built in the late 1950s. Ida and Norman Grace bought it brand-new. It had an empty swimming pool that hadn't been filled in a decade, and a long, narrow driveway that led to a pink one-car garage, and a front door that was the same color.

Right around the time they'd bought the house, Magnolia's mother, June Butler, gave birth to Magnolia. June actually lived three streets down in a rented house on Plantation Boulevard. But just when Magnolia reached four weeks old, they brought her to live with them after June had her breakdown, which her mother blamed on baby blues, but everyone on the outside knew she had issues. Issues that her parents hoped being a young mother would cure. But it only made it worse.

Being that it was the anniversary of Magnolia's birth, she was right where she wanted to be.

Magnolia sat in the family room on the contemporary brown sofa she'd bought her grandmother, the oversized sofa that rested on the new ivory ceramic tiled flooring she had put in for Gigi last month. Magnolia also wore the silver link chain with the black angel charm her grandmother had given her when she was a teen. She never took it off.

Gigi wore her usual red-rimmed eyeglasses. She leaned back in her two-decade-old tan recliner with her feet propped up. "Oh yes you do, baby girl. I never believe you when you say you don't care. You care."

Magnolia gave a certain look. "This time, please believe me."

Gigi's age-defined hands rested in her lap, fingers interlocked. She still wore her emerald-cut wedding ring. Never took it off either. "I felt the same way after your mom's dad ended up being a rolling stone. But your Grandpa Norm came into my life and proved me wrong. He was a good man, Magnolia. We were together for more than forty-two years before he died." She wore fluffy house shoes, her legs crossed at the ankles.

"Oh, I know he was. But I've found Grandpa Norm to be the exception to the rule, unfortunately. These men have the mentality of *too many women, too little time*. I have no *time* for that."

Gigi pointed her light brown eyes as if they were fingers. "Now don't you talk like that. You can't put all that mess in your head, otherwise you'll start bringing it to you. You have to be positive. God is getting you ready for your ordained mate. All these other men are part of the preparation. You have to pray, baby girl. And just when it looks like you're getting more of the same, pray some more. The right man is out there and God will bring him to you when the time is right."

Magnolia brought her bare feet up onto the cushion

beside her, tucking them to her side. "That sounds sweet. But, Gigi, at this stage in my life, I'm just not having much faith in all that. I'm forty. I thought I'd have three kids by now. And only one husband."

"Baby girl, you've been busy with your education and all that you do at that bank. You didn't make vice president overnight. You've had relationships before, and you'll have more. The babies will come in time if it's the good Lord's will." She reached over to the timeworn TV tray and picked up a piece of peppermint candy, undoing the wrapper and popping it into her mouth.

Magnolia leaned her head back along the cushion. "Not from this body."

Gigi smiled at her granddaughter big, exposing her tongue working her mint. She spoke and sucked the candy at the same time. "You're funny. Young as you are, you're acting like you're ready for a cane or something. Forty is nothing." She shook her head as though amused. "I'm the one who can speak on old, not you." Gigi looked serious but winked at her granddaughter. She reached back behind her head and fiddled with the worn and nearly torn rubber band that held her shoulder length hair into a ponytail. "It's funny. You know your mother called the other day, which rarely happens. She called from who knows where. And she asked me that very question, about whether or not I thought you'd make her a grandmother. I told her it's all up to God." Gigi placed her hands back on her lap.

Magnolia looked unenthused. "Please. With all due respect to you, my mom's got some questions to ask God about herself, not about me. Besides, what would make her think she'd even deserve to be a grandmother?

What does she know about babies? God blessed her with a daughter she couldn't even show up for. Considering how much you and Grandpa taught me, I'm wondering how she missed out on the basic skills like, first you get your own husband, not someone else's, then you have children, in that order." She took a breath. "I'm sorry. I just want a normal life, not a life of havoc. Not a life filled with mistakes like she made."

Gigi bit into her mint with her back teeth, cracking it into pieces and crunching, but talking with her mouth open like her words just couldn't wait. "Now I just know you're not using the word *mistake* when it comes to you, right? I'm not even going to sit here and let you talk like that."

Magnolia looked down, rubbed her feet, and was expressionless. "No ma'am. I didn't mean me in particular."

"Baby girl, I've always known how you've felt about your mom. She's had some serious problems, and yes, she still does. But that's why we took you in. Whatever it is she didn't get, you did. Whatever it was you needed, we got for you. She may have never known how it was supposed to be, but you do, and that's what matters."

Magnolia looked over at her grandmother. Her face agreed with what she heard. "You're right."

Gigi lowered the footrest of her recliner and came to a slow stance, wearing a light blue housedress with deep pockets. "That's what I like to hear. Come on, baby girl, let's eat this birthday dinner I made for you. Your favorite fried turkey wings with cabbage with brown sugar yams. And cheese biscuits, of course."

Magnolia rubbed her hands together. "That's what I'm talking about." She stood and walked barefoot over to her grandmother, and they walked slowly toward the long, narrow kitchen, holding hands.

Gigi told Magnolia, "Just because we didn't have enough precious times with your mother, doesn't mean we can't cherish the times we have with each other."

"Times with you are enough," Magnolia said, while Gigi stood at the stove, removing the lid from a large cast-iron pot, grabbing a large spoon. A cell phone sounded near the sofa. Magnolia stepped to it. "I'm sorry, just one second, ma'am."

"No, it's okay. You go ahead and get your phone. You never know who's trying to reach you."

Gigi kept mumbling and Magnolia quickly reached inside her bag, checking the caller ID with a puzzled look and connecting the call. "Hello."

"Hey, Mag."

She sighed a large sigh. "Hey."

"How are you?" Neal asked with energy, as though extra glad to get Magnolia live for once.

"I'm good." Magnolia was bland.

"You busy?"

"I'm at Gigi's house."

"Oh? How is she?"

Magnolia watched her grandmother add her magic spices to the pot. She skipped right over his question. "Why'd you block your number?" she asked, trying to contain her voice.

"Honestly, I knew you wouldn't answer unless I did."

She gave a sarcastic nod. "You were right about that. We're about to eat."

"Okay. I understand. Real quick. I just wanna know if

you got my Happy New Year text at midnight, and the one this morning wishing you a Happy Birthday."

"Uh-huh." She rubbed her forehead.

"But you didn't call back. Why?"

Magnolia turned her back from the kitchen. "Because. It's my birthday. And even if it wasn't, I still wouldn't." She walked out of the family room and down the long hall leading to the bedrooms. The volume of her voice then kicked up a notch. "Why are you still calling me anyway? Besides, isn't your girl gonna see this call on your bill?"

He sounded puzzled. "Why would she see my phone bill? It's not like that."

"Whatever." Magnolia stood with her back against the hallway wall.

"Mag, I don't live with her."

"Live with her or not, what you need to do is stop contacting me. Try being faithful to someone for once in your life. And next time you call, I promise you, I won't answer."

"Mag, why are you still mad after all this time?"

She stepped toward the back bedroom. "Do not call me that. Stop acting like it means something just because you think I'm still mad. What happened between us wasn't that long ago. You just need to stop doing this." She paced back in the other direction. "It's bad enough I have to see you during the week. Now please. Leave me alone. You need to live with the choice you made."

"Have you ever thought that maybe seeing you at work is making it harder for me? Maybe just a little bit harder for me to move on? I do care about you, Mag."

Magnolia shook off his words. "Well you shouldn't. I'm fine."

"Okay. Is it safe to assume you're not seeing anyone? I mean, do you have a date tonight for your birthday?"

At that moment, Gigi yelled from the kitchen, "Baby girl, we can eat whenever you're ready."

Magnolia said loud back, smiling while lowering the phone to her side. "Okay, thanks. I'll be right there." She frowned just that fast and spoke to Neal. "Listen, I've gotta go."

"No worries. Can we go to lunch next week? I really want us to get an understanding, and ahh, I guess, close the book once and for all. We just never discussed it face to face. With you being so mad, I sent the email, I was all messed up. All of what went down was so fucked up on my part. I just want to talk to you in person. Please."

She gave an *oh please* look and spoke fast. "I've gotta go. I'm hanging up."

"Mag." He rushed his word.

"Bye, Neal." In a hurry she disconnected the call and walked back into the family room. She turned off her phone, placing it in her purse, and then went into the kitchen. She pulled out a chair.

As soon as Magnolia sat, Gigi approached with two steam-seeping plates and set them down. Her eyes were curious. "Neal?"

Magnolia looked surprised that her grandmother's hearing was that good. She nodded and scooted her chair in. "Grandma, I apologize for that. That man keeps trying to stay in touch. It's just his ego, that's all."

Gigi took a seat across from Magnolia, pressed her eyeglasses closer to her face, and grabbed the hot sauce, shaking it heavily over her helping of cabbage. "He's trying to keep an eye on you to make sure you're still available, just in case it doesn't work out with that woman. He is still with her, right?"

"Yes."

"And you don't want to talk to him? Or does the fact that he's calling do something for your ego, too?"

"Oh, not even. Not in the least."

"Okay. Then change your telephone number, baby girl," Gigi said, as if it should be easy.

"Why should I? Besides, I see him at work every day anyway."

"Well then, get yourself a new job."

"Gigi, I'm not about to get out there and look for a new job in today's market. I like my job. I was there first. Plus, I've got a retirement plan and benefits. Let him get a new job." She unfolded her paper napkin and placed it on her lap.

"Okay, then I guess you run the risk of hearing from and seeing him. Not much you can do, I guess." She shrugged her shoulders and then stood, walked to the cupboard, and took out two drinking glasses.

"I'll get the drinks," Magnolia offered.

"Oh no. I've got it. This is my kitchen. You know better. Lemonade, right?" she asked, opening the fridge.

"Yes, thanks." Magnolia surrendered. "I think once I get a new man in my life, I'll let him pick up the phone when Neal calls. I bet he'll stop then."

Gigi spoke as she poured the lemonade into the glasses along the counter, "I guess he would. Or it might make him try even harder. There's nothing like an ex having a new love to make people act up. For now, if you really want him to stop calling, it's up to you and you alone to be firm, and consistent."

"You're right."

Gigi put the full glasses on the table and then sat, but left the pitcher of lemonade out, and the refrigerator open. "I'm almost seventy-three years old, baby girl. I've seen enough to know enough, as my momma used to say."

Magnolia stood and grabbed the pitcher, placing it in the fridge and closing it. "Yes, I suppose you have."

Gigi said, "But there is one more thing I know."

"What's that?" Magnolia asked, sitting back down.

"You're not over Neal yet. That's unfinished business for the both of you."

Magnolia giggled and put a hot biscuit on her plate. "I think you're about to ruin your record on this one then. Because I could care less about any man who cheats like he did, especially right under my nose with a co-worker. There are no second chances on that."

"Okay. You say so."

"I do know one thing. If I was anything like Mom, I guess I'd start seeing Neal behind his girlfriend's back, wouldn't I?"

"I guess you would, huh? Though whichever road you take, one day you'll find out what it's like to be cherished. To be protected. To be valued. To feel safe. To be with a real man who gives and cares about your feelings before his own. I've told you about that before. But you must believe your happiness is just around the corner."

Magnolia's eyes looked as if they only wished. "Your mouth to God's ears."

They put their heads down and prayed, giving the

sign of the cross, and began eating, talking the entire time.

An hour later, after she convinced Gigi to let her help with the dishes, Magnolia went into the den and Gigi headed toward the back bathroom.

On the way she yelled, "Just making sure you're okay spending your birthday with your old grandma. If you have a date or something, I understand."

"No, Gigi. You are my date. And I love it."

"Okay now. We'll dig into that cake later," Gigi said as she closed the bathroom door.

"Can't wait." At that very second, Magnolia hurried to take her BlackBerry from her purse, turned it back on, and scrolled through her speed dial numbers. One read, Neal's Voicemail. But he'd already changed the code. Another read, Neal's Facebook, but he'd changed that password, too. She switched to her phone's browser application and logged into Neal's account at Ocean Bank. She perused the listing of his recent transactions.

Neal had paid for flowers from Beach Side Florists, made a purchase from Victoria's Secret, and had been to a few restaurants., One in particular was their favorite, El Rancho Grande.

Her heart skipped a beat.

She frowned, logged off, disconnected, and remembered how her grandmother would tell her, *what you don't know won't hurt you.*

But still, for Magnolia, it was both the feeling of knowing and not knowing that was killing her.

Her grandmother was correct.

She was not yet over Neal the Heartbreaker Graham.

Four

"Try It on My Own"

Darla

EXT.—DARLA'S CAR—DOWNTOWN MIAMI—LATE
MORNING
January 2, 2009

The powder blue skies were barely tickled by the slight playful morning breeze.

It was the second day of almost summer-like temperatures, so soon after the chill of the last day of 2008. It was another day of oddly sudden, orange blazing sunshine that had won its fight with the clouds, shining the warmth of its light on Southeast Florida with a bold glare.

Riding along the northern streets of Miami in her midnight blue Maxima, Darla, wearing her Bluetooth headset, paid close attention to the street signs and street numbers as she said to her friend Rebe, "Hey, sis."

"Cool. So what's up with you?" Rebe was at home, voice sounding like she could have been soaking in the luxury of a warm bubble bath.

"I'm good. The question is, what's up with you?"

"I'm good, too."

"I guess you are. Running off with a strange man and all. Magnolia and I got two little text messages. One that you were in the VIP area with him, and the other that you were on your way up to his hotel room."

Rebe's voice was low and slow. "Darla, he had a room at the same Fontainebleau hotel. No big deal."

"No big deal that you didn't call the rest of the night and all day yesterday."

"You know I texted you both yesterday, and again to say Happy Birthday. I was home all day yesterday, making gumbo for the New Year, hoping Trinity would come home, but she was out all night, again. Besides, I'm calling you now so can we talk, please? "

"Okay. But if it were me, I would've called first thing yesterday morning, if not sooner. Screw a dang text. Whatever happened to picking up the phone?" Darla asked, still watching every street number along the way.

Rebe paused. Her sigh was audible. "Darla, why is it you act like Mother Teresa all the time? Especially after we sat there on New Year's Eve night and agreed to lighten the hell up, and here you are, the second day of 2009, still with your panties in a bunch. I'm gonna start calling you my energy vampire. You suck all the fun right out of me."

"Well, excuse me for giving a darn. All I can say is at least he wasn't an ax murderer. I mean, you are still alive." Darla sped up a bit, realizing she had a few more blocks to go. "But believe me, I listened to every word of that conversation we had about our resolutions. That's why I'm driving around looking at places to open my store right now."

Rebe's voice sparked. "You are? Very good."

"Somebody's gotta be good."

"Yeah, yeah. Where've you been looking?"

"Right now I'm in Miami." Darla ducked her head to see the addresses. "Downtown on Northwest 40th between 1st and 2nd, looking for this one place that's somewhere over here, suppose to be a corner spot. And then I'm headed over near Midtown."

"I'm really proud of you for not wasting any time."

"Well thanks. You didn't waste time either, obviously. I'll let you slide, though. So what happened anyway? Magnolia said you beat us to the punch in getting deflowered for 2009."

"Yeah." Rebe spoke with more energy. "And I'll tell you this, just like I told her, for the first time in my life I went back to a man's place. In this case, a man's hotel room. A man who I'd just met, and we had sex. And when I say sex, it was a freaking sex extravaganza, Darla. This man went all night long. I swear he must've been on Viagra or something."

Darla had a momentary impressed look on her face. "Oh my. Who is he?"

"His name is DeMarius. DeMarius Collins, he told me. And girl, the trip is, he told me he's actually an escort."

Darla waited at the traffic light. "An escort? Rebe, you had sex with an escort?"

"I did. And it was the best sex I've ever had in my entire life."

"That's total TMI on his part. Unless he was trying to get you to pay him, I can't believe he even told you that. That's not something I'd imagine a person admitting."

"I can tell you for sure he was not trying to get paid with money. He was getting paid with pussy dollars, maybe. Girl, I thought he was gonna eat me alive." Rebe laughed and then moaned in remembrance.

Darla replied, "I'm sure that man gets all the sex he can handle. Why was he sitting at a bar on New Year's Eve all alone?"

"He was in town for a job and it just so happened to be around New Year's."

"I would think New Year's Eve would be a big money making night for escorts. With all the single women who don't want to bring in the new year alone, fine as he was, he should've been booked."

"Whatever. As they say, he was cute for a drive-by, but not a vacation. It was a one-nighter. All I know is, I got mine and it didn't cost me anything."

Darla proceeded as the light turned green. "I guess not. But did you even ask him if he lives here?"

"He's from New York, actually here for an interview. A track coach position at our old alma mater."

"Track, huh? As tall as that man is. He'd tip over try-ing to run a dang relay. That'd be a funny sight." Darla giggled.

Rebe sounded serious. "Oh, please. I've seen some pretty tall guys running track. Usain Bolt is like six foot five." Rebe waited a second. "You trying to say he was lying to me, or what?"

"Just sounds odd."

"Why would he lie about something as simple as in-terviewing for a coaching job? Especially after being open enough to admit he's an escort."

"You did at least exchange numbers, right?"

"No. After he told me what he did, I was like, let me just cut my losses."

Darla slowed down again and then stopped at a crosswalk, allowing the plentiful weekend crowd of pedestrians to cross the street. "I can understand that."

"Yeah." Rebe's voice was again relaxed.

"So anyway, what about your pole dancing classes? When does that start?"

"I'll have my first class tomorrow."

"Maybe that's what I need to be doing. Rebe, honestly, my ass is getting bigger by the day." Darla proceeded on cautiously.

"You should come with."

"What I need to do first is get this weight off me before I can even begin to go sliding down some doggone pole."

"You look great to me."

"Thank you. Like Mo'Nique says, 'I'm skinny fat.'"

Rebe laughed. "No."

"The only reason you don't say how big I am is because you love me, right?"

"Yes, I do, in spite of your annoying motherly ways. But you also know the best way to get on my bad side is to keep acting like a mother. Keep it up."

"Speaking of a mother, I just wonder sometimes if you're curious about how she's holding up. I mean, she's been in jail for what now, more than twenty-five years?"

"Next topic. You talk to your mother-in-law lately?" Rebe asked.

Darla pulled over. "I did yesterday. She called me, not texted me, mind you, to wish me a happy birthday. Always cries when we get on the phone. Lost her only child. When I hang up I feel like crap."

"I'll bet."

Darla parallel parked along the curb in front of a newer shopping complex. "Well, Rebe, I guess I'll go ahead and get out of this car. Maybe I can peek in a few windows to see what these places look like inside." She put the car in park and eyed the brand-new development, in particular, the store on the corner with the white brick and tan stucco. "It looks pretty nice. But I doubt I could afford this."

"You never know. Go ahead and check it out. I'm gonna take a nap. I'm still worn out from marathon man."

"Yeah, you do that. Plus, you're going to need your energy for your stripper class tomorrow." Darla turned off the engine.

"True."

"You be good."

Rebe's voice was half asleep. "I'll try."

Darla rushed her words, speaking louder. "Oh, and Rebe."

"Yes."

Darla took a deep breath. "I wanted to ask you."

"Uh huh."

She took an even deeper breath, searching for the words and the nerve. "You know, I just might need a, well, I have this, what I'm saying is, I might need, need to call you back after you get some rest, once I see these places. You know, get your feedback."

"Sure. Call me back."

"I will. Bye."

Darla hung up, grabbing her purse and taking the keys from the ignition, ready to get a closer look at the storefront.

The store she had the nerve to even look at, considering she'd almost just asked her rich friend for a loan. A loan not only to open a store, but also a loan to help her pay her most basic of bills.

Because unbeknownst to her friends, Darla Clark was flat busted broke.

Five

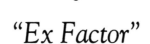

"Ex Factor"

Rebe

INT.—REBE'S CORAL GABLES HOME—COCONUT
GROVE—EARLY EVENING
January 3, 2009

It was the next day, a Saturday, and Rebe sat down after devouring leftovers of her traditional New Year's chicken and sausage gumbo. The smell of her spicy stew still lingered in the air.

She had upgraded the oversized chef's kitchen with all-black cabinets, dark hardwood floors, and the best brand of fitted stainless steel appliances. The empire cherry island was so big it could have served as a queen-sized bed.

Rebe's custom-built estate home was in an elite section of a city called Coral Gables, compliments of one cheating ex-husband named Randall.

Rebe didn't come from money, but for the moment, she was swimming in it...eight million dollars' worth of swimming. Two million for each year they were married.

Wearing a yellow pair of tights, a hoodie, and track shoes, Rebe sat on a leather barstool at the island, thinking about her life as she rummaged through a stack of mail. She looked around at her beautiful home and thought about the small house she and her brother grew up in. Her thoughts were dark. Her mood dipped.

It was a run-down, two-bedroom apartment, in a public housing complex in Ocala, Florida. It was the place where all hell broke loose.

Just like her daughter Trinity did after her birth father died, Rebe had learned to live without her father, who moved back to Hawaii once Rebe got pregnant and moved in with Trent. He'd never even met his own grandchild. Never made an attempt.

But Rebe wanted to be all that Trinity didn't have as far as extended family. She made sure to be there for her daughter, almost to the point of being overprotective. And Rebe had no choice but to learn to live without her mother, who was locked up. The woman whom Rebe called the she-devil.

Right out of college, Rebe worked as a customer service representative at a bank with Magnolia, but all Rebe ever wanted to do was be a dancer. Though never encouraged at home, she loved dance class in high school, and one thing she made sure to do in college was take modern dance and ballet. Dancing was her passion.

Back in 2001, when Trinity was fourteen, Rebe attended a tryout for the Miami Dolphins cheerleading squad. She didn't get the spot, but she did catch the eye of one of the guys on the practice field, Randall Richardson, who back then was a star tight end for the Dolphins. Within one month, she quit her job and she and Trinity moved in with Randall, though some warned Rebe it was way too soon. But the whirlwind romance led to them getting married six months after that. Five years later, she was awarded alimony after filing for divorce. It was not nasty. He gave her what she wanted in the divorce, but not his fidelity in the marriage.

According to Rebe, their marriage fell apart because Randall arrived back in town after an away game and called to say he'd be home in a few hours after he made a stop by the coach's house. Well, he did go by his coach's house, but when he left, he didn't head straight home, and Rebe was hot on his trail, following right behind him in her Benz, straight to the W South Beach.

Rebe watched him pull up to the front of the hotel and hand the keys to his silver Porsche to the black-vest-wearing valet. He went inside as Rebe and her nervous heart waited. And waited. Adrenaline was in overdrive.

Halfway into the second hour, Randall came out hand-in-hand with a woman, a woman with platinum hair, whom Rebe recognized as one of the team's cheerleaders. The valet pulled around the woman's brand-new black Mustang and then stood with the door ajar, and by the time the woman finished hugging Randall, ready to scoot her narrow hips into the driver's seat, Rebe came booting it along the circular driveway in her Adidas, like she was Flo Jo, and she commenced to swinging. Swinging at Randall, at the woman, and toward the valet who stepped forward to try to block the door so the woman could get in her car. He shut the door, and she drove away. Randall restrained Rebe, grabbing her arms while she shook and kicked and squirmed to release herself from his grip.

"You bastard ass muthafucka. I'm so sick of you telling all these damn lies. You're never where you say you are. You flew into town and lied as soon as you landed, knowing I'm waiting for your sorry ass to come home. And I recognize that scrawny bitch anyway. Isn't her name Kandi? What the hell?"

Another valet pulled up who was driving Randall's Porsche and Randall shoved Rebe away, hopped in, and sped off, all without saying a word, pedal to the metal. Rebe went sprinting down the street, trying to get to her car fast enough, but by the time she did, he was out of sight.

Rebe breathed hard like it would be her last, and pressed redial on her cell in a repeated panic, but Randall didn't pick up. She yelled so loud her ears popped. "Pick up the phone, Randall. You fucking dog ass punk, you!"

She hurried home and waited, crying, pacing, imagining, and dialing again for over two hours, all while Trinity slept down the hall.

Then, Randall simply walked in the bedroom with a stroll, calm and casual, like nothing had happened. He never even gave her eye contact. But her angry eyes made precise contact with him.

Rebe was seated on the bed, legs crossed, bouncing her foot, focusing on his every move. Her nose and upper lip were sweating and she was shaking like a crack addict.

He went straight to the closet, packed a small suitcase, and casually walked out of the room.

Rebe begged her bad side to stay right where it was, though she wanted to handle him so bad she could taste it. She counted to three, stood, and screamed toward his exit, "Horny ass bastard. That'll be the most expensive pussy run of your entire life." Instead of hurrying down the stairs, chasing behind him, as much as her nerve tried to convince her to, she ran to the bedroom window, parting the ebony pleated curtains and eyeing him again, praying looks could kill.

He approached his Porsche, which was parked in the circular driveway, and tossed the suitcase inside, jumping in, revving his engine, and driving off.

At her side as she watched him leave, Rebe was holding a large red hammer she'd hidden behind her back, and as much as she had it in her to throw it through the window like a heat-seeking cheater missile, something made her drop it onto the hardwood floor. It hit with a thud and chipped a strip of mahogany, and she crumbled to the floor, fighting with all her might to chase away the feeling of wanting to kill him with one blow. It was in her.

That night Rebe realized what it felt like to want to kill someone.

Him.

Or herself.

Also that night, Randall Richardson's W hotel mistress, who was indeed named Kandi, the woman whom he'd just bought the new Mustang for, got pregnant. She since went by the name of Mrs. Kandi Richardson.

Included in the divorce settlement was Rebe's white CL-Class Benz, which she traded in for a brand-new one, sunset red; and she was awarded the home they'd shared, which he quitclaimed to her.

In spite of Randall's unwillingness to fight for Rebe,

he did care for her twenty-one-year-old daughter Trinity. He was the only father Trinity had ever known, and she loved him something deep.

To Trinity, the breakup of Randall and her mom was all her mother's doing, even though Randall was the one who cheated. To her, it was her mother's own fault that she was, as Trinity put it, a lonely and bitter divorcée.

Speaking of Trinity, she had just walked downstairs from her room.

Rebe quickly shook herself from her recollection of her marriage breakup drama.

"Where're you going?" Rebe asked her daughter, holding one particular letter in hand.

"Out." Trinity placed the keys to her new silver Mustang on the island right where her mother sat. It was the Mustang that Randall bought her, which matched his new wife's car. Trinity, very thin, very tall, very light, with very long hair and very big eyes, was very pretty. She opened the door that led from the kitchen to the backyard, leaning down in her tight jeans to pet their chocolate Labrador named Randi. She was given to Trinity by Randall as a birthday gift. And she named it after him.

Rebe often joked she felt it appropriate that a K-9 was named after a dog like Randall. She couldn't even stand the sound of Randi's name, let alone the sight of her.

"And who are you going *out* with?" Rebe asked with an impatient glare.

Trinity's tone shifted to a high pitch, definitely not intended for her mother. "Hi, baby, that's my baby. Such a pretty girl. That's my Randi. Yep. That's her."

Randi ran circles around Trinity's feet and tried hard

to sneak past her into the house toward Rebe, but Trinity blocked her way. "Come back, now. Stop." Trinity pointed and Randi ran back outside into the grand backyard. Trinity closed the door and locked it. She stepped to the island and picked up her keys, giving a quick look to her mom, who only stared at her. Tapping her foot. Hand now on her hip. Waiting.

Trinity spoke with the tone she saved only for her mother. "Why do you even ask? You sound like I'm still in middle school."

"I ask because you *act* like you're in middle school. Like school is still free. I'm paying for you to go to college and you end up letting your grades slip again like this, after all this time?" Rebe held up the letter.

"Mommy, I'm the only one of my friends whose parents get sent a copy of their grades. Why are you still all up in my business, like that? Dang." Trinity popped her tongue from the roof of her mouth.

Rebe turned her ear toward her daughter. "Like what? Did I hear you right? Let's say like because the last time you messed up we decided I'd be copied on your progress reports. The day you pay your own tuition, and move from under my roof, I'll get out of your 'business.' But for now, you're throwing money in the trash every time you fail one of these classes, Trinity. This is supposed to be your senior year and you're a junior. Now what is really going on with you?"

Her eyebrows lowered. "Why do you always remind me that you pay for my school? Don't you think I know that?"

"It seems to me you need to be reminded of it. And I'll tell you what's going on. What's going on is you're hanging out too much. You and your friends are always on the run. You were out almost every night last week. Now here it is the second day of a new year, and you're trying to start it just the way you ended 2008, by always going somewhere in that fast car Randall bought you. You've gotta do better than this once the spring semester starts."

Trinity's arms were folded along her chest. "I'm fine, Mommy. And please don't remind me that I have the same car Kandi has." She rolled her eyes and all but rolled her neck. "Anyway, it's still Christmas break. Everybody's having fun. You're making it a much bigger deal. It's normal."

"You should be about to graduate. Being on the brink of academic probation is not normal at this point."

"I'm not going to let it get that far, Mommy."

"How do I know that?"

"Because I'm telling you it won't."

"So I'm supposed to just take your word for it? I don't think so. We need to make a plan for these next five or six months. I think you need to meet with another counselor." Rebe looked down at the letter, perusing it for more information.

"I am meeting with one. On my own. That was part of the agreement when this year started. Meeting with a counselor and a tutor. I only failed one class. Lay off, please."

Rebe looked up, eyes big enough to pop. "Lay off? No, I will not lay off. You need to appreciate the fact that you've got a mother who can afford to pay for your college. You don't work. And you live rent free."

Trinity let the weight of her head drop, and then she

looked back up. "Why do you keep saying a mother who can afford it?"

"And what does that mean?"

"Isn't Randall paying, really?" She said *really* like it had sixty letters instead of six.

Rebe pointed her index finger Trinity's way. "You listen to me. Randall isn't paying for anything that has to do with you, other than that car, which he seems good at buying for just about anybody. He's not your father and you're not a minor, so there's no child support order. He's paying alimony because I deserve it. It's my money. And besides, that's none of your damn business, Trinity. You need to be grateful that you can live in a home like this. And as far as you talking back to me, I don't know where the hell that came from. My mother would've beat the shit out of me if I talked to her like you talk to me."

"I'm sure." Trinity all but mumbled.

Rebe bit her lip, squinted her eyes, and then balled up the letter, lobbing it straight into the trash can near the sink, like a free throw.

Trinity put one hand on the island, and one hand on her hip. "Mommy. Let me get a job and get a place of my own. I can get hired at Starbucks tomorrow."

"You know the deal. You working a job and going to school will not mix. Your grades are bad enough as it is."

Trinity crossed her arms again. "Have you ever thought that maybe I just might do better on my own?"

"No."

Trinity gave her mother a *you get on my last nerve* look. A look that Rebe was very familiar with. It was the same look she used to give her mother. Rebe heard her inner voice telling her to take a breath and downshift, and so she asked her daughter again, "So, where are you going?"

Trinity tossed her keys back onto the island. "Nowhere now." She gave a fake smile.

Rebe stood. "Oh, so I ruined your going somewhere mood? That's funny." She headed toward the front door.

"Umh."

Rebe slowed down her step, and wanted to turn back so bad she could taste it.

"Where are you going?" Trinity's words were marinated with sarcasm.

"To the gym. I'll be back." Rebe took her purse from the wooden coat rack near the front door. She waited to hear a response. All she heard were her daughter's weighted footsteps headed up the stairs. The footsteps of a daughter who had no idea her mother was going to pole dancing class.

Going to a pole dancing class with the dream, and New Year's resolution, of being a paid exotic dancer.

INT.—CRUNCH GYM—MIAMI BEACH—EVENING
That same day

It was just after seven that same evening. There were six brown women, three red poles, and one dirty-blonde instructor with what looked like four-inch eyelashes and six-inch platforms. She was mid-thirties and had a non-impressive body. No chest or backside, average legs and face. But, when she made the pole her friend, she was a sexpot, jackpot, seductress.

As everyone sat on the floor in their platform stilettos, in the large exercise room of the popular, state-of-the-art gym, the instructor anchored the pole and then did an around-the-world spin move, grinding in the air and sliding her body up and down, along her back. She broke out into a full split, and kicked her leg around to come to a stance, standing against the pole with her hand gripping its width. Her voice was feminine and steady. She looked around at her new students and then took a seated yoga position among them. "Now, first thing. Relax. Just sit like this for a minute and breathe, in through your nose, out through your mouth, and get your body to simply go limp. Do that now because once you start working that pole, you're going to need those joints and muscles to be all loosened up and ready to work. Bottom line is this is exercise. It's a workout. And judging by the looks of you ladies today, this just might be my best class yet. Now, let's get started."

After the ten minute warm-up, three of the ladies stood and leaned their backs against the pole, keeping their hands about waist high, following the instructor's lead. They bent their knees slightly, pushed their hips out to the right and then forward and in a circle, again and again, in a sexy grind.

Rebe flung her braids forward with her hand and rubbed the middle of her back up and down the pole.

The instructor stopped before her and said, "I see you're having fun."

Rebe nodded, staying focused, and smiled, keeping up the movement.

They each slid down a pole and reached upward, using upper body strength to lift their feet and press their legs to the side.

Within another half hour, after more moves were taught, the instructor stood next to Rebe and leaned in toward her as Rebe completed a complicated pole trick. "You're a natural. I can see it already."

"Natural what?"

"You've danced before. That much I know."

"Oh, yes. I have. Years ago."

"It shows."

One of the other students overheard, a butterican, toasted-pecan-looking young girl who turned up her nose and walked away.

Rebe said softly, "Thanks. Just trying to get in shape. I think a few more times doing that move and it's gonna hurt right around here." Rebe rubbed the inside of her right thigh.

"Oh it will. And every other place too. You will have bruises. It's no joke."

"I can tell."

The instructor said in an even more private tone, "Listen, if you ever think about doing this to make some money, let me know. As you can imagine, I get a lot of calls from strip club managers looking for dancers."

Rebe's thought was that this was too easy. "I'll bet you do. I need a whole lot more work, even if I did decide to try it out."

"What are you, like, thirty-two?" the instructor asked.

"Ahh, close." Rebe realized that indirect dishonesty was in order.

"Nice," she said, walking away to speak to the group, grabbing on to the pole again herself. "Okay ladies, next we'll do what's called the martini spin. You stand beside the pole, like this, with your inside arm up high and your inside hand at chest level. Bring your outside leg in front of the pole. Now extend your leg straight out while spinning and hook it around while shifting your body weight forward. Make sure to bring your leg up quickly, shoot it straight out, and slide down slowly. Then tuck your leg to bring yourself back up. Now try it."

The ladies went through about another forty-five minutes of learning that and other moves, and then headed to the locker room to get dressed. As Rebe sat down, her dance instructor approached.

"You've got a lot of strength. I have this friend who owns a place in Fort Lauderdale. I'll tell him about you. If you want to do this on the side of your normal job, he just might be willing to hire you."

"Oh, I don't work," Rebe said, trying not to sound like a millionaire with issues.

"Really? Are you married?"

"No."

"Single is better if you think you might try this out."

"I might be interested."

"I'll see you in a couple days for the next class. I'll tell him about you."

"Okay."

When the instructor walked away, Rebe glanced up at the ceiling and said in her head, *Lord, my mother would beat my ass for even thinking about doing something like this. And dammit, that's all the more reason to give it a try.*

Six

"Computer Love"

Magnolia

INT.—MAGNOLIA'S BEDROOM—MIAMI BEACH—
LATE EVENING
January 26, 2009

Neal still called.

Magnolia still didn't answer.

He still sent text messages.

Magnolia still ignored them.

He found excuses to get in touch. Like asking if she'd watched the historical Presidential Inauguration six days before.

She didn't reply.

She had, but was determined to not act like they were simply old friends.

Though she ignored his repeated initiated contact, she still checked his online account balance, trying to figure out his spending habits, just as she did when they were together.

Magnolia took a sip of Pinot Noir from her leopard wine glass and then talked to herself.

Why is this man still in my head? I haven't slept with

him in months. Maybe it's my ego. Maybe I just like the at-
tention. Maybe I'm a hopeless romantic. A dumb, foolish,
hopeless ass romantic.

Magnolia spoke to her confused self after midnight,
up way too late for a Monday. While sitting in the executive chair at her large desk in her pale-purple bedroom,
walls adorned with pricey floral abstract artwork, she
searched the web on her laptop.

She lived in a sprawling, twenty-eight-hundred-
square-foot, three-bedroom ranch in the Miami Shores
area of Miami Beach. It was more than enough room
for a single solitary bachelorette. The pale yellow stucco
house with the red clay roof sat neatly at the end of a
cul-de-sac. The side entry, two-car garage had white car-
riage doors.

Her diffuser burned Thai fruit scented oil all through
her bedroom suite. The amber nightlight near her dresser
was subtle. The screen of her computer shined light on
her curious face. She had the overhead fan at medium
speed to cool the effects of another warm day in January,
including the warmth exuding from her heated loins.

Heated because the words *meet, real, sex, partners,*
tonight, filled Magnolia's eyes, all the result of her viewing the website GrownFreakyFolks.com, the site she
kept getting emails about, especially lately.

The tagline said "Swingers, Free Adult Chat, and
Adult Personals." The home page offered links for live
webcam viewing of videos in every category from guy-
on-guy, to Latin love, to whatever. GFF, as it was called,
was a freakazoid's playground.

Magnolia's newbie heart skipped one beat after another. Anticipatory.

She sighed a virgin sex-site sigh, taking in the X-rated screen before her. Photos of members named LickitySplit, HeadLover, and BlackSugarDaddy were exposed before her in graphic nude poses with sex dripping from their heads to their toes.

She sat up straight, only wearing an orange bra and matching lace boy shorts, scooted closer...and clicked Join, typing her new screen name as if she'd thought of it beforehand, MaggieVirgin. "Never use your real name," she said aloud, recalling what some dating expert said one time on television. Forcing her thoughts to get a grip and shift to the land of the wild, brave, and sexalicious, she deleted MaggieVirgin and tried TightandRight, then CurvesAhead. Taken. SomeSkill. She shook her head and said, "Not."

TastyTangie. Her adventurous brain gave a finger snap. "That's it. But how the hell would I know if I'm tasty or not?" She hit Enter. Accepted. Welcome TastyTangie. Credit card information entered, and she was an official online adult friend.

After twenty minutes of filling out her profile, setting preferences, revealing boundaries, detailing turn-offs, turn-ons, and turn-outs, and such tantalizing bits of info, her profile was nearly complete. All but the photo.

Damn. Can't put my headshot on here. Nothing but ladies' body parts and men's dicks. Oh boy. Well, Magnolia, you need to quit playing. You've gone this far. She made up her mind to play nice.

Grabbing her digital camera from the bookcase above her desk, she got up and stepped along the cool bamboo flooring, and headed straight to her queen canopy bed. She lay back on the black and white flowered comforter with the mauve covered pillows, and pulled off her boy shorts. She positioned the camera right between her legs and felt a flutter in her stomach. She sensed the beat of her shocked heart against the mattress. "No way I'm showing my landing strip vagina for the world to see." She sat up and took off her orange bra. Her heavy breasts hung free and she looked down at them as if she was waiting for them to perk themselves up and participate. Magnolia lifted one up and it drooped back down. She put her bra back on. "This is gonna have to be a bra cleavage shot."

She stood in front of the dresser mirror, turned off the flash and took the picture, but it was too dark. She turned the flash back on and again aimed the camera toward her, looking at the viewfinder through the mirror. Click. She got a shot from her neck to her upper belly that she thought made her breasts look two sizes larger, but she said, "That's gonna have to do."

Within an hour after adding her sexy pic, TastyTangie was already invited to accept a chat with five members, in particular, Carl10Inches, who lived within ten miles. Thirty minutes after chatting with him back and forth, she blocked the number to her cell, grabbed ahold of her nerve, and made her virgin call to a stranger she'd met on a sex site.

"Hello." His voice was deep and slow, sort of like a Barry White baritone.

"Hi. Carl?" she asked, talking fast. Her voice was shaky.

"Yes. Tangie?"

"Uh-huh." She said it as though she just might be lying.

"How are you? You nervous?"

"A little."

"Don't be. Just first-time jitters."

She nodded as if he could see her. "So, you're used to this, I see?" she told him, making it sound like a question.

"Yeah. Sort of. I found GFF about a year or so ago."

"I see." There was a lull. Magnolia cleared her throat.

He spoke up. "So. What are you looking for on a site like this?"

"I don't know."

"Just curious?" he asked.

"You could say that."

"I will tell you one thing. You need to be careful, especially if you do end up meeting up with anyone. Make sure you don't take valuables with you, and maybe if you have a friend you can trust, you can tell them where you're going. Don't go to anybody's home. Only hotels. And even then, as a single woman, be aware. Make sure no one is using his or her cell or laptop to tape you. You know, all I'm saying is, be careful."

She smiled, barely. "Okay. That's nice of you to tell me that."

"No problem. You really sound sexy."

"Thanks."

"Kind of sultry."

"Really?"

"Really. Making my dick hard the more I hear you talk."

"I see."

"Tangie."

"Yes."

"Is your pussy wet?"

Damn, he got right to it. "I don't know."

"Check."

Magnolia went from the desk chair to her bed, sat on the end and parted her legs a little, inserting her finger, playing along. "Yeah. It is."

"Wetter than usual?"

"Yes." She cleared her throat like it would clear her mind. "I'm not used to talking like this with someone I don't know."

"Then think of me as someone you do know. Pretend I'm an old friend. A friend from college, and now we've connected. Pretend you're going to see me this weekend, but until then, we talk about the good old times together, like how you'd sit on my face every morning."

"I would?" Magnolia found herself leaning back.

"You would. We'd call it the good morning hello. And you'd let me eat your pussy till you'd damn near smother me when you'd come. How you slid down to my dick and rode me, bucking like you were pumping for dear life."

"Ummm." She rubbed her thighs, and then her pussy lips.

"And then you rose up from my dick and faced the other way, getting on your knees, and you raised my legs and backed it up so I could watch your ass clap."

"Uh-huh." She again stuck her middle finger inside. Her wetness was seeping.

"You do have a big ass, don't you Tangie?"

"Uh-huh."

"Good. Do me a favor. Put the phone up to your pussy and finger-fuck yourself so I can hear it."

Magnolia found herself doing just as she was told, placing her cell to her opening with one hand, and sliding her finger in and out to the sound of her creamy juices. Loud juices. Louder than she thought it would be. She put the phone back to her ear. "Did you like that?" Her tone was suddenly X-rated.

He moaned deep. "I did. I almost nutted. But first, I want you to taste it for me."

"Taste it?"

"Yeah. Stick your fingers in your mouth and tell me what it tastes like."

She immediately licked her own juices from her finger. "It tastes sweet. Different. And it smells good."

"Good. Now suck your finger like you're sucking my dick. And let me hear that shit."

She did.

He sounded as though he was in pillow talk overdrive. "See, I'm about to. Damn, Tangie. Suck it. Suck that big dick. Uggh. Uggh. Aww." And Carl came for Magnolia, or Tangie, or whomever, over the phone. He kept groaning and made the sound of a deep, yanking grunt.

Magnolia kept listening as Carl10Inches flowed through his solo ecstasy. Her mind was surprised at how loud and turned on he was. She lost her erotic groove for a minute and waited until he stopped.

Within one minute, his voice was instantly normal. "Good girl. And next time, we'll get on the webcam. You do have a webcam right?"

"I do."

"Cool. I'll be in touch online. Good night Tangie."

"Good night."

And he hung up. Magnolia sat up and said, "Well I'll be damn. What if I'd wanted to get mine? His ass could've cared less."

She heard a chime on her computer and stood up, noticing another chat icon that had popped up. She spoke to her kinky laptop. "No. Not tonight. Let me get over that shit first." She prepared to turn it off as she stood over the screen, pantieless, and saw that it read, LeanAndJean. A couple. "Bye, LeanAndJean." Magnolia shut it down. She looked over and glanced at herself in the dresser mirror.

"Dammit, I took that picture with my chain on. Duh."

Seven

"Let's Get It On"

Darla

INT.—DARLA'S CONDO—MIAMI BEACH—EARLY
MORNING
January 30, 2009

Once Again.
    Bed by ten.
She lay in a fetal position.
Mind on her money.
Money on her mind.
Darla's body was barely covered by a peach, lace-trimmed negligee with elbow length sleeves, front ties in black, and black panties. It was only one of a ton of lingerie she had in the cedar chest at the foot of her walnut sleigh bed.

She lived in what was a $450,000 condo four years ago when she purchased it, but it was now worth a little more than $300,000. The eighteen-hundred-square-foot condo was nestled on the eleventh floor of a fourteen-story building. It had been revived to contemporary standards, but still had all the old charm and glamour of the 1950s in Miami, a city also called New York South.

Her taste was beige and black, and every piece of her décor reflected the classy contrasts. The fully tiled natural floors were beige with black borders. The corner balcony exposed the full nuance of downtown Miami, and the Atlantic Ocean, which served as her backyard.

Darla's mind luxuriated in the grand fantasy of what the possibilities of her new business could be. And also, she stressed about where she'd get enough money to open a business, let alone to catch up on her expenses.

She'd found a couple of places she knew were a little too pricey, but the notion of location, location, location kept running through her head. She kept envisioning her store and what it would look like, who would be the first customer, and how her "lingerie boutique" would be the talk of the town, curing her from her money woes, if she could just get a loan.

She was thrilled that it was Friday, and that she had the whole weekend ahead of her, which meant two whole days of not having to deal with the people at the dental office where she worked.

She'd been there for over ten years, working as a dental technician, and even though she had a bachelor's degree in merchandising, at the encouragement of her now deceased husband, she went back to get her two-year education at a dental school where she earned her certificate in dental technology.

But she hated working in the dental field. She was way too creative for that. She loved fashion, and the sexy lingerie she wore under her clothes. She loved unusual, comfortable, pretty, girlie undergarments. The fabric and look made her feel like a sex goddess. It made her feel desirable, framing the curves of her queen-sized body. Her unmentionables were not mentioned. They were on the down low, her own little secret she didn't dare share.

When Aaron was still alive, she only worked a few days a week, a few hours a day. But once he passed, she had no choice but to work full time in a field that didn't fit her. And the day-to-day drama at her office was weighing on her heavily. Even causing her to eat more, sit around at home and think, simply working during the day and spending time with herself at night, and occasionally with Rebe and Magnolia. Other than that, she was alone.

The one person she should've been spending more time with was her father. But she seemed to make excuses not to see him. As much as she wanted to spend time with the man who was her heart and soul, for her, it just seemed like they were two pathetic widowed souls, surviving but not living, experiencing life alone against their will, vowing to be true to the one that God had other plans for. It sometimes made her sadder. Just like with her mother-in-law, it reminded her of what once was, but now wasn't.

And of course she didn't date. She didn't even have date options. Last summer there was a man, a handsome Hispanic, who came in for an appointment. When she walked past him in the lobby, he tried to hit on her. But to Darla, he was half the size she liked her men to be. He was thin and short. Darla liked them almost heavy, and very tall. Not a man who was one-quarter her size. It only reminded her how big she was. She liked them to look just like Aaron did. Big.

But now, to her, it seemed as though she couldn't

even get a starving man to look at her even if she had a pork chop dangling from her neck.

Darla, aside from her financial problems, was lonely.

And as much as she fought the very feelings that sometimes, more than others, slapped her on the ass...she was horny.

For some reason tonight, the tall stranger Rebe met on New Year's Eve named DeMarius, was on Darla's mind. Rebe joked that he fucked her so hard that if she'd gotten pregnant, she would've had twins. And the fact that he wore Rebe out till the break of dawn was taking up Darla's imaginary mind. She felt the call of the wild tonight. And it was loud.

Darla threw the white cotton sheets off her body, leaned over to look under her bed, and opened her trusty old shoebox where she and Aaron used to hide their grown-folk toys. She'd gotten rid of some of the items, too many memories she thought. But she replaced them with a few movies she'd watch from time to time. The one she hadn't watched before caught her attention. It was called *Three the Hard Way*.

Darla took it out, got up, placed it in the DVD player on her dresser, and grabbed the remote, snuggling back into bed, propping up the bed pillows behind her head.

Darla pressed Play and fast-forwarded to the real action. The shot of two men and one woman. The woman was sitting on a sofa in an office, one man was going down on her, the other was on the couch next to her, on his knees, and she was sucking his long, thin dick. The young woman with short red hair could barely get all his length down her throat without gagging, and he seemed to enjoy the sound and sight of that even more, placing his hand behind her head to align her mouth for her precise deep throat.

The man on his knees got a good steady tongue groove going, and the woman, who looked like she just couldn't help herself, paused her sucking to focus on the supreme oral sensation. She quivered, shook, and bumped her vagina toward his face, threw her head back with one hand still on the other man's dick, and she ripped a fast orgasm, shouting to the sex powers that be, saying, "Thank you. Yes."

Darla squinted and said, "Damn." Her eyes, and mind, continued.

The man who'd made her come traded places with the man on the couch, who got between her long legs and inserted his dick all the way back to her cervix, and she took it, deep inside, all while the pussy eater's dick was in her mouth. He wasn't as large as the other man, so she handled it better, but he gave conniption-fit sounds like he just couldn't take it. He revved up, and at the same time, the man between her legs revved up.

By now, Darla, who had pulled her nightgown up and her panties down, had two fingers deep inside of herself, finger-fucking her pussy slow and deep, trying to get a good angle as deep as she could, and with the other hand, she flicked her right nipple and twisted it, feeling it get stiffer and stiffer as she played with herself. Darla grinded toward her hand and watched the two men wind down from their ecstasy.

She closed her eyes for a moment and thought about what Rebe must've been feeling, being done by the big man, and she started to warm up, getting wetter, and the more she pictured them, him inside of her, her taking all of him, the more Darla began to feel the build up of her own excitement and it felt forbidden.

She slowed down and the fantasy vision was replaced. All she could think about was Aaron, on top of her, grunting and groaning, exploring the pussy he'd known for so long, that belonged to him and him alone, getting her in a deep missionary, working Darla just like the last time they had sex. He moved faster and faster, frantically digging inside of her tightness, sperm shooting from his penis into the crevices of her vagina, when he made a sound like he was swallowing hard, and his mouth flew open. To her, Aaron was growing heavier and heavier, and more still, and he stiffened from head to toe. She looked at the side of his face and could tell that his eyes were bugged to the extreme.

He looked shocked and pained.

And he collapsed on top of her.

Dead.

Just as he'd died in real life five years ago.

Tonight, two minutes later, it was panties up, video off, and under the sheets in a fetal position.

Darla's sex life, even her masturbatory sex life, would have to wait once again.

As well as the exploration of experiencing an orgasm.

Which she'd never had in her entire conservative life.

Eight

"Seduction"

Rebe

INT.—MAKE IT RAIN GENTLEMEN'S CLUB—FORT
LAUDERDALE—LATE EVENING
February 4, 2009

The hot pink sign outside flashed a neon busty bur-
lesque girl with shapely long legs. It read, *Make It
Rain Gentlemen's Club* and was located on a dead-end
street of an older Fort Lauderdale business park.

It was a Wednesday night, the most popular night,
and the parking lot was full. It was the night when the
virgin amateur dancers would get their introductory exhibitionist chance. And Rebe would be one of them.

The place was speaker-bumping loud.

It was fantasy-mood dark.

And it was cigarette-burning smoky.

The main room was big and round with a circular
stage. Three rows of padded stackable chairs surrounded
it. Up against the walls were royal-blue velvet sofas with
curvy dancers straddling the laps of hungry men, and
hungry women, at twenty dollars a pop and more.

The music was funky and fast, soulful and trendy,

talking about drop it, pop it, bend it, and make it clap. Fit females worked their moves, making love to the pole while their fans with penis-poles between their legs wished to be her sole focus of desire.

As pasties and rhinestone G-string wearing, six-foot-one Trixie Blue left the stage, Lil Wayne's "Lollipop" began at full blast, and Rebe, aka Queenie, who'd been hired the week before, strutted on next, with her long, lean body adorned by a shimmering silver thong and thick clear platforms. Her mocha skin had a thin glossing of silver body glitter, and she wore a hint of an insecure gleam in her huge eyes, which were lined with royal blue and black, extreme false eyelashes.

Queenie stood tall at the very front of the stage. She fought to not drop her chin at the sight of the lustful twinkle in the eyes of those who took in her scantily clad vision. She shook it off by poking out her chest, shoulders back, while flinging her long braids from left to right, and then she turned her backside toward two suit-wearing businessmen sitting front and center. She had a mental moment with her old self. *You can do this. You need to do this. It's okay.* It was her way of talking to the preacher's kid inside of her, or as Rebe would call it, pseudo-preacher. It was her own personal self-esteem pep talk that she'd been doing for years whenever she needed to brace herself for what she was told would send her straight to hell.

She took a deep breath and bent over, sliding her thong down her hips, dropping it to her ankles, and kicking it off near the pole. The club's policy was that it was sexier to not take it all off, so what she wore underneath was a skinny black G-string that was barely enough fabric to shield her fat, waxed, brownish-red pussy lips. She stood still for a moment, again taking in the full attention from all eyes on her, and forced a major breath through her nose along with a forced weak smile.

Though to her the word *sinner* buzzed in her head, her heart told her she was the woman. It actually pounded beats of excitement for her as though giving her two thumbs-up like it was enjoying the powerful adrenaline that was rushing through her veins. It hadn't felt the feeling enough.

And her admirers agreed with her heart. Just as she accepted the odd feeling of her own thirst of the moment, their naughty faces spelled a matching hunger of approval for more. When they hooted and called with dollar bills in hand, she took three big, sultry steps to the golden pole that awaited her skills, and leaned back along it, immediately doing her mastered, martini spin move, sliding her limber body around and around, then lifting her legs higher and higher toward the top until she was upside down. Her braids hung and swayed and her scissor move exposed a tad bit of what she was working with, even her new, gold-studded clitoris peeked through and winked. She pulled her legs together and flipped to her feet, rubbing on herself with passion while she approached a young man on the side of the stage who was holding a crisp new twenty.

Queenie got down on her knees and crawled closer like a cautious feline, arching her back and poking her ass out as far as she could. She felt a sensation that made her flinch all over. The heated turn on was foreign but friendly.

She pressed her tits together and eyed him down while he examined her cleavage. His green-eyed gaze was locked. He had a face like he was barely old enough to drink, no facial hair whatsoever, and his hair was short and curly. His skin was so light, he was banana-beige. He wore chocolate diamond studs in his ears.

She admired the sight of him and moved in even closer.

He inhaled the smell of her skin, the scent of Escape, and folded the crisp bill, inserting it in and out between her breasts like a credit card, like the twenty was getting its own tittie fuck. He then placed the bill inside the string of her skimpy undies, just along her hip bone and said, "Damn. Umm, umm, umm." He unglued his eyes and scooted them to her face. "If I could have you to myself, I swear I'd never set foot in here again."

She grinded her hips and replied, "Oh, you wouldn't, huh?"

He spoke low. "Never. And just so you know, there's more where that came from. When are you on the floor?"

"Hang around and find out. I'll find you," she whispered.

"You do that, Queenie." His sights shifted toward her pussy. "You got the right one there." And then to her ass. "Your body is so sick. You are definitely the queen of this place."

She blushed and blinked. "Thanks, Babyface." Queenie slowly backed up her crawl and rose to her feet, pulling the twenty from her G-string, stepping to the pole where she placed it along the floor as she began rubbing her hands along her nearly forty-year-old flat stomach, making sure to glance back at him, giving him a look as if to say she could take him right there on the stage if he'd dare to try. Her eyes spoke the dirty actress dare only for a few moments, and then she looked away at the waves of men who gave lustful stares, men sure to use her visual image for their own sexual mind-rendezvous later. Some shook their heads like she was the goddess of their worlds, and some whistled like she should come to them and give them a whiff as well. There were even three women who sat in the second row with their legs crossed, saying nothing to each other, just admiring, one looking at Queenie's tits, licking her lips.

A few of the men in the front row stood and all at once released their handfuls of cash onto the stage in front of her, literally making it rain. She watched the money fall to the floor and said inside her head, *Damn. That was easy.* She felt an odd sense of approval.

The song wound down and she ended her striptease with a money stroll, sexily picking up all the cash that was sprinkled along the floor of the stage.

The DJ spoke loudly from his booth by the door. "Let's hear it for Queenie. Our newest dancer here at Make It Rain. She looks like a sexy pro if you ask me. No amateur there. And up next we have Loveliness, who sure is that. Give her a big hand of appreciation," he yelled, as if the next contestant, who was a pretty, butch dancer, were coming out for an *American Idol* audition. He played "Seduction" by Usher. The ladies in the crowd, especially, stood tall, bills ready.

Rebe looked over at her baby-faced friend.

Her first-time admirer.

He gave a wink with his thick, long lashes.

She winked back.

And in one second she was backstage. "That shit made me hot," she said to another dancer who was bent over in the mirror backward to check the correctness of the opening of her own vagina.

"Oh, you must be new," the tall, tanned dancer—a mix of German and Sudanese—sounded totally amazed, almost disgusted.

Thirty minutes later, the champagne room was occupied by four other men, and Babyface. The men were getting private dances from their chosen ladies, at least for the current song, "Sexual Seduction," by Snoop. And Queenie was Babyface's choice.

He asked while sitting on an armless chair, scooted back, strategically wearing loose gray sweatpants without underwear, with his legs spread wide open, "So, where've you been?" in a low, slow voice to the curve of her long back as she did a reverse cowgirl, moving her shape in a dance of erotic, simulated intercourse.

"What do you mean? Like why haven't you seen me here before? Is that what you're asking?" She worked her ass cheeks along his crotch. His member was at full attention, and she could feel every inch of it. Queenie was wet.

He said while fidgeting as though battling himself to not put his hands along her slender waist to guide her X-rated grind, "Exactly. Newbie. This is amateur night."

"Okay, so then why did you ask where I've been then?" She had a hint of a smart-ass tone to her words, like she'd been around.

"I meant all my life." His vision stayed on her cheeks

that pressed against his lap. He looked like he had imaginations of his dick deep inside her while he'd play lazy, letting her do all the aerobic work.

"I've been in my skin, how's that?" She still spoke spunky, and raised her body inch-by-inch, enough to bring her leg around to straddle him, facing his torso. Her neck was right around the area of his mouth. He got ready to speak, but instead she said, "You talk too much."

"No rule against talking. Makes it seem more like you're my girl, for real."

"Okay." The tone of her reply hinted that his words were corny, but her body moved like he was a stud, saying all the right things. She readjusted herself so she could feel his total thickness between her legs. He smelled like manly mango. She breathed hard and exhaled soft. In her mind she said, *Please song, don't end yet.*

"Yeah, you're new all right." He pumped back and rubbed back as she slid along his dick. The fabric of his sweats was moist, and not all from his seepage alone.

She talked near his ear, pressing her full breasts along his chest. "Well, I guess you'd know because I'm willing to bet you're a regular."

She could feel his breath along her collarbone as he spoke. "You could say that. Been coming here for years."

She backed her chest away slightly and gave his virgin face a good once over. The full-grown occupant living below his waist didn't match the puberty-like look above the neck. "Since you're what, about twelve? 'Cause you certainly don't look legal."

He raised his bushy eyebrows, looking assured. "I'm old enough, believe me."

She put her hands on her own thighs and raised her hips up and down, shoving her vagina to his dick, and moving it back, shoving it forward again. Her thighs flexed. "Just barely, I'll bet."

"Speak for yourself." He looked at the definition in her legs. "Youngster."

"Please. I've got bras older than you." Queenie adjusted herself to turn around again and bent down to the floor with her hands grasping her ankles, making sure the exact point of her opening met his shaft.

He sucked his teeth and said, "Ooooo." And then spoke after a sigh. "I doubt that. But even if you do, I'm down for what I see. I'd put a ring on this, no doubt."

She giggled softly.

He groaned and let her do her thing, looking like he could simply explode in his pants.

She leaned her back against him, bringing her hands to the back of his neck, interlocking her fingers, with her long micro-braids draped behind the both of them.

He smiled and sniffed her again, and his dick pulsated. He said with his eyes closed, "You like me, don't you?"

Her eyes were half-closed, "Feeling what's in your pants, I'd say *you're* the one who likes me." She sat straight up just as the last beats of the song wound down. "But like I said, you talk too much. You're done." She stood and ran her fingers through her braids, readjusting her thong.

He reached into his Nike shirt pocket and pulled out a hundred with a Post-it stuck to it, folding the bill into quarters. "I'll see you later." He handed it to her. "Take this and make sure you keep the note. Queenie."

She did, and kept it up in her hand. "Maybe so."

He looked down at himself, shook out all three legs, and stood up, readjusting his placement.

She asked, eyes looking baby-girlish, "You aren't leaving, are you?"

"Yes."

She walked on and he followed. She knew it.

His eyes zoomed in on her orgasm-prompting behind. He simply watched, looking like he was taking a mental snapshot.

Rebe's eyes said without blinking, *Oh no*, to him leaving, but Queenie simply said a carefree, "Bye."

Nine

"Whenever, Wherever, Whatever"

Magnolia

INT.—MAGNOLIA'S HOME AND WORKPLACE—
MIAMI BEACH—MORNING
February 9, 2009

Magnolia awoke on Monday morning after a relaxing weekend, getting her head right to go back to what she called the slave factory. She joked about the concept of working for the master, but loved her work and always seemed to head to her office with the realization that she was happy to be employed.

She'd usually lie still for a moment after turning off the alarm clock. She liked to listen to the birds singing outside her window. When she was young, her grandmother would tell her to take the time to listen. That it always seemed as though birds sang in the early morning. That it may have been because at dawn, sound broadcasts can be more effective than at midday. But also birds use song to communicate, and that it's usually the babies who awake to the light, looking for the mothers who've gone off to forage for food for their younglings upon the rising of the sun. It would make

Magnolia think of when her own mother left. She wasn't the type to come back, though. In her heart, she wanted a chance to be the "coming back home" type of mother. The type whose babies would anticipate her nurturing, and sing to cheer on her return.

Still, with no husband or children after all these years, she accepted her reality and got up, placing her bare feet on the floor. She made her usual, slow trek to the walk-in closet to pick out one of her many business suits to wear to the bank. Today, it would be the black skirt and blazer with the yellow and blue watercolor print blouse. Teal pumps. Metallic bag. Hair back into a long ponytail, as usual.

She was the vice president of branch operations for Ocean Bank in its Miami Beach office on Arthur Godfrey Road, a newer building that served as the southern headquarters. She'd worked there for over a decade, making her way up from opening new accounts, to regionally supervising branches, to being assigned as a director at a branch near her home, and then overseeing the regional branches. Magnolia had earned her own spacious office, with a spectacular ocean view from the eighth floor.

A half knock sounded while Magnolia was at her oak desk at work, sitting in the brown ergonomic chair. Her door was ajar.

His Old Spice body wash hit her nose a second before her eyes could manage their journey. She looked up and her heart thumped while she gave a large swallow, and then scooted her eyes back to her work.

"Hey." Her ex-boyfriend and co-worker, Neal Graham, stepped inside after saying the one word. The forty-two-year-old assistant director for the real estate team serviced the southern Florida residential lending division.

Clean shaven with keen features, Neal was the color of coffee with a lot of cream, six-foot-four, black low-cut hair with a tinge of gray, and had the physique of a model, long and slender.

He wore his signature good-guy smile, flashed his perfect teeth and stood with one hand in the pants pocket of his Burberry, pinstriped two-button steel blue suit, looking as friendly as ever, as if nothing had even happened between them.

Magnolia had managed to avoid him since their last conversation on her birthday, until now, nearly five weeks later.

But still, she'd failed to ignore him emotionally.

"Hi," she said as bland as she could, on purpose.

"How's it going?"

"Fine." Pen in hand, she looked up for a second and noticed the colors of his tie matched her blouse.

"You've been avoiding me on purpose, huh?" His words were extra suave.

"Don't flatter yourself."

"You used to come over to the other side near my office once you got off the elevator. You'd even pass by my door when you'd go to the kitchen."

"What are you talking about?" A vertical line formed between her eyes.

"It's just that I never see you anymore. Just wondering if it's on purpose. Seeing if you're avoiding me."

"Wherever I need to go when I'm at work, I'm surely not thinking of, nor worried about running into you.

Believe me." She looked back down and began writing on a notepad.

"You say so."

"I say so."

He stared.

She gave him the evil eye. "What? What do you want?"

"I want you."

She put her pen down and began talking with her hand. "Neal, do not start this with me at work. I've got a job to do eight hours a day, maybe even more today than usual, and I am not trying to fool with you."

"How about after work? Can we meet? I've been trying to call you ever since the last time we spoke."

"No. I said no then, and I'm saying no now."

He removed his hand from his pocket. "Look, all I wanna do is talk. That's it. I think enough time's gone by. I mean, we can just sit down and take a moment to understand each other from where we are right now."

"Nope. Sorry." She sliced the sight of him and flipped though some papers.

"Mag."

"No. What I do understand is that you need to understand that I don't want to talk to you. Another thing I understand is that you have someone, someone you chose to be with. That's all I need to know."

His face looked serious. "Maybe, but I didn't want her more than you."

She flexed her hand. "You know, you really need to stop talking to me at work, I'm telling you."

"Then let me talk to you later. Please."

"No."

"Mag. I love you."

She pushed her chair away from her desk like she was prepared to stand. She struggled to keep her voice down, but her face looked like she was yelling. "Neal, cut it out, now. Don't make me start to complain to corporate about you. I'm telling you I will. Now, this is hard enough on both of us, but I'm asking you nicely, just like I would with anyone whose conversation is unwelcome. Please stop."

He took a step closer. "I can't believe you're acting like what we had is gone."

She stood. "Neal."

"Mag." He looked at her around her hip area, and then back up at her face. "I'm beginning to think even if you did tell HR, it'd be worth it. I need to talk to you. And I'm going to keep trying at work, on the phone, email, telefax, telephone, tell-a-friend. We are gonna talk. I'm not gonna stop trying."

She crossed her arms. "Well that's pretty dumb considering you already got your boss on your tail for screwing your secretary. I doubt you'd want them to know you're harassing me, when everyone knows what happened. They all know you live with her." She sat back down and closed a file folder.

"I do not." He licked his lips and looked out the window for a second, then looked back at her. "And Mag, I'm telling you now, I don't give a fuck what they think, to be honest with you."

Her tone grew louder again. "Yes you do." She shook her head and downshifted one notch. "You walk around here telling jokes and acting like you're campaigning for president. You don't want anyone to know your dirt."

"You think so? If I need to, I'll stand right here in front of your desk until you tell me we can talk away from work."

She pointed at him with her stare. "Neal, stop it. I'm warning you. Besides, your words are like a dull knife, baby. It just ain't cutting. You're talking loud, and saying absolutely nothing."

"Okay James Brown. But what you need to say is yes."

"No." She fought off a smirk.

Just then, a red-headed, stocky woman walked in, grinning from ear to ear. "Magnolia. These came for you at the front desk." The woman moved a large flower arrangement away from her own face so she could see in front of her. "I told the front desk I'd bring them to you. They're beautiful." She held a tall vase of a dozen red roses in her hands. And randomly mixed in between the roses were Magnolia's favorite flowers, white magnolias. "And they smell great."

Magnolia managed a small smile. "Thanks, Lynn. That's sweet of you. You can set them right here." She made room on the corner of her desk for the burgundy vase by moving a stack of papers.

"Sure." Lynn set the vase down and looked back, "Hello, Neal."

"Hi, Lynn. Those are nice." He kept his eyes on Magnolia.

Lynn stepped away and waved as she said, "See you later, Magnolia."

"Thanks."

Neal took a step closer. "Look at you. Somebody loves you."

She ignored his face and took the tiny card from the tiny envelope. It read the exact same thing. *Somebody loves you. Happy Belated Birthday. Neal.*

She gave him a quick glance, and no smile at all. "Thank you."

"No problem. I know what you like."

Her eyes told him to give her a break. "You really shouldn't have. You should've sent these to your woman. But I'm sure she gets flowers from you all the time."

"I sent these to you."

She put the card back in the envelope, taking a second to sniff one of the velvety roses, and then scooted the vase over farther, again looking down at her work.

Neal gave a lengthy clearing of his throat. "I'm still here."

She closed her eyes and exhaled. "Okay. Yes." And then she stared at him.

"Yes, what? Yes, you'll talk to me?"

"I said yes." Her eyes said don't push it.

"Good girl."

"Bye." Her voice sounded like a shove.

He faced the door and took one step with each word. "Tonight. Eight. My place."

"Fine."

"You'd better come."

She again resumed her work.

He gave a tug on his jacket lapel and walked away with a GQ stroll.

She looked over at the flowers and shook her head. *What in the hell am I doing?*

INT.—NEAL'S TOWNHOME—UPTOWN MIAMI—
EVENING

"Why are you so uptight?" Neal asked his ex-woman,
Magnolia Butler.

It was half past eight that evening.

Magnolia took a sip of Moscato d'Asti, placing the
gold-rimmed wine glass back on the clear Lucite coffee
table. "I'm not." Magnolia sat on Neal's white leather
sofa in the great room of his one-bedroom townhome.
The fifty-eight-inch plasma television was on, muted as
usual, showing a *Martin* rerun, and Neal played the An-
thony Hamilton CD, which was on "Can't Let Go,"
with Kem as his CD backup. Random candles were lit
and it smelled like he'd sprayed his pumpkin pie air
freshener, which mixed in the air with the smell of
seafood and garlic from the kitchen.

He lived on the fourth floor of the all-glass, swanky
twenty-eight story Onyx on the Bay condos on 25th
Street. His was a split-level modern unit with vaulted
ceilings, skylights, white floors, white countertops,
white furniture, and white marble stairs, on the water's
edge with a direct view of Biscayne Bay.

Neal, barefoot, who'd already changed into shorts
and a T-shirt, checked out Magnolia's body language—arms crossed, legs crossed, sitting forward, looking around. "You are uptight. I know you."

She suddenly sat back farther, in the same clothes
she'd worn to work, only she had on high, sexy, black
slingbacks. "Oh, you know, huh? Okay." She tapped
her foot, midair. "It's just that last time I was at your

place, I was your girl. And now, I'm not. So forgive me for seeming uptight as you say." She looked around at the subtle changes, like the large palm tree near the window, and a few random chrome knickknacks and non-bachelor-like mink sofa pillows. She told him with authority, "This is the place of some other woman's man. Not mine."

He nodded but looked as if she could possibly be mistaken. "Understood." He walked from the CD player to the other end of the sofa and sat. He eyed her. "You look good. Showing those legs nowadays I noticed. Even at work. The last two times I saw you it looked like those skirts were getting shorter and shorter. Nice." His pleased eyes went from her ankles to her thighs.

"I wear what I wear." She took in the moonlit window view of the beautiful bay.

"You wear it well. You don't want to take your shoes off?"

"No." Magnolia replied with an air of rude, and then said, "Thanks, though. I'm just here to talk." She looked toward the open kitchen. "So you cooked yourself dinner? Smells like shrimp something."

"No." He said as though matter of fact, "Keyonna cooked."

Magnolia turned her head askew. "Keyonna? When?"

"Tonight."

Magnolia heard the sound of footsteps in the loft and glanced toward the stairs. "Neal, what was that?"

He came to a stance and reached out his hand. "Come with me. I wanna show you something."

"What?"

He motioned his hand toward her. "Just come with me. To my office."

Magnolia stood only because her mind was too busy trying to figure him out to resist. She reached out her hand with caution, still.

He took it and led the way to the stairwell.

They got to the top and made a left into his office. He stepped aside and Magnolia heard, "Hi Magnolia."

Magnolia instantly dropped her hand from Neal's, jolted her head back, and pressed a breath through her lips as she pointed her index finger at the woman, while asking Neal, "What is she doing here?"

Keyonna sat at Neal's large desk in his office, turning away from the monitor of his desktop, aiming the office chair toward Magnolia and Neal. "Don't be mad at him. I insisted he let me be here. I know Neal and I know what he likes." Keyonna, who spoke her words with a casual cadence, was medium brown, with shoulder-length hair and short bangs. She had a young-looking face and flawless complexion. And she had on a short blue robe, tied tight at her twenty-four inch waist, bare shapely legs extended.

Magnolia asked, frowning, "You know what he likes? Well that's good. Because the only thing I know is that, as usual, he likes lying." She gave a stabbing stare at Neal. "You didn't tell me you had company." Magnolia turned her back to walk out.

Neal took her by the upper arm. "Mag, baby, hold up."

She snatched away. "Don't you dare call me baby. Your baby is right there." Her eyes skipped to Keyonna. She asked, "Is this an ex-girlfriend hater setup or something, because I'll tell you now, I do not want your man, so you can lighten the hell up. All this wasn't necessary."

Neal then placed his hand on Magnolia's shoulder and squeezed. "This is not anything like that. We both want you here."

Magnolia moved his hand by bumping his forearm with hers. "You what?"

Keyonna said, "We wanted you to come by for dinner."

"We?"

Keyonna continued, still talking with an easy breezy softness. "So we could bury the hatchet. You know. Get to know each other better."

Magnolia gave much neck-ti-tude. "I don't wanna know you. You got with my man when you knew he was taken. I was your co-worker. All that's fucked up, Keyonna. I have nothing to say to you."

"Wait," Neal told Magnolia, trying his best to get her to take his hand again.

Then Keyonna stood and knelt down before Neal, pulling down his shorts, and within just a few seconds, she took his saluting penis into her hand.

Neal looked straight at Magnolia, who looked down at Keyonna like she'd seen a hundred-twenty pound hoochie snake. "What the hell?"

Keyonna sucked his brown penis, licking his mushroom tip, bobbing her head, like it was as normal to do in front of someone as coughing.

Magnolia forced her mouth to close so she could swallow and then talk. "Oh hell no. You are some crazy ass fools. You can do all that nasty mess when I leave. Which is in about thirty seconds."

"Wait," Neal said again. "Come here."

"No," Magnolia yelled.

But Keyonna kept sucking.

Neal tried again. "Come here. Kiss me. Now." He eased his feet out of his shorts.

Magnolia raised her hands and shook her head like she was dreaming. "No, Neal. If you think I wanna be in the same room with you and your new girl while you two freaks freak, you are sadly mistaken."

Neal began to say a word, but the sounds of Keyonna sloshing and moaning as she went down on him grew louder, so he looked down and so did Magnolia. Her eyes then met his.

She took a deep breath and her shoulders dipped.

Keyonna's eyes rose to watch Neal pull Magnolia closer. He opened his mouth and met her lips, and he led her through a deep tongue kiss, pressing lips like they definitely knew their way around each other's mouths.

Keyonna raised one hand and placed it on Magnolia's hip and then squeezed Magnolia's plump backside. Her hand made its way to Magnolia's thigh and up her skirt. Then Neal lifted her skirt to expose her rear end. The rear end he always said was sitting on 22's.

Neal and Magnolia stopped kissing.

Keyonna stopped sucking. She stood and lifted her robe and lay pantieless on the white carpet with her legs up and her knees almost to her ears.

Magnolia could see it all, landing strip and runway. And she was stunned. Her jaw dropped to her belly.

Neal got on his knees to position himself between Keyonna's legs. In one quick move, before Magnolia knew it, he'd penetrated Keyonna and was fucking her, right in front of his ex.

Neal groaned. Loud.

Keyonna groaned. Louder.

A cat had Magnolia's tongue. She looked traumatized.

Neal began to pull down Magnolia's thong and scooted her closer. Being on his knees, his mouth was in a prone position, right at her vagina. He got her thong to her knees, just when she leaned down so she could pull it back up.

Her hands were shaking.

She awkwardly wiggled herself back into it and readjusted her skirt.

Neal looked up at her with an expression that was half ecstasy and half worry.

A tear rolled down Magnolia's cheek in slow motion.

Though Keyonna was grinding fast, Neal ceased his stroke.

Magnolia said with a soft voice, "I can't." In her high heels she high-stepped around her ex and his new woman and walked out the office door.

"Mag," she heard Neal say.

And then, "Magnolia, it's okay," Keyonna yelled her way.

By the time Magnolia reached the bottom of the stairs, she could hear fast footsteps behind her. It was Keyonna, adjusting herself, closing her robe. "Magnolia. I'm sorry you're uncomfortable. But please don't go."

"You've got to be kidding me." Magnolia looked at her, astonished.

"Seriously, we don't want you to go. What you don't know is that Neal has you in our bed every damn time we have sex. Your name always comes up, or his eyes are closed and I know what he's thinking. He's thinking of you."

Magnolia had her purse in hand. She shook her head, not believing what she was hearing.

Keyonna continued. "I'm someone who's fine with fantasy. I'm pretty okay with a lot of things as long as it's with my man. But I will admit, you're constantly in his head. I figured I'd join him with you. Getting with you and him, threesomes are not new to me. He knows that. And I'm quite sure you know it's not new to him, either."

"I know that. But that's no longer my problem."

"He and I have been with other women before. But I know you're the one he fantasizes seeing me with. It gets him off, fast. It's simple. Neal wants us both."

"Yeah, well I don't want him, you, none of this shit. This madness is insane. I mean, it makes no sense whatsoever. What is wrong with you? Excuse me but it really doesn't look like he's your man now. You're just a participant in him living out all of his fantasies."

"It's not that big a deal to me."

"Wow. I really do feel sorry for you. You're giving him a license to cheat. What is that about?"

"A lot of people do it. I'm okay."

Magnolia looked over and saw Neal standing at the foot of the stairs with his shorts on. She said to him, "This was fucked up, Neal. Plus, you're trying to be with two women you've been in relationships with. That's just straight up messy."

"I'm sorry."

"You should be. You set me up. Not to mention the

fact that you're using her." She pointed at Keyonna with her head.

His eyes were blank. "Honestly, I just thought maybe, maybe you'd come out of your shell a little. I guess I was wrong. No worries."

"Yes, worries. What made you think that? And if I ever did, you can bet you'd never see any side of me out of my shell. Not with you, not with Keyonna, not with anyone you set me up with. If I do end up out of my shell, the person I enjoy my new sexual freedom with will not be Neal Graham. And Lord only knows what made you think I've lightened up." She stepped to the door and said to Keyonna without looking back. "Good-bye Keyonna. I sure hope you wake up one day."

Keyonna nodded. "Magnolia, I hope you do, too."

Magnolia took one final look back, this time cutting her eyes more at Keyonna than Neal. "Oh, I'll get out of my damn shell all right."

Magnolia slammed the door.

She drove home traumatized from watching the man she still had feelings for, penetrating his new younger woman right before her eyes.

And the anger from the visual made her feel just a little bit more anxious about the challenge of her own resolution.

Just a little bit less okay with being missionary.

Ten

"Ain't No Sunshine"

Darla

INT.—BRADLEY DENTAL—MIAMI BEACH—LATE
MORNING
February 12, 2009

Darla, line two is for you."
It was a Thursday.

The tone of Darla's co-worker was rushed and dry, like maybe Darla shouldn't have had a call at all. Darla knew her co-worker's attitude all too well, and had grown to expect it.

"Thanks," Darla told her, walking by without taking the sight of the petite girl into view. Darla headed down the hallway, straight to her desk in the back office.

Darla had nine co-workers, and half of them were younger. As far as Darla was concerned, most of them were unprofessional gossips. The customers had often complained regarding the frontline customer service. And Darla was never surprised. She kept telling herself she was only passing through, but year after year went by and it was weighing on her like a ton of bricks, on top of everything else.

The small, red brick office of Dr. Tracy Bradford's dental practice was located on Lincoln Road, less than four miles from Darla's condo on Collins Avenue, which allowed Darla to walk to work whenever she wanted. She'd been walking every day of the new year thus far, aware of her need to trim down her thicker-than-thick frame. Thus far, she didn't see any effects from her daily strolls, which she attributed to her high level of stress, and otherwise sedentary lifestyle.

Darla picked up the receiver. "Hello. May I help you?"

"Mrs. Clark?"

"Yes."

"This is Maggie Kinnear with the Florida Dental Credit Union."

"Yes."

"You applied for a small business loan with us, correct?"

"Yes. I did."

"I wanted to ask you a few questions if you don't mind. Is now a good time?"

"Sure." Darla turned her back from the front door.

"We pulled your credit file and, while your score is on the low end, it is right at the bottom limit that we require. It's just that I see some collection accounts, mainly medical and it looks like some charge cards. Oh and a tax lien. Can you please give me an explanation as to what went on?"

Darla paced the width of her desk, back and forth, as she talked. "My husband died five years ago, and some of the medical bills we had weren't covered because he'd lost his job just before, and we didn't have COBRA. He wasn't even sick, really, he just collapsed from a heart attack and died. And I did get some life insurance money but not a lot, so I paid off some things but his credit cards were maxed out, and the ones that show up on my report are the ones that were joint accounts. I had to use some of those for some car repairs and other things we owed. But the biggest was the federal tax for 2005. I filed head of household for the first time and got hit hard. I did sell our house and paid it off, and got a condo. I'm pretty sure the only accounts showing a balance owing are some small collection accounts."

"I see. Do you have any savings?"

"No, I don't. Not anymore."

"You know, in order to get a business loan you need to have some liquid assets or seasoned funds that would equal a percentage of the loan. I see your checking balance is low. I don't see that your mortgage payment came out of your checking account for last month. Your report doesn't reflect a problem lately with your mortgage company, but it looks like it was behind before, right?"

"It was." Darla's reply was dry.

"There's quite a bit we'd need to make sense of. Honestly, I'm sure you can understand, but when we see reports like this it makes us a bit nervous."

Darla looked down at her feet and then stood before her desk, leaning her hand along the desktop. "Excuse me. So, obviously you're disapproving me, right? I mean, everything you've said sounds very negative."

The woman spoke a bit more rushed. "I just needed to ask for your explanation and take notes. Usually we ask you to put it in writing once we hear the reason, and then we have a better idea as to whether or not our underwriters might consider it for approval. Though I must say, you're probably right. The likelihood of you being able to survive until your sales are in the black looks bleak. Especially that first year."

"I thought that was what some of the loan money was for. I mean, you call me at work and make me go through all of this, only for you to tell me you can't help me. You knew when you ran my report you couldn't do it."

"Mrs. Clark. No, I didn't actually. But I really am sorry."

Darla paced again and moved her hand about. "Okay, so what are my options then? I mean, if I can't go through the SBA, through my own credit union, whom I've been with for nearly twelve years, what can I do?"

"I suggest maybe you borrow the money from a friend, if possible. Again, I'm sorry. You'll be getting a letter in the mail."

"Well, thank you, Ms. Kinnear, was it?"

"Yes."

"Yes, Ms. Kinnear. Thanks a lot." Darla's cynicism was loud as she hung up without exchanging good-byes.

From behind her back Darla heard the same co-worker speak. Darla turned her way. "Darla, the doctor is looking for you. You know the prosthesis you built for the lady who complained last week that her veneers were loose?"

Darla looked like her mind was elsewhere. "Yes."

"Her husband is here. He's not very happy. The doctor wants you to meet with him as well."

"Please tell her I'll be right there. I just need to make a phone call."

The woman cut her eyes toward the ceiling and walked away without replying.

Darla picked up the phone again and dialed. "Magnolia."

"Yeah. Darla. How are you?"

"Okay." The sound of her voice disagreed.

"I didn't recognize your work number on the display. Are you okay?"

Darla cut right to the chase. "Magnolia, listen. Do you think I could get a business loan at your bank?"

"I can try. How much are we talking about?"

"Eighty thousand."

"I don't see why not. You do know one of the first things we'd need is a business plan?"

"I've got that."

"Okay. I'll have the branch manager email you an application. Would that work?"

"It would. But I'm telling you now, my own credit union turned me down."

"Were they trying to do an equity loan?"

"No. I've only been in my condo for four years. No equity. If there was some before, it's depreciated now, like everything else."

"Let's see what we can do. I'll talk to you later. Maybe we can meet, too, for breakfast soon. For now, just email me your last two years' taxes. We can pull your credit right away. "

"Thanks, I appreciate it."

"And Darla, girl, I just wanted to ask you. Did Rebe tell you she got a job stripping already?"

"What? No."

"Yes. I got an email from her last night telling me

she started working at this club, and she said she's loving it."

"Oh my goodness."

"She'll tell you, I'm sure."

"That Rebe. What are we gonna do with her?"

"Beats me. But hey, she told us she wanted to so can't
be surprised I guess, right?"

"Well I am." Darla scooted her thoughts back. "But
anyway, I'll see you later. Gotta get back to work."

"Okay. Bye, girl."

"Bye." Darla hung up, gave a cleansing breath, and
headed straight to the dentist's private office.

At the end of the day, at the height of rush hour,
Darla headed down the busy street, Collins Avenue,
taking the last block toward her condo, people all
around, mainly driving but some pedestrians as well.
With her work shoes in her shoulder bag, she wore her
walking shoes and took it slow. Her mind had zigzagged
its way into an official headache. The patient was not
upset about the loose veneers, it was the infection that
had set in her gums after the extraction. Though Darla's
boss asked Darla to make an adjustment to the veneers
anyway, as though that might have made a difference in
the beginning. Darla agreed to do that once the swelling
went down, though she didn't agree that her work was
part of the problem.

After an overcast day, with the early evening wind
on her skin the entire walk home, Darla arrived at her
building and entered the lobby, giving a quick smile to
the doorman.

She stopped by the mailbox in the lobby, using her
key to open it, adjusting her purse, and then rummaging

through the envelopes. There was one from American Express, past due. One from Chase Bank, thirty days overdue. She took the few steps to the elevator, pressed 11, rode up to her place and walked up to her front door, seeing that there was a notice posted for the world to see. Notice of Intent to Lien from her overdue home-owners' association dues.

Darla snatched the notice, jammed her key in the door, opened it, and stormed inside, catapulting it closed. She untied the shoestrings of her tennis shoes and tossed each shoe with strength. They both bounced with dull thuds, landing across the room near the sliding glass door, one on its side and one right side up.

Darla, who never ever cursed, screamed at the top of her lungs, "Fuck!"

Eleven

"Sex Me"

Rebe

INT.—ARMANI'S APARTMENT—HOLLYWOOD,
FLORIDA—JUST AFTER TWO IN THE MORNING
February 14, 2009

It was Rebe's fortieth birthday. A Saturday.
Trinity had left a generic Happy Birthday card on
the kitchen counter at home, but said she'd be out for
the evening.

Rebe briefly talked to Darla and Magnolia.

A girlfriend breakfast was set for later.

But for now, the apartment Rebe was in smelled like
day-old supreme pizza with onions and extra cheese.

They walked in together after she followed him from
the club.

The man Rebe called Babyface turned on the floor
lamp to illuminate his bachelor pad, and immediately
picked up a can of Meadows & Rain Febreze, aiming
randomly, pressing the lever in every direction like he
was spraying an attacking swarm of killer bees.

Rebe made her cautious entrance, closing and lock-
ing the door behind her. Her better judgment said,

Speaking of spraying, what you need, Rebe, is that can of pepper spray you left at home. She told him with a reserved look, "I'm not supposed to be doing this."

He walked into the kitchen area, which was more like a small L-shaped closet with a three-foot counter that he used as a bar. "Yeah, yeah. You women are so hard on yourselves, with the whole good girl, bad girl, routine. What's up?"

Rebe looked around for a barstool that might belong to that counter but there was none. Or something to sit on that didn't have clothes strewn all over it. She asked, "Oh, we women are, huh?"

"Yep, you women," he said, pushing his trash deep into the bag and securing it with the drawstring.

"What would you know, Babyface?"

"Oh, I know. And it's Armani."

"Armani. Okay, but you still have a baby face."

"You say so."

"So I guess it's no big deal for you since you're a man. You don't need to worry about being bad or good. And also because you bring dancers home all the time."

"You assume, I see. One thing you need to know is that with me, if you want to ask, ask. But don't assume."

"Okay. Do you? Bring girls home all the time, that is?"

"No, I don't actually, Queenie."

"It's Rebe. So I'm the first one, is that what you're saying?" She looked at him like surely he lied.

"Yeah, Rebe. Lucky you. You get to see my bachelor pad. Or bachelor room." He tossed his Nike hoodie and a couple of pairs of sweatpants from the black futon onto the back of a wooden chair.

"It's fine." She eased herself down onto the thin cushion of the raised, framed mattress.

"It's cramped, is what it is."

"You're young. You live alone. I had a small place when I was your age, too."

"Am I gonna have to keep hearing about how young I am?"

"You might. You are young."

"I see I'm gonna have to show you a few things to shut you up."

She furrowed a brow. "Like what?"

He just gave her the eye.

"You sure are edgy. Nothing like the Babyface back at the club."

He walked back into the kitchen. "You want something to drink."

"No. I don't drink. But thanks."

"Why not?"

"I just don't. You didn't answer my question, like what?"

He reached inside the tiny, round fridge and grabbed a cold bottle of Corona. "Like how a man handles things. A man is gonna be a man, no matter what the age. Manhood is judged by what a person does. And I'll tell you one thing about me. I am not a boy."

"I see. So I shouldn't trip on the fact that you're probably my daughter's age."

"No. And I won't let the fact that you must be just a year or two younger than my mother trip me out. Your wisdom is sexy. But underestimating me, is not."

Rebe nodded. "I feel you. So, since we're estimating, how do you estimate me?"

"All I know is that you dance like a goddess. And you have a sharp ass tongue. That's it."

"And? What do you think about the fact that I'm sitting here in your apartment? Old enough to be a year or two younger than your mother."

He walked back into his living room. "Just hope to get to know more about you."

She watched his bowlegs and what looked like a round butt through his jeans, and examined his facial structure and green eyes, all while simply asking, "Why?"

"Because I like you."

"I'm fully aware of what you'd like to do with me."

He swigged from his bottle, swallowed with an *ahhh*. "I've done that in my mind a few times already. If I don't get to, oh well."

"Oh please. Why are you playing off the whole reason I'm here? I say let's get it over with." Her eyes grew playful.

He stepped to her. "Hold up. You'll take all the fun out of it."

She stood and faced him, eye to eye. "Armani. You know what? You are my fantasy. You are young. You are hot. I'm feeling hot for you like it's a new me. Something about the smell of that club, and the look in your amazing eyes when you see me on that stage, and the feeling I have running through my body, is like an aphrodisiac to me. It's like a drug. It's making me high as a kite. No lie." Rebe's eyes looked like she was sex drunk. Her words spilled from her mouth like water and she barely blinked, only putting one hand on his shoulder, and one hand on his forearm. "I want to go ahead and fuck you before it all slips away. Before I have to deal with what it would be like to again feel the guilt of this lust or whatever it is, versus jumping on your dick, right here, right now, in your apartment." She lifted up her top and pulled it over her head, and then reached back to unsnap her bra, never telling him it was her birthday.

He took a slow sip of his beer and looked serious as a heart attack.

"Now I'm going to undress. And I want you to do whatever you want to me. I won't stop you. Just do me a favor and dim the light a little, maybe put on a slow love song, and then get your fine ass back over here, Armani." She had stepped from her skirt and purple panties, and was buck birthday-suit naked.

Armani lifted his chin from his chest, his eyes stuck on the sight of her bare vagina. He put the empty beer bottle who knows where and hurried toward the floor lamp like a kid on Christmas, goofy and excited, turning the dimmer switch down to almost off, and awkwardly shuffling through three CDs, picking out Johnny Gill and pressing Play on the title track.

Rebe's face was cool, but her heartbeat was quicker than even when she was on stage in front of a room full of horny men.

Armani took off his jeans, shirt, socks, and underwear in two point two and approached her again, taking her into his arms, meeting her face with his, and he kissed her, sucking her tongue while pressing his lips and his bare body against hers.

"Let's get the mood right. Turn on your heart light."

He led her and her heart into a slow dance move to the music and kept kissing.

She held on to his arms, and then stretched her arms around his back, massaging his muscles.

The mood was sexy.

He eased his lips away and leaned over to adjust the futon to a flat position.

Rebe told him with a whisper, "I don't want to lay down yet."

He spoke fast. "I do." His penis high was obvious.

"I want you to do something different. Something you've never done before."

Armani twisted his mouth and began to think, giving in to her demand and picking her up like she weighed two pounds. He placed her on the counter.

She scooted her bare ass back along the tan laminated surface. Armani knelt down just enough so that her pussy met his mouth at its exact point. She leaned back just as he pulled back her pussy lips, exposing her clit stud, and went to work. He licked and flicked his tongue while holding on to her hips, pressed his face closer and used his fingers, index and middle, to enter her upward, adding pressure toward her G-spot, pressing against it with a strong force.

Already, Rebe felt her head spinning but braced herself, one hand on the edge of the counter, and one hand on his head, though the sight of what he was doing to her, along with the pressure on her undiscovered internal spot, was too much. She took a deep breath and focused to allow the feeling to take her away and then, he stopped.

He said, as Johnny Gill continued to serenade their mood, "I want to make you come with me inside of you."

"Baby. Wait." She fought to not have to come back down from her ninety percent acceleration.

Armani picked her up and in a rush, his dick standing up so tough it looked like it could walk, he laid her hot body on her stomach, upon the futon and ran to his desk, reaching in the drawer for a foil packet, securing the condom, and hurrying back. She arched her back and raised her hips in the air at just the right level. He immediately inserted himself into her, going in little by little, first to halfway while she flinched inside, and then the other half. His hands were on her waist for cooperative guidance.

With each grind she groaned in a way that sounded like a porn movie was being watched or made.

The CD played subtle female moans in the intro of the next song, "Bring It On."

"Girl the night is so young, girl you look so ready."

Armani was talking shit from behind her. "Your body's so damn fine. And your pussy is on fire. It's hot just like an oven. Damn."

Her head was turned back toward his face, watching him do his thing.

He dug deep and kept poking the upper part of her insides. She mumbled inaudible sentences as he said, "Yeah. Your freak is on tonight. Young ass dick got that pussy surprised, huh? Tight pussy don't know how to act with a dick that knows its way around. Come for me like you made me come after I met you that night. When I came home and jacked the fuck off in your name. Come like a bad girl. You know you're a bad girl. I sure know you are."

"No, I'm not."

"Oh yeah, you are. You've been a bad girl, Rebe. You know you have. Showing all of us horny men your stuff up on that stage. Teasing us. Sounds like a bad girl to me. Does it to you?"

"Uh-uh." She played along, knowing he was right.

As his dick dug in and then out at a fast pace, you could hear the wetness of her insides, as well as his pubic area slamming against her ass cheeks. "I can feel that pussy clenching up. Dang, got a grip on my shit. Girl, you need to stop lying. Pussy don't lie. You're about to come for me, aren't you?"

"No." Her eyes began to tear from the full penetration pounding. She looked straight forward, riding the rhythm of his fuck current.

"Yes, you are. Me too. Come with me, Rebe. Get this young ass dick. Come."

"Ahh, Ahh. Oooh. Ahh. No. No. Shit."

"Oh fuck," was all he said.

And they came together, unraveling from the plateau of their muscular contractions.

His post-orgasm face went from tense to serene.

She slipped into deep thought, wondering how she'd, for the second time suddenly in her life, and this time on the very night of her birthday, managed to be turned on and turned out, again.

She collapsed onto her belly and looked behind at the flawless sight of his toned body, and gave him the stud salute with her eyes out of respect for the intensity, his skill, and his nasty shit-talking.

With him still on her back, his breathing downshifting from his massive expulsion, their bodies breathed the same. He said, "Happy Valentine's Day."

She'd forgotten. "You, too." She sounded spent.

All was quiet except for the slow serenade "It's Your Body."

And then his cell rang from the floor near the futon.

She glanced at it halfway through the first ring as her head hung over the edge of the futon.

Just as the BlackBerry screen lit up, she turned her head the other way, adjusting her neck to get comfortable.

He reached down to press the Ignore button, and turned back to adjust himself along her backside.

It had read, Trinity calling.

Twelve

---♦---

"That's What Friends Are For"

Girlfriends

EXT.—THE NEWS CAFE—MIAMI BEACH—MORNING
February 16, 2009

Magnolia and Darla and Rebe planned to meet for breakfast on President's Day just to have some girl chat time, and to celebrate Rebe's birthday, though Magnolia and Darla needed to follow up on the business loan talk, so they arrived a few minutes early.

Darla walked up, looking like it was summer in her jean shorts, tank, and flip-flops. Magnolia, in black pants and a white blouse, had already about finished her cup of coffee, and was seated at a cozy courtyard table for three. Her tiny red clutch rested on the edge of the square table.

Their meeting place was the News Cafe, a quaint sidewalk restaurant on the corner of 8th and Ocean Drive in Miami Beach's Art Deco District.

The sun shone strong, even though it was February, offering a bit of spring heat upon the many restaurant patrons who filled the tables, enjoying the energy and ambiance of the well-known eatery.

Located along the glittery stretch of coastline, originally the café was known as a local news kiosk, and heralded for its award-winning breakfast dishes. It was a cozy, garden-like spot with white trellises adorned by shiny green ivy. Large clay pots of pale flowers aligned the white cement ledges.

Darla, who had to duck her spiked pixie cut to keep from hitting the dark green table umbrella, took a seat next to Magnolia.

"What's up, Foxy Brown?" Magnolia joked, checking out her conservative friend who was wearing those shorts extra short.

"Hey sis," Darla offered a kiss on the cheek.

Magnolia returned it to the air, making a smooching sound, still eyeing Darla down. "Look at you, showing those shapely legs."

"Big legs is what they are. I just felt like, whatever. A little bit of sun today. I'm wearing these."

"I see. One thing about you, you have quite the waistline, girl. You look good."

"Well thanks. The thing for sure is, red beans and rice didn't miss my butt." She joked, but still, her mind was focused. "So what's the verdict?"

Magnolia shook her head and looked sorrowful. "Girl, I couldn't get it done. I talked to the branch manager and she said it was your credit score. Suggested you wait a year or two and work on repairing it. I can't pull strings when it comes to that, any more than I can with income requirements. The underwriters are way stricter than ever before. It's just the times we're in, with all of the failed loans. It's tough."

"I figured." Darla adjusted her hips and sat back.

"What happened? I mean, was your score always an issue, even back when you bought your condo?"

"No. Just stuff since Aaron died."

"Darla, now, I know you. I know how private you are, so I won't delve, but there's got to be another way for you to start a business. Some type of program where the state allows more flexibility. There should be more government-type programs for those who want to be business owners. I know there's the Ladies Who Launch organization for female entrepreneurs. I can check it out and let you know what I find out." Magnolia reached into her handbag and pulled out her BlackBerry, making notes on her to-do list.

Darla forced a smile. "Thanks. Bottom line is, I think it's about time for me to get a second job and clean up my mess." She took a deep breath and shook her shoulders. "Heck, maybe I'll start stripping with Rebe. She did send me an email, too. Said something about some place called Make It Rain or something? What the heck does that mean, anyway?" Her tone was a bit lighter.

Magnolia pointed near the walkway. "Speaking of Rebe."

Rebe came over and pulled back a chair. "Hey ladies. Smooches." She gave air kisses, too, wearing white Dior sunglasses. Her peach, sequined tank matched her lips and cheeks. Her floral sandals were tan. Her linen trousers were bright white. She sat.

Magnolia said, "Hey Rebe. We were just talking about you."

"Really? Talking about me literally?"

Magnolia replied, "No, not *about* you, about you. Happy belated Birthday."

Rebe said, "Thanks. Hey, Darla."

"Howdy. Yeah, Happy Birthday, girl."

"Thanks."

"This is for you," Magnolia said, taking a tiny blue gift bag from beside her chair and placing it before Rebe.

"And this too," said Darla, reaching into her purse and putting a small box on the table.

Rebe adjusted her studded bag along the back of the chair and removed her shades, placing them on her head. "Oh, you two are so sweet. Wow." She grinned. Right away she reached inside the gift bag, underneath the baby blue tissue paper, and inside to find a sterling silver BFF key chain. "Awww, how cute. Where'd you find this?"

"This little store in the mall. They engraved the back."

Rebe turned it over. It read, *R,M,D 4ever*, the letters of their first names. "Oh, how sweet. Thanks, Magnolia. This is adorable. Muah," she said, leaning to her left to give another smooch.

Darla eyed it. "That is cute. Where's mine?"

"It's no longer our birthdays, Darla."

"Oh, okay. So I'm gonna have to get my own, I see. Or wait until next year. I got it. So, it's like that, huh?"

"Ah, yeah." Magnolia gave her a comical, *duh* look.

"And what's in here?" Rebe asked, lifting the top of the small white box. "Ohhhh, excuse me. Sexy, sexy." She lifted a frilly pair of pink ruffled panties, and looked proud.

Magnolia looked around to see who saw. No one.

"You can leave them in the box," Darla said, looking around, too.

"Oh who cares? Adorable."

"Anyway, they're from Marshall's. Nothing too fancy."

"They're hot. I like. You've always had the eye for lingerie. Thank you." She leaned to her right and smooched Darla's way. "Muah. Thank you both." Rebe tucked the panties back into the box and placed it in the bag just under the table. She scooted forward. "So what exactly were you two talking about?"

Darla came right out and asked, "So you're really truly stripping already?"

"Really truly." She picked up the menu. "Do you mind if I order first? This working girl is starving."

Darla said, "Oh Lord. Anyway, I already know what I want."

Magnolia glanced over her menu, too, while fingering the hairs of her ponytail along her shoulder. "I can't wait."

The young, apron-wearing, sandy-haired male waiter approached with a smile. "Welcome. Can I get you ladies anything to drink before you order?"

"Iced tea," said Darla, glancing up at him.

Magnolia told him, "Orange juice for me."

He asked Rebe. "Would you like some water, ma'am?"

Rebe replied slowly, putting down the menu and then twisting her vintage Lucite bangle along her wrist as she looked up at him with caution, "Yes please." Her skin crawled. She hated the word *ma'am*.

Magnolia kept looking at the menu and said, "Go ahead, we can order now. You can go first, Darla."

Darla did. "I'll have the eggs Florentine with spinach."

"Sure. And you, ma'am?" he asked Rebe.

Rebe flung her braids back as she spoke. "The steak and eggs, scrambled. Wheat toast."

"Sure. And you?" He looked at Magnolia just as she closed her menu.

"The scrambled eggs with smoked salmon and onions. And some more coffee please."

"Coming right up," he said taking their menus and stepping away.

Rebe looked in the direction of the waiter, and then cut her eyes. "Did you hear him call me ma'am? Not once, but twice."

Darla waved her hand. "Oh Rebe."

"Oh Rebe what? I didn't hear him call either of you ma'am."

"I'm sure he didn't mean it in a negative way," Darla told her, seeming certain.

Rebe gave a heavy exhale and worked hard to stay cool, calm, collected, even though her mind tried to rewind. "Well, he needs to give us a little equal opportunity with those manners. Directing it all to me when I'm younger than both of you."

"By a little more than a month." Darla gave a tiny laugh.

Magnolia said, "Actually, come to think of it, that did happen to me last week. Being referred to as ma'am for the first time is...well, noticeable to the one who's called ma'am."

Rebe replied with a tone that said she was giving Magnolia a verbal high five, elongating the second syllable of her one word. "*Okay?*"

Darla leaned forward and put her elbows along the table. "So, back to your stripping, or dancing, whatever. You're really doing that?"

Rebe was honest. "Yes, I am. The lady who taught my pole dancing class referred me to the owner, and he hired me the minute I walked in. Believe me, I didn't expect it to happen that fast myself."

"Amazing." Magnolia was all ears.

"What's it like?" asked Darla.

"I just get up there and move my body like it's no big deal, feeling free, much more uninhibited than I thought I'd be. I mean, it feels wrong, sort of, but I do it almost because of that, if that makes sense. This whole thing to me in the first place is about being comfortable with being uncomfortable. But the trip is to see the kind of people who come in there. All types. Executives, athletes, fathers. One guy, from what one of the dancers told me, is actually a preacher."

Magnolia said, "Uh. Why am I not surprised? Though I'm still trying to imagine you, on stage."

"Then maybe you guys should come on by and see for yourselves."

Darla spoke up. "Oh, no thanks. I'll just imagine. That's good enough."

"So, the guys. Are they weird?" Magnolia asked.

"Not so far. Funny thing is, I met this guy the very first night I worked. My name on the stage is Queenie. I just made that up, just because my neighbor had a dog named Queenie when I was little. But he knows my name now. And I called him Babyface, because he looks so young. Well, actually, he is young. But his name is Armani. I spent my birthday at his place."

"How old is he?" Darla asked, angling her head.

"He's twenty-one."

Even Magnolia had to ask, "What? Twenty-one?"

Darla gave a snicker. "Uh oh. Cougar."

Rebe leaned in to speak softer but sounded like she had a news flash. "Yep. The cougar has her cub. And listen, we fuck like horny ass pussycats." She sat up straight. "Thank you very much."

Magnolia said, "Uh on. Hold up. Don't you go giving that young boy all the freak, now. You're old enough to be his mother."

"Exactly." Rebe looked like he could have it all and more.

"When did all this boy-toy loving start?" asked Darla.

"The first night I met him. Thing was, when I gave him a lap dance I could tell he was packing, and I was shocked."

"You do the lap dances, too?"

"All that. So for my birthday the other night, I went by his apartment at like two in the morning, and I'm telling you, that young man has energy. He can go right ahead and use me until he uses my ass right on up."

Magnolia looked impressed. "Hold up. How is it all of a sudden you end up with all the sex-machine men?"

"See, I am not playing, whereas you two, my dears, are. Plus, these younger men out here are bringing their A game. I remember when the young guys would say they wanted an older woman so she could show them a thing or two. Hell, they already know a thing or two, three, and four. I can't teach him a thing."

Magnolia said, eyeing down her friend, giving the cuckoo sign, circling her hand near her head, "Okay, Rebe, you have totally flown over the cuckoo's nest and lost your marbles. Or maybe it's your pussy that's lost it."

Rebe looked at her like that was a dud. "Very funny. If so, it needed to be lost. But I know one thing, I sure don't feel forty. Even if this sorry ass waiter is up in this place calling me ma'am."

Darla told her, "Ma'am or not, don't start acting like you're twenty-one, too. You need to be responsible still. You know there are a whole lot of perverts out there."

Rebe put her fingers to her temples like she felt a headache looming. "Here she goes again, Magnolia. Make her stop. Please."

Darla said, "Okay now. You asked for the fast lane and you got it. That's on you."

Magnolia only looked back and forth between the two of them. She then asked, "So Rebe, honestly, what do you know about this guy, Armani, anyway?"

"He said he works at the Miami airport. I think for Transportation Security or something. And he spends a lot of time in the club. The girls tell me he's in there five nights a week. He's a pseudo-model. Showed me some of his hot ass pictures before I left the next day. And oh, yeah, this is what I wanted to tell you both." Rebe looked impressed with what she was about to say. "He's a swinger. He goes to this new swinger's club called Erotic City."

Magnolia said, "Oh, so he's a real freak."

"Are you thinking about going?" Darla asked.

"I am."

Magnolia admitted, "One of Neal's friends went there. From what he told him, Freakazoid City is what they should have named it."

"Well, I'm going. And he invited you guys, too."

"He invited us?" Darla raised her eyebrows.

"Yes. He knows the owner who's some former boxing champ." Rebe was perky. "So what's up? You two wanna go, or what?"

"I don't know," said Darla. "I doubt it."

"You know, I think I would." Magnolia sipped her last sip of coffee.

"There ya go." Rebe nodded.

Magnolia said, "But I'd probably just stand there in shock. Traumatized."

"Armani said the first time, we should just watch and take it all in. Then, if we decide it's not for us, we don't have to go back. No harm."

"Okay." Magnolia gave a thumbs-up nod.

"So, we'll go soon. Maybe next month so we can build up the nerve."

Darla said, "We've straight out all lost our minds."

The drink girl approached with their water, juice, and tea, and poured more coffee for Magnolia.

"Thanks," Magnolia said for them. She eyed her friends back and forth, again changing the subject. "I joined an adult site." Her words spilled.

Rebe asked, "You did?"

"Yep. And I had phone sex with this guy. It was a trip."

Rebe smiled. "With a stranger, huh? Good girl."

"You put a photo up?" Darla asked, putting a straw in her tea.

"Just a boob shot."

"You are brave," Rebe said.

"I told you I was curious. But not too curious, because wait. Neal..."

Darla jumped in. "Oh no. There's that name again."

"Listen. Neal tried to pull a fast one on me. Well, my dumb ass agreed to come by and talk, and he had the nerve to have his new girl upstairs. They tried to set me up for a threesome."

Rebe said, "Now that is some kinky shit there. You did say tried, right? You didn't."

"Ahh, no. Of course not. If I were ever to decide to be with two or more people at the same time, he would not be one of them. That, I can tell you for sure."

Darla shook her head. "Ahh, that's messed up. So they tried to ambush you?"

Magnolia explained, "Yeah, and her sad ass is so pathetic. These women just do whatever these men want them to. She's cool with him having me on his mind while they screw. Not."

Rebe picked up her water. "That is a trip. I hope you never see him again. Really. That's just so disrespectful."

Darla joked, "Magnolia, you know you were probably hoping to get laid by him when you went over in the first place. You're not fooling me one bit."

"Well if I was, he ruined that for sure."

"Man oh man. Slick old Neal. Kinky dude."

"Yep. We knew that." Darla sipped her tea.

Rebe said, "Just when you try to get a little bit wilder, he one-ups you."

"And so Darla, what's your status update anyway?" Magnolia asked.

"None. Just still trying to open this store."

Rebe asked. "Did you like any of the spots you saw?"

"Yeah. Just still working it out. It takes time. Gotta get things lined up."

Magnolia said nothing.

Rebe sipped her water and put the glass back down. "Okay. No extracurricular?"

"None."

"Still got Aaron on the brain?" Magnolia asked.

"That. And even when I was having sex, I still had the orgasm thing. I'd probably bore a man to tears. I'd be better off just doing the battery operated boyfriend thing."

Rebe told Darla, speaking closer to the table, "See, you need to read up on why you're not being able to come. I heard that not having an orgasm is either a libido thing, or an issue you might need to get checked out, like blood flow. Or . . ."

Magnolia spoke up to complete her own version of the sentence. "Or, you're not asking for what you want in bed."

"Oh really? Well, what if I don't know what it is I want in the first place?"

Magnolia continued, "I'll tell you one thing. I'm no expert, but Darla, a man can play around all he wants to down there, and there's one main spot that's only for the purpose of a woman having an orgasm, and no other reason. And that's the lovely clitoris."

Rebe nodded, uncrossing and then crossing her legs. "Heck yeah, I know that's right."

"Darla, there are a lot of women who don't even come vaginally, but orally, now that is a must. And it's a beautiful thing." It seemed she had a flashback.

Darla thought back. "I can imagine. I think I'd gotten just about there before, but I admit, I pulled back."

Rebe looked unconvinced. "Believe me, if someone was doing it right, there'd be no pulling back."

Magnolia said, talking like she had a cure for cancer, "Darla, here's what you've got to do." She had one hand on her orange juice and lowered her tone. "If you notice him licking it, or missing it, or close to it, whatever, tell him to take that bad boy in his mouth and suck on it. 'Suck' is the magic word. Suck. I promise you. I may not know much, but that I do know. A man who has those skills is a valuable asset to any woman." She scooted her hips. "Hell, I'm getting horny. Where's our food? I need to eat and go home and get on my play site."

Rebe said, "I know that's right. I'm starving."

Magnolia said, "So, Rebe, Darla wants to know what Make It Rain means."

"I do not. Don't even lie. That's your question," Darla said, giving Magnolia a look.

Rebe answered, "Whoever asked, that's when the customers throw the money in the air and it falls down like rain."

Magnolia said, "Oh, I thought it meant, like, to come all over someone. Like skeet?"

"Oh no. Even I knew that. You are old," Darla joked and then asked in a lower tone, "Rebe, what I do want to know is, is it true what they say about the champagne room? Do they have sex in there?"

"Yes."

"But you don't."

"No."

"Okay, so if someone wants you to, then what?" Darla asked.

"I'll say no."

"You're not even curious?"

Rebe said, "Even I know that sometimes curiosity can kill the cat."

Magnolia laughed.

Rebe asked her, "Magnolia, so, are you trying to find a man online to marry and have kids with, or what?"

"Oh, hell no. And as far as having kids, I'm sure my eggs are dead anyway. They say by the time you're forty, the three-hundred thousand eggs you had at twenty-one are down to like nine thousand, and you haven't got a snowball's chance in hell at getting pregnant."

Rebe said, "I heard that madness. But I think it's not the number of eggs, it's the quality. You could still have some good ones left."

Magnolia looked around, back toward the direction of the waiter. "Speaking of eggs. Really. Where is our damn food?"

"For real." Darla caught the waiter's eye and flagged him down.

Magnolia continued, "I say, expecting that picket fence, fidelity, two and one-half kids, and a dog, or cat, or frigging hamster, is just a mirage. Be glad you have a roof and a job and your health. Life ain't but a minute. Screw the rest."

"I plan to," Rebe joked.

Magnolia said, "I'm starting to believe you will. Making up for lost time. What are you on, some kind of Viagra for women or something?"

As they laughed, the waiter came up and said, "Yes, ma'am."

Darla pointed toward the kitchen. "Young man, where's our food?"

Rebe watched Darla's facial expressions, inching to a frown.

He said, looking hurried, "I apologize. We're just very busy. I'll check on it now. I'll make sure we bring it out right away, ma'am."

Rebe got ready to say something but Darla beat her to it.

"And young man, listen to me. Please don't use the word *ma'am*. You wouldn't know what we mean unless you were a forty-year-old female and someone said it to you. But, please, take our word for it. It's not good." Rebe and Magnolia nodded at him.

He spoke fast and almost bowed. "Oh, okay, please know that I apologize. I had no idea. It won't happen again."

"Good," said Darla.

"Sorry." The waiter turned around just as their food was brought over by another server.

Darla watched them pass out the plates, steam doing its dance off the hot entrees, the smells of green peppers and butter and salmon made themselves known. The potent smell intoxicated Darla as she inhaled and savored the aromas; however, it was not enough to make her forget about her other hunger. Darla said in a low voice, still on the previous topic, "Suck it, huh?"

Rebe's mouth dropped and she laughed. "Uh oh. Seems like you're ready."

All Darla did in reply was bow her head. The others did as well. She said, "God bless this food for the nourishments of our bodies."

"Amen," they all said together.

They grabbed their silverware and began to eat, while

Darla gave each of them an unbelievable look like they were all going to burn in hell.

All because of a sex promise.

She also prayed that Magnolia picked up the tab for their breakfast meals.

Thankfully for Darla, her prayer was answered.

Thirteen

"*I Wanna Be Your Lover*"

Magnolia

INT.—MAGNOLIA'S HOME—MIAMI BEACH—
EVENING
February 28, 2009

It had been a minute since the drama of Neal inviting Magnolia over for a threesome with him and his new woman. Magnolia had been online every night since she first signed up for GFF. She was bound and determined to spill over into the world that she'd for years talked herself out of taste testing. She felt sad for Keyonna, but also a little envious that Keyonna was not jealous or rigid. It made Magnolia wonder if exploring beyond the boundaries was so bad after all.

Magnolia searched through the naughty videos and watched women with women, guys with guys, big breasted, big dicks, different nationalities, and fetishes. At first she was in amazement at what was out there in the world, and with what people were willing to do. Some women squirted their liquid orgasms like water, some sat on fake penises that had suction cups secured to a coffee table or against the wall, and some inserted foot-long dildos in every orifice, while most of the members just wanted a sex partner for the evening.

Magnolia, once again, for the fourth time, had phone sex with Carl, and even did a webcam chat with HungHenry, and then with BigBoom. She'd had her sixth request to play from LeanAndJean. She denied, again. The new Magnolia was willing, but just wasn't into couples.

She searched and selected and watched, and then another chat request chimed. LeanAndJean. She clicked deny, and then sent them a message. No thanks, LeanAndJean. Maybe when it's Lean without the Jean.

She chuckled to herself. *Even then. No.*

She turned to her cell and thought about maybe calling someone over who she knew from her past. Someone to do her the way she could possibly now be open to. But the ones in her past were so-so at best. She scrolled through some numbers and got to the G's, and then saw Neal's name. A thought came to her head. To again log on to his account at Ocean Bank.

Don't.

Don't.

She did.

Curiosity took her by the hand and squeezed. Before she knew it, she'd clicked the browser and logged in, reading about a debit in the amount of seventy-three dollars and four cents at Charlotte Russe, and a debit in the amount of twenty-nine dollars and ninety-five cents to Grown Folks Finder.com. Magnolia's antenna shot straight up. She closed down the connection.

Her computer chimed. LeanAndJean replied to her

message. That can be arranged. Ding. Ding. Ding. Ding. A bell went off in Magnolia's swift brain that told her maybe, just maybe the name LeanAndJean was really Neal and Keyonna. Neal spelled backward. She looked closely at her own photo and remembered that she wore the black angel charm in the shot. She spoke as if she was not in her bedroom alone. "That sucker is a member of this site. Could he have figured out it's me? Maybe that's why he tried that mess and invited me over. He knew I was on this damn site."

This time, it was Magnolia who initiated the chat request. The chat box expanded, accepted. And someone typed.

Hello sexy.

She typed, Hi.

Thanks for requesting.

No problem. I've been overwhelmed by the site. It's hard to maneuver.

We see. We knew you were pretty new. Never saw you before the other day.

Yes I am new. Who am I talking to?

This is Lean.

Lean, huh? Okay. So you got rid of Jean?

She's not home right now. But she liked your photo, too. She's a breast woman.

Oh really?

Yes. But I can tell from your profile you're only into men. It's cool.

Okay. So, you play alone.

Yes. But you'd like her.

Really? So why do you call yourself lean?

I'm tall. Low percent body fat. But I'm a big guy.

Uh-huh. Big all over, I hope?

I am.

Nice. You're not going to ask what I look like?

No. I saw enough. We're both into breasts.

I see. Well, I do have enough to feed the needy. So you live in Miami.

Yes.

Good.

Do you think we could meet?

Maybe.

He just went for it. Like tonight?

Possibly.

Say the Holiday Inn Miami Beach. At eleven.

Magnolia replied as though she couldn't wait. Sure.

Cool. Check the front desk. Ask for the room number for Jean Lean. They'll tell you. I'll tell them Tangie will ask. No worries.

Got it. See you then.

Bye, Tangie.

And that quick, Magnolia got so excited she couldn't contain herself. *See. This is gonna be good. No worries my ass.* She'd set a date to meet a stranger to have sex, only this stranger was her ex-boyfriend. But this time, Magnolia just may have been one step ahead of him.

INT.—HOLIDAY INN—MIAMI BEACH—LATE
EVENING

Four knocks on the door.

"Just a minute," a female voice said.

Footsteps.

Magnolia heard the door unlock and the knob turn. The door opened.

She, a white woman with golden eyes and platinum, shoulder length hair, fake black lashes, and skin so brown one would've thought she applied an entire bottle of bronzer, stood before Magnolia. "Tangie?" she asked.

"Yes," Magnolia said, and then she remembered. *Oh no. I just know this is not who I think it is.* She gave a cautious sigh and braced herself.

"I'm Jean," the platinum woman said. "Come in." She stepped aside wearing a short red dress, and opened the door wider.

Magnolia counted to three and crossed the threshold, aligned her canvas bag over her shoulder, and prepared for what lie ahead, holding her inhale and then forcing a release of air.

The platinum-haired woman told Magnolia, "Glad you came. I know you're probably a little nervous coming by yourself. I know I would be, too."

"Yes," was all Magnolia said as she stepped inside the narrow entryway, her feet cooperating but her mind suddenly told her not to go farther, yet the large off-white room was before her, and lying across the king poster bed at a six-foot-six angle, wearing only boxers, with the remote in his hand, looking like Michael Jordan himself, was lean Randall Richardson, Rebe's ex-husband.

There was the sound of the door closing, and the audio of Fox Sports on the flat screen.

"Hi, Magnolia." His voice was deep and friendly, and slow. He smiled like they were at a family reunion.

That damn face. That damn voice. Damn. "Randall." She nodded. Her expression was even more stressed than her voice.

"Surprise, huh?" He had to have known her answer.

"Yes. To say the least." Magnolia stood still. "What in the world are you guys, I mean you and Kandi, doing here? It is Kandi, right? Not Jean," she asked, expecting Randall to answer.

"It is," Kandi said from behind her.

Randall said, "Small world."

Magnolia blinked her sight back to Kandi. "I knew you looked familiar. I've only seen you in photos from when Trinity came by for your daughter's birthday party."

"Yes. I saw you on Trinity's Facebook page."

"So you knew who I was when you opened the door?"

Kandi nodded and gave a soft grin, looking like she wanted to say more.

Magnolia looked at Randall as she readjusted her purse strap. "I'm going to go."

Randall spoke up. "You don't have to." A half-empty bottle of bourbon was on the nightstand. He sat up along the corner of the bed. His muscular legs went on forever. His chest was defined and hairy. His six-pack was an eight-pack. His biceps were chiseled.

Magnolia looked down to fight the sight, and then looked at Kandi and then back at him. "Oh, yes I do. This really is not turning out the way I thought it would. I mean, I'm open to new things in my life, but being here. No."

"Magnolia, as far as Kandi and I are concerned, it turned out just the way we wanted it to."

"So, you knew it was me?"

"Your description, your breasts, and that ladybug on your neck."

Magnolia touched her neck. "You are kidding me. You saw that in the photo."

His speech was unsteady. Almost a slur. "Barely. But if not for the tattoo, I'd be able to draw your cleavage in my sleep if necessary. I've noticed everything about you from the first day Rebe brought me to your house to meet you."

Magnolia was half surprised, half not. She glanced over at Randall's wife, ready to duck if necessary.

Kandi added, "I saw you online first, and then he looked closer. He wasn't one-hundred percent sure but, actually, I'm really glad he was right." Kandi kept her sights on Magnolia's chest. "Nice."

Magnolia noticed her notice. "Oh my goodness. Really, I have to go."

"Please don't," Randall said.

"You of all people know that Rebe is basically my sister. I just can't." She turned back toward the door while her devotion skills were still intact.

"Don't run away. Stay. Just for a minute."

"Please," Kandi said, now sitting on the settee at the foot of the bed, spreading her legs, pantieless.

Magnolia faced them and paced her breaths, eyes saying she was in a place where she didn't belong. She watched, and Randall came to a tall stance and then knelt down to his wife, meeting her waxed vagina as she opened her legs. And he went to town, keeping an eye on Magnolia, who looked frozen in place. Randall kept up his mouth between Kandi's slender legs and ate her.

Her white tan surrounded his dark, bald head. He did his oral thing and she squealed, tossing her head back. And by the time they changed places, Magnolia had dropped her bag onto the floor and stood closer to the bed, watching Kandi suck Randall's tall dick all the way down to her tonsils.

The sight was forbidden.

Magnolia watched the kinky goings-on, similar to Neal and Keyonna getting freaky, and this time, she asked permission for her internal self to let her witness the act for herself. Seeing two people get down like that had her absolutely mesmerized.

Randall's eyes were filled with lust. "Touch her back. Just put your hand on her back while she sucks. Go ahead," he urged, looking at Magnolia's hand and then at his wife, as if drawing an imaginary line to guide her.

Magnolia took a deep breath and placed her fingertip on Kandi's lower back, standing behind her, and then she used her whole hand. She noticed the smoothness of Kandi's skin, unlike any man she'd ever touched before.

She had a bird's-eye view of Kandi's dick-sucking skills, and preferred to look at the deep throat action as opposed to into Randall's familiar eyes. That would have ruined her self-talk, speaking to her better judgment, trying to convince it that it was not really Randall. It was only a black dick, getting some head, that it really wasn't the dick of her best friend's former husband.

Within thirty seconds, Kandi was on all fours, backed up to Randall who was deep inside, delving and pumping his stiffness, looking back at Magnolia, who watched closely. Kandi's lower back was tramped out with a scripted stamp that claimed her as his, that read, *Randall's*.

Now caught up in the allure of erotic voyeurism, Magnolia was at the point of no return, and she lifted her own dress, put her hand inside her panties and fingered herself. She was soaked.

Randall reached back and took her hand, placing it on his back. He found her other hand and placed it on his shoulder and brought her closer to him so that her full breasts pressed against his back. He smelled of alcohol. She smelled of gardenia.

She found herself moving in the same motion as his fucking.

And it was as though another person, a vixen disguised as Magnolia, suddenly said, "Fuck her. Get that pussy. Let me see how you fuck her. Show me what that big dick can do." She'd gone further into the sin den, and played along.

And Kandi moaned a long moan like a cat in heat. She looked back with her golden, bedroom eyes, and arched her back, taking in the sight of Magnolia behind her man. Kandi fucked Randall back faster and harder. Her intense wetness meeting his thrusting penis made sultry sloshing sounds.

Randall grabbed the back of Magnolia's head, bringing her face to his neck. He instantly yelled. "Ahh, yeah. Ummgh. Ummgh." His frame tensed up and he lost control.

Magnolia spoke along the skin of his shoulder. "That's it. That's how you come inside of that pussy." Her words came from a mind that was caught up. Caught up into the newness of the freaky.

Randall wound down his release and also wound back up just as fast.

Magnolia rose from the bed behind him and stood, shaking her head. It was like at that very instant, her guilt had gotten over its amnesia. And her sanity hit hard again.

Randall reached out his hand toward her to see if he could again reach her new side. His eyes, half-bloodshot but lust filled and hopeful, invited her out to play just a little longer.

Kandi lay still, rubbing her pleased vagina and offering a look of *you're next, you lucky girl.*

Magnolia looked at Randall's large right hand and saw the bling of his Dolphins Super Bowl ring on his long, thick middle finger.

And she was gone just as quick as he came.

Completely and utterly bothered.

Fourteen

———— ⌘ ————

"Better Days"

Darla

INT.—DARLA'S FATHER'S HOME—DAYTONA BEACH,
FLORIDA—LATE MORNING
March 7, 2009

Darla's father lived in Daytona Beach, Florida, in the same mid-century home Darla grew up in.

She hadn't actually taken the time to drive up and see him in about five months. And she knew better. It just seemed that each time she had intentions of seeing him, she just couldn't motivate herself to go. Seeing him lonely reminded her of what it's like to be frozen in time.

The day was in the mid-seventies. Not a cloud in the sky. The perfect day for a four-hour drive to the place she'd called home. A drive away from her life of trying to make ends meet, trying to find a way to live her dream.

In her black jeans with a coral top and bronze sandals, Darla walked in after her father opened the screen door.

Wearing khaki pants and a dark plaid shirt, he

headed back barefoot across the parquet floor to his favorite place in his house, the right side of his hunter green sofa in his sunroom, the side with the cushions that, through the years, had conformed to the shape of his backside.

"Hi, Daddy," she said, with a sweet tone.

Though he walked like he was forty, he sat back down in slow motion and gave a grunt. His sciatic nerve had always acted up, radiating down his right side for years. He stretched out his legs. "What's going on with you, darlin'?" His television was tuned to a gardening show.

Darla's father had robbed the cradle. Her mother was about ten years younger. But gray hair just barely made its visit, even though he was almost seventy. He was a sepia tone, almost five-ten, and had a slight beer belly.

Darla walked to him and leaned down to kiss his high forehead that matched hers. "Missing you. I need to get by here more. And missing Mom."

"Me, too," he said, offering a sad smile. "You want anything to drink or eat? There's some Kool-Aid and orange juice, and some leftover turkey chili."

"Oh, I'm fine, Daddy. Thanks." Darla took a seat next to him on the sofa, patting him on his thigh. "So. You look good."

"Thanks. I feel good. You look good, too. Still wearing your hair short I see."

"Yes. It's easier." She patted the back of her head and then fluffed up the top strands along her forehead. "And you know I love my bangs."

"It's nice."

"Thanks." She inhaled his compliments, which was his usual nature to offer. The nature she'd grown to love. And another thing she loved about him was that he never talked about her weight. She was getting to be about the same size as her mother, but he never said a word. He liked a woman with a little meat on her bones.

Darla exhaled, wondering why she didn't make the drive more often, and slipped off her shoes, crossing her legs at the ankles.

He looked back toward the TV screen.

Darla watched him closely. "Do you get lonely sometimes? Any friends or anyone you spend time with?"

"No. I don't get lonely and I don't have any friends."

"Okay. And no ladies?"

He looked at her with a raised brow. "Especially not that."

"I know." Darla glanced all around. It was a three-bedroom house with the master on the main.

He rarely even went upstairs. It was basically going to waste, but the home was paid for and he took care of himself fairly well. Even when she was little, he was always the one to cook and clean. He loved to barbeque so he grilled all the time years ago. Today, his place looked tidy, but his furniture, drapes, and televisions were old. They were the same items he and Darla's mother had when Darla grew up. He was old school. He'd never think of getting a cell phone or a computer. In his mind, he lived just fine. He was just missing his wife. It was just that simple.

Darla asked, almost as though she was just checking, "Daddy, if I needed to move in with you, could I?" It was her plan B solution. She dared not ask him for money. He'd worry.

His bushy eyebrows reacted as he looked at her. He asked, "Why? Are you okay?"

"I'm okay. It's just that I'm thinking about opening a store, or some type of business. If I do, I might need to save as much money as I can, and staying here would let me do that while I run the store and see how it goes."

"What kind of store?"

"A clothing store."

"Really? I didn't know you knew anything about that."

"Other than a merchandising class in college and that summer job at the Gap years ago, not much experience, but I think I could do it. Didn't you and Mom own a burger joint for a minute when I was born?"

"We did. Your mom knew about the restaurant business from managing one before we met. And me with my accounting, we worked it out, darlin'."

"That must be where I get it from. My independent spirit."

"Yes, you do have that. Where would you open the store?"

"I was thinking Miami, but if I moved in, it would be a place out here. Not sure if it'd be cheaper. Just thinking though."

"I see. The answer is yes. You know that. Having you here would breathe some life into this old house."

"Well, thanks. Looks like this house is just fine though." She sat back and crossed her legs, facing him. "But who knows, maybe I'll settle down again and won't have to bother you."

He resumed his focus on the TV screen, but took her hand. "Maybe."

She looked down at his wide hand, his aging fingers and pronounced veins that ran from his wrist and up the back of his hand. And he still wore his gold wedding band. She held his hand with both of hers. "One thing's for sure, I won't be having any kids, so, sorry I never gave you any grandkids."

"You and Aaron weren't meant to have any, so being that God took him home, it wasn't meant to be."

"True."

"Don't apologize to me for that. I'm fine. You just do what you need to do to make yourself happy. And if that's opening a business, then fine."

"I'm trying. I'm trying to do the right thing. I'm trying to make you proud."

"I'm already proud. And your mom's proud too."

"Daddy. Seriously though, I think maybe I might want to marry again."

"You do?"

"Yes."

"Why?" he asked.

"I get lonely. It's been five years."

"I get lonely, too. But in honor of your mother, here I'll be. Now what you do is up to you. You're a grown woman. I can't tell you what to do. All I can say is be true to your heart."

"My heart is the reason I haven't moved on. It's my head that tells me it's time to be open to meeting some-one new."

"Then that's what you need to do. Just do the right thing."

"The right thing. Wow. That sentence sounds simple, but sometimes, Daddy, haven't you ever done something

you knew was wrong? Didn't you ever give in to tempta-
tion? Just throw caution to the wind and be crazy. Wild.
Take a risk."

"Not much. I pretty much had drama-free years with
your mother. My life with her was spent living according
to our vows, and my life after she passed has been spent
according to my devotion to her memory. Now if something is telling you to move on, that's your decision, just
the same as whether or not you open a store. Your heart
will keep you faithful. Listen to your heart. Not faithful
to someone, but faithful to yourself. I'm being faithful
to myself based on who I am. You be faithful to yourself based on who you are. All the rest is just part of the
learning lesson of life."

"I hear you, Daddy." She focused on the words of wisdom he'd spoken, and his handsome profile. "You really
do look good."

"I feel good, darlin'."

"Now that makes me happy."

He picked up the remote and aimed it toward the TV,
pressing off. He turned toward Darla. "So, you're forty
now, right?"

"I am." She turned toward him a bit more.

"Then it just might be time to start living. You were
a good wife. Aaron will always be with you in spirit.
Only you know what he'd be okay with, but you're the
one who's still here. Being here makes me happy. You do
what makes you happy."

She smiled. "True. I understand."

"And when you're ready to move in, just say so."

"Okay, Daddy."

"You look beautiful, Darla. Your mother had you

when she was twenty-four. She died when you were sixteen. When she passed away, she was forty like you are now. Live."

Darla's heart thumped. "Yes, Daddy. I will."

His eyes were in mourning. "Darla, do you ever wish heaven had a phone?" He stared at the wall, at a photo of him and his devoted wife.

"Yes, Daddy. I surely do." Darla looked at the photo, too. "I'd dial that number every single day."

He nodded and said, "Me, too."

After an entire afternoon of talking, heading to Home Depot for the new patio furniture he'd had his eyes on, a new gas grill he'd been wanting to buy, and then to lunch at one of his favorite places to eat, Applebee's, Darla and her father arrived back at his home, and said their good-byes as she left.

Darla kept an eye on her father, who watched her walk to her car. She got in and pulled out of the driveway, and kept looking back at him, watching him stand in the doorway, just as she did every time she left, never knowing if it would be the last time she'd ever see him. He'd promised to grill for her soon. She looked forward to that. Unlike some females', her father had been there from day one, and she was thankful for that. He raised her with values and unconditional love. And he was all she really had.

I love you, Daddy.

Fifteen

---❧---

"Sexual Healing"

Rebe

INT.—REBE'S HOME—MIAMI BEACH—MORNING
March 10, 2009

After another night of hanging out at young Armani's bachelor pad, the sexual athlete himself, getting smacked up, flipped, and rubbed down, bachelorette Rebe walked away at a snail's pace under the new morning sun. She wore a royally sexed up look on her face, doing the *morning after I got some* walk of shame, stepping barefoot to her car with her teal blue high heels in her hands. Her head hurt and her stomach cramped. But she had a smile on her face.

She drove home at ten in the morning, blue skies and zero traffic, listening to the most appropriate song on her radio, "Sexual Healing," by Marvin Gaye.

Releasing her mind was just what Rebe needed. She was finally able to feel what it was like to go beyond the thoughts her mother had put in her head, or to be more exact, forced into her head, since she was a child, always labeling Rebe a sinner who equated to a whore.

Now it was all about Rebe's own, grown woman sexy healing.

Rebe looked ahead, not worrying about the past, just being whoever she wanted to be and doing whatever she wanted to do, without criticism, judgment, or repercussions. She was a stripper, soon she'd try out a swinger's club for the first time in her life, and she was having regular fuck sessions with a man young enough to be her son.

Still, she'd made a point of not having Armani over to her place, just because of his age.

Her no's were now yes's, on her terms.

And the new medicine she was on didn't hurt either.

When Rebe arrived home, the garage door trundled up and she pulled her car into the garage, parking next to Trinity's Mustang. Every time she saw that car it still reminded her of Randall, but nonetheless, she hummed the Marvin Gaye tune, even after turning off the ignition, and walked into the house through the door that led from the garage to the kitchen.

"Trinity," she called as she entered.

"I'm in here," Trinity said from the family room.

Rebe followed her daughter's voice and the sound of the television, and then her eyes leapt. "What are you doing?"

"What do you mean?" Trinity sat on the micro-suede sectional without looking up.

"What is Chyna doing here?" Randall's one-and-a-half-year-old daughter was sitting in Trinity's lap, playing with a toy telephone.

"What do you mean what's she doing here? She's your stepdaughter." Trinity angled her eyes toward her mother, looking as though her own actions were routine. Her tone did have a sly bit of sarcasm.

Rebe noticed, and her antenna went up even higher. "Oh no, she's not." She placed her keys in her purse and tossed it onto the sofa chair.

"How can she be my stepsister and not your stepdaughter? Come on now Mommy, did you take your manic meds? Or maybe it's those new ones your gynecologist prescribed for your low testosterone. And also, you're on Avitan, right? Did you skip a pill? "

Rebe wondered if her ears were playing tricks. "Trinity. I'm gonna count to three." She took a grip of her mind and waited for it to rewind, looking away and then back, as though it made a difference. But her flushed skin said it didn't. "Trinity, maybe when you get your own place you can make these decisions, and talk like that to whoever is in your house, but this is my home, and as much as I don't want to feel like this, I do. That is trifling Randall's baby with the white girl he left me for. Actually, the truth is, he left us for."

Trinity giggled as she held her sister. "Mommy, please. He didn't leave me. And that night you went looking for him and found him, if you hadn't gone off and kicked him out, he'd probably still be here. It's just that you went berserk."

Rebe's blood pressure was rising. She could feel it. "You know what? I did not go berserk. I don't know what he told you. And I'm telling you now, you'd better be glad this baby girl is here, because I don't think I've gone upside your head in about six years, but today would be just the day. And it just might be if you keep flapping your lips out of disrespect to your mother. I'm not having that." Rebe stood over them both.

Chyna looked up at Rebe and so did Trinity. "Mommy. You..."

Rebe took a half step closer. "Mommy, you, what? Say it, Trinity. What? Please say it. Because I'm about ready for you today."

Trinity ducked her head and shielded Chyna's face with her hand. "Mommy, don't hit me. I wouldn't want to end up getting my head split open like your mother did to you. Are any of those bottles labeled chill pill?"

Rebe bit her lip and balled up her fist. Her voice was big, and it was pissed off. "Bitch." She took a deep breath, looked at Chyna's on-edge expression, and spoke one tone lower. "Trinity. Put that child in the room and come back in here. I give you two minutes." She stepped in the direction of the stairwell.

"No."

Rebe's jaw was tight. "I give you two minutes to come in my room. And if you don't, I'm coming back down here and your ass is mine, Chyna or not." Rebe's head seeped smoke from her ears. Her mind was on fire. She stomped her heavy feet that carried her heavy heart upstairs into her bedroom, and slammed the door with a force reserved for a WWE wrestler.

All that could be heard from downstairs was evil shouting. "Your own mother's in jail for killing your brother. My Uncle Maestro, who I'll never ever meet, other than in heaven. Don't you think you should learn to curb your temper?"

The three sentence-missiles hit as if seeking a double target. Rebe's heart and her back.

Rebe's ears shook. Forehead was sweaty. Eyes blinked like a tornadic wind was in the room. Nostrils flared. Goose bumps formed on her skin, even on her fingers. She could feel the tattoo with her brother's name on her shoulder bubbling up like it was boiling syrup. Her mind insisted that she sit on the end of the bed, where she found herself panting, forcing herself to breathe normally. Heart arrhythmia was in overdrive. The video in her head shifted from the fantasy of her beating the hell out of her daughter, and the reality of her mother beating the shit out of her. Rebe couldn't turn it off, and found herself reeling with anxiousness. She leaned forward with her elbows to her knees, and shielded her face into the palms of her hands, and she cried as a voice asked, *Where's that hammer? Get it.*

Two seconds later she hopped up and yanked the door open, sprinting back into the family room with a red face and a deep frown, ready to put her daughter in her place. Ready to teach Trinity a lesson for having such a fast mouth.

She entered an empty room. No Trinity. No Chyna. The TV was still on, but they were not there. "Trinity, where the fuck are you?"

Nothing.

"Trinity." Her words reverberated in her head and it shook.

Nothing.

"Get the fuck in this room, now." Her own ears popped. With tears still flowing, she ran through the house, looking in every room, and ended up heading out the front door. The garage door was open, but Trinity's car was gone.

Rebe screamed up toward the sky and felt a rumble in her stomach, suddenly running to the side section of the lawn where she vomited, repeatedly, and violently. She heaved and gagged and remained bent over and waited. Her breaths got shorter. More tears flowed from the forcefulness of her expulsion.

She stayed in place with her mouth open, working hard to catch her breath, her nose running.

While she wiped her lips with her hand, she said the same four words she'd said every single solitary day of her life. "Mother, I hate you."

Sixteen

"Worst-Case Scenario"

Magnolia

INT.—MAGNOLIA'S HOME—MIAMI BEACH
March 14, 2009

Guilt was kicking Magnolia's butterscotch ass.

She'd tossed and turned for two weeks straight and just couldn't bring herself to tell Rebe that she'd had a freaky night as sexual cheerleader with her ex-husband and his new wife.

She wondered if maybe she was having such a hard time because she couldn't believe it herself. Did it really happen, or was it just her imagination? Did she watch Randall eat pussy and get his dick sucked by his wife and screw her doggy style, the enemy, the other woman who'd stolen her best friend's man? The man who said "I do" to Rebe, who stood beside her and Darla, Rebe's maids of honor on Rebe's wedding day years ago. Yet she'd seen the spectacular penis of the man who crushed Rebe's heart by cheating on her.

How could I let myself do that?

Rebe's my girl.

She's been to hell and back.

Who the hell am I?

Magnolia piddled around the house, straightening up and washing clothes, doing mindless things, which were about all her brain had room for. She fixed herself a lasagna dinner with a spinach salad, and then sat on the sofa in front of her television, trying to relax, fighting to chase away thoughts of her newfound online hoochie life, and her staying true to her promise to Rebe and her new lover to go to Erotic City soon.

She flipped through home design channels, CNN news, the movie *New Jack City*, which was showing on BET, and a variety of reality shows. Her thoughts shifted to what was possibly awaiting TastyTangie online, on GFF. Part of her was curious. She leaned forward to brace herself to stand, and something pushed her back down when she remembered that Randall had known it was her. She shook her head at herself. *I'm shutting all that crap down.*

Magnolia refocused on the television screen and switched back to the Wesley Snipes movie, just as Wesley asked, "Am I my brother's keeper?"

She crossed her legs, swaddling herself with her leopard Snuggie, when her doorbell rang.

Magnolia got up and went to the front window, peeking through the thick slats of her wooden living room blinds, but there was no sight of a car, or anyone at the door.

She walked to the door and looked through the peephole. "Who is it?" Nothing.

She headed back to the couch, and the doorbell rang again. Along with the voice, "Magnolia, it's me. Neal."

Oh hell. With an angry forehead, she headed back to the door and spoke close to it. "What, Neal? And don't just show up over here unannounced."

"I know. I know. I'm sorry. I just need to talk to you. I've been trying to reach you. I need to apologize. I didn't want to approach you at work, and since you won't take my calls, I decided this is the best thing, just come on by."

"Actually, no, it's not. I just looked out and you weren't there. What's up with you?"

"I knew if you saw me you'd pretend to not be home. I needed to make sure you were here. Please open the door. Please."

"Dammit." She unbolted the door and jerked the knob, pulling the door toward her. "What?"

"Mag. Can I come in?"

She stepped aside, he stepped in wearing a sweat suit, she closed the door and turned her back to it, shifting her weight to one leg. His scent was his usual Old Spice bodywash.

He stood in the dimly lit entryway and glanced into the family room.

She said right away, "And no, you can't. This is as far as you get."

"I was just making sure you were alone." He looked straight at her. "Mag. Why are you on GFF?"

"Oh Lord."

"Really. I want to know. Why?"

"I'm not."

"You are."

She shifted her weight onto her other leg. "Dammit, Neal. Even if I was, that would be none of your business, now would it? Obviously you're on it or you wouldn't ask. And I don't give a damn anyway."

"Yes, I'm on it. Keyonna and I are on it. And so are you. Same city. Same age. Same height. Same damn orange bra I bought you. Same titties. My titties. Same fucking red tattoo on your neck." His words grew bigger. "Not to mention the fucking charm you had on. See the problem is, she and I are supposed to be on it. You, Mag, are not."

She snickered at him for using the word *my* anything. She knew he was already a member, but didn't know he'd found her on there for sure until now. She tried to play it all off. "And what makes you think I'm not supposed to be on a freak site, Neal?"

"You're not like that."

"Oh, I'm the good girl, huh?"

"Exactly."

"Well, actually, I have found that bad girls like Keyonna finish first. So I wanna try and see what that's like. I'd say it's way past time for me to be first. You chose Keyonna over me. Randall chose Kandi over Rebe. Maybe being wild in bed has its advantages."

"Mag, there's nothing but trouble on GFF, I'm telling you now."

"So why do you pay for it then?" She found herself about to get caught. She rephrased her question. "I mean, you spend money to be on a site that you know is trouble?"

"I'm part of a couple. The single women on there can get into trouble."

"So how many single women have you two gotten with? Did they look like they were afraid of trouble when you and your girl had threesomes with them? That's what all this is about. I guess I'm trouble, too, then, since I'm a single member. But you've finally got what you wanted. You've got a freak in the sheets. Remember, you said I was class in the streets and class in the sheets. You said that's not how it works. So, make it work. I now plan to make it work for me."

"See, I don't understand. Didn't what Keyonna said give you enough of an idea of how I'm still stuck on your ass? Can't you see I'm not over you? If I was, I wouldn't still have you in my head when I'm with her. And I wouldn't be here now."

"You having some woman in your head when you have sex with someone else is no big deal for you. I know when I was with you, you always had someone else in your perverted mind. You think I didn't notice? I wasn't as clueless and square as you thought. You were somewhere else in your mind with me then, just like you are with her now."

"I don't know what you're talking about. You're in my head, and in my heart." He looked to the side and let out a large exhale. He aimed his sight back at her and took a step closer. "I want you back, Mag. I want you back in my life."

She looked away as she replied. "You only want me because you don't have me. Once you got me back, then what? You'd do to me just what you're doing to Keyonna, trying to get some new pussy, old pussy, some pussy other than what you had. Never satisfied. Face it. You're not a one-woman man, Neal. And it's okay." She put her hand on the doorknob. "Now please, if you don't mind, I'm going to get back to my evening. Alone."

He tried to aim her face to his with his stare. It worked. "Mag. Look at me. You can't deny how you still feel about me. I see it."

She sounded like she was amused. "Yeah right. You can't see a damn thing. Sparkle gone!"

He grinned. "Sparkle there!" he said, speaking adamantly.

She looked away again.

He said, "Baby, please. This is the worst-case scenario. I don't want anyone else but you. I don't care about Keyonna. I don't care about Bambi, or Trixie, or anyone else. I want you back."

"Neal." Magnolia's cell phone rang, light blinking from the coffee table. She stood looking down at the floor, and crossed her arms.

"Baby."

It rang again. And again. She opened the front door for him to leave. Her cell rang again.

He looked over at it. "Someone looking for you?"

All she did was step fast to the table. "Hello?"

She heard, "Let me talk to Neal."

"Who is this?"

"It's Keyonna. I know he's there. Let me talk to him."

"Keyonna, have you lost your mind calling on my number?"

Neal went from standing with his arms crossed before him, to dropping his hands and moving closer to Magnolia.

Keyonna was loud. "Why would you have my man over? As nice as I tried to be to you."

Magnolia was louder. "Oh, now see, let me tell you something, bitch." She pointed her finger in the air and moved her head about. "You don't call on my cell and get nasty with me. Actually, don't you call me at all. If you ever do again, I promise you I'll file a police report for harassment."

"I don't give a shit. Put his ass on the phone. Now."

Neal stood right in front of Magnolia and moved his hand toward her to take the phone. She pushed away his arm and turned her back. "What you can do is call him in about two minutes. On his damn phone. I guarantee you he'll answer it then."

"Fuck you."

"Fuck you, you dyke ass ho," Magnolia screamed.

"You're the one who—" Click. Magnolia pressed the off switch on her phone and slid it across the table. "Neal. Get the fuck out now." She pointed to the door. "Don't bring your silly ass drama into my life like this. Acting like you're done with her. Get out of my house."

"But—"

She hurried to the door. "Get. The. Fuck. Out." Her face was disgusted.

He followed. "Mag. I love you. I'll handle her." He took two steps to the other side of the doorframe and prepared to turn back to her. His mouth prepared to speak.

Magnolia slammed the door and double locked it, turned off the porch light, turned off the TV, and headed for her master bedroom.

She turned on her laptop, immediately logged on to GFF, and canceled her membership.

TastyTangie was no more.

It was enough just handling Magnolia Butler.

She spoke aloud, "That Negro has some nerve. Bitch

calling on my fuckin' phone. I've got enough shit in my life, I don't need no mess like that crap. I don't think so."

She shut it all down, climbed into bed, and laid her head down in the dark.

That night, Magnolia once again tried to fall asleep.

But just as she did the other nights since she'd played with Randall and Kandi, she failed.

And it, along with Neal's nerve, were eating her alive.

Seventeen

"Secret Lover"

Darla

INT.—DARLA'S BEDROOM—MIAMI BEACH—EARLY
MORNING
March 19, 2009

Darla begged, "Nine. Stop." His body was very short,
and very thick, but he was very, very hung.

The tawdry, muted porno movie called *Kinky Kiki*
played on the TV screen, but nobody was watching. It
was an expert ménage scene gone to waste.

"Relax, baby." He rubbed her firm, thick legs while
on top of her generous frame. His words were greedy,
like he was hungry for every pound. "Yeah, those are
the thighs I saw when you walked past me earlier
today. The closer you got I was like, yeah, that's a
goddess there. I'm a leg man. And I like 'em just like
this. These sweet, shapely legs got my dick hard from
the first second I saw you. And now my dick is digging inside of this fat, juicy pussy. Sweet like mango
juice."

Her eyes squinted and she winced. "Nine?" Darla said
his name as a question.

He was named after the size of his dick. "Wait, just one minute, baby. Hold up."

"Nine. It's too long."

He ground a couple more times and then paused. "Are you okay?" he asked, sounding like he might not really care either way.

Darla spoke from underneath him. "It's just that it feels like it's all up in my stomach. Like it could end up in my throat."

"I can just do it slower, or maybe not put it in all the way. Know what I'm saying?"

Darla scooted back to make his penis come out. "It just feels like, maybe I'm dry, or, I don't know. It feels like every time you pull back, and then in again, like my vagina's going to split open."

He spoke close to her face. He had sweat on his forehead and his eyes were red. His breath was warm and stale. "Oh. Well, how about if I eat you again? I can do that."

She shook her head along the pillow. "No. It's okay. That part was good. But, I just can't do this."

Nine reached down to make sure his condom was still secure and not inside of her, and then he turned over onto his back. "Okay. Let's just lay still for a minute."

"Sorry," Darla said as if it was all her fault.

"No problem. Maybe another position. Maybe on all fours. Know what I'm saying?"

"No," was all she was saying. She closed her eyes.

"Are you okay?" he asked again, not looking at her.

She turned her head toward him and looked down at his still hard dick. "I just thought I was ready for it, or for this. It's different from what I was used to. It's been a long time. Five years."

"Really? So you haven't been with anyone since 2004? Is that what you're telling me?" He still looked away.

"Yes. That's what I'm telling you. My husband was my one and only lover for almost twenty years. Well, I did have one other, but only once."

"Wow. I mean that's good. You're a queen. A real lady. Know what I'm saying?"

"I don't know about all that, but I know for a fact that he was nowhere near as large and long as you."

"I'm the one who's sorry. We don't have to."

She looked down at his size again. "I've never even seen a condom on a man, other than the movies. And how do you fit that on you? What size is that anyway?"

"Durex XXL."

"Wow." She looked in shock.

"You'll be fine. You just need someone to take their time and break you in. Know what I'm saying?"

Darla gave a small laugh and looked up at the ceiling. She said in her mind, *If he says, "know what I'm saying" one more time* . . . "You make it sound like I'm a virgin."

Suddenly, his tone changed. He now looked at her. "That's exactly what you are. A damn virgin. Know what I'm saying? How the hell you gonna be a virgin at forty? With a pussy that damn tight. What the hell is your problem?" She looked over at his face and suddenly saw the devil himself. "Are you some kind of sexually repressed, closet lesbian or what? And you just lay there like a damn corpse. What you need to do is take all this dick and get this shit over with, with your fat . . ."

"Ahh," Darla pressed the breath she'd been momentarily holding while she slept and her eyes burst open like they'd popped. In her head she could still hear, "Know what I'm saying?" It rang like a doorbell. She caught her exhale in time to force a sufficient inhale and grabbed her throat and tried to calm her chest.

Her room was dark.

She was alone in bed.

And she was sweating like a first-place marathon runner in Zimbabwe.

"Oh my God." Inhale, exhale. "What was that all about? That young man was a trip." She drew another deep breath, let it out fast, and saw the omniscient red light from her alarm clock that read 4:44 in the morning.

It was the same time of the morning that she and Aaron would joke they'd always awake automatically just before they'd adjust sleeping positions for a final hour of slumber. And there she was in her solo bed of one, dreaming about having sex with another man.

A man who her shy vagina would not accommodate.

"What in the world is that going to be like? God forbid it's with someone like that. I'm a pretty sad case. Aren't I Aaron?"

In her spinning head, she convinced herself that Aaron brushed the side of her cheek with the back of his hand as usual. She felt it for sure. And smiled. All was easier to take for a minute.

Within the next hour, Darla was up and showered, dressed in her work uniform and tennis shoes, and in her kitchen brewing her morning black coffee. She grabbed a vanilla Slim Fast shake from the fridge, popped it open, and sipped.

After a swallow, she asked herself, "Why do I drink these when all I do is stay the same size?"

She stepped to the balcony of her condo and leaned against the white railing, looking out along the majestic, first morning vision, and eyeing the aqua waters of the Atlantic Ocean. The fresh sun shone its tangerine highlight in flickers of light that spanned across the water's horizon like a gigantic fan.

How did I end up alone? A widow by the time I was thirty-five. No credit. No money. A job I hate. And still I have the nerve to want to open a lingerie store. Who in the hell is going to give me a loan?

She found herself headed to her built-in bookshelf in her living room where she found her cherished, black study Bible that her mother gave her on her twelfth birthday. It was even signed "Presented to Darla, By Mom, On January 1, 1981."

She set down her shake and flipped through the pages of the Bible, opening it to a section that was bookmarked by a long, thin, ivory crucifix. Darla noticed some scribbled notes alongside the explanation of the verses. Her mother had written, *It may be late, but it's not too late. It only depends on how hungry you are. Get hungry for purpose. If you're not hungry, he won't come with food. A fast will sharpen the things of God. Empty yourself, for yourself.* The writing was on a particular highlighted page, *Isaiah 4, verse 4—The Lord will wash away the filth of the women of Zion; he will cleanse the bloodstains from Jerusalem by a spirit of judgment and a spirit of fire.*

Darla took in the words, read them again, and it was like she could hear her mother speak to her. Darla sniffled and then her eyes filled with tears, and they flowed heavy and fast until she could no longer see the writing from the water-clouds in her eyes.

She clutched the Bible close to her, just as her home phone rang.

Darla walked to the kitchen phone and said a nasally, "Hello."

"Mrs. Clark, it's Ralph, the concierge from downstairs. We have a delivery for you that's been at the front desk since yesterday. It's a certified letter that we took, but you need to sign the card. I don't know if anyone called or put a slip in your mailbox. I know it's early, but would you like to come get it on your way out, or we can bring it up?"

Darla sniffled again and patted her cheeks. "Yes, please bring it up. And don't worry about it being early. I don't think I'm going in to work today."

A knock at the door ten minutes later was answered by Darla, who was now in her nightgown and slippers, with a white silk robe wrapped around her. Her hair was brushed straight back.

With her red nose and makeup-stripped face, she opened the door and took the envelope, signed the green confirmation card, and handed the man a few dollars.

"Thanks, Ralph."

"Surely. Have a great day, Mrs. Clark."

Darla shut the door, examining the letter front and back, expecting it to be another letter from the homeowners association, or the bank.

She opened the letter, headed to the kitchen for that cup of brewed coffee that had her name on it, saying aloud, "Oh please. This is all I need right now."

She read.

Mrs. Clark,

We have been unable to locate you since December 2004. Your husband took out a supplemental life policy one year before his death. We'd been trying to verify that his medical records did not indicate a pre-existing condition that was not noted on his application. When we cannot locate beneficiaries, we sometimes check public notices to verify the whereabouts of unclaimed benefits. Enclosed please find a check in the amount of five hundred thousand dollars. Please contact me if you have any questions.

> Sincerely,
> Rita Walters,
> Life Insurance Disbursement Manager
> Allstate Insurance Company

Darla was careful to examine the check, which was attached to the letter via paper clip. She saw her name, but it didn't seem real. She saw the numeric amount, but she couldn't believe it.

She put her hand over her heart and her head spun. Darla dropped the letter and the half-million-dollar check onto the floor, and stood. She was completely still, not wanting to awake from what could have been an amazing dream.

She turned her face toward her Bible that she'd left open, which was sitting on her dining room table and she had a look of disbelief, and then the look of a woman blessed with a dream come true.

Darla, shaking, dropped to her knees, clasped her hands, lifted her head up high, and said to the heavens above, "Thank you, Mom. Thank you, Aaron."

That next day, she gave her two weeks' notice and quit her job.

Her dream could now become a reality.

Eighteen

"Erotic City"

Magnolia

INT.—EROTIC CITY SWINGER'S CLUB—DOWNTOWN,
MIAMI—LATE EVENING

March 25, 2009

Out of feeling an internal need to concede to Rebe, just from the sheer feeling of the loud voice of her wrongdoings, Magnolia agreed to keep her promise and go with Rebe and Armani to the new swinger's club in Miami called Erotic City. She'd agreed mainly out of not being able to say no, but also because she was a little bit curious.

Darla had decided to pass, telling both Rebe and Magnolia the good news via three-way call. She told them she was handling her necessary business, including going back to one of the locations to sign a lease for her new store. They cheered Darla on and agreed to celebrate later.

Tonight, though, was a big step toward Magnolia's and Rebe's New Year's resolutions, and they convinced themselves they were ready to try the lifestyle, if only for one night.

Magnolia sat in the passenger seat of Rebe's
Mercedes, and Armani rode along, sitting in the backseat. Magnolia kept her mind on the topic of Randall
and Kandi rather than think about what awaited her
at the sex club. She'd actually called Rebe from work
the day before to tell her what happened, but chickened
out. She changed the subject once the words just
wouldn't flow right. She didn't know how to tell her
friend who'd been through more than enough her entire
life. Magnolia believed telling her what transpired with
her ex-husband deserved a face-to-face, and she was just
going to have to be a big enough woman to do it. But
not tonight.

They valet parked and Magnolia looked up at the
purple neon sign that read, *EC Miami*.

From the outside, you couldn't tell what was really
going on behind freaky closed doors. It was owned by
Milan Kennedy Lewis and Lavender Lewis, a couple
who had a very successful swinger's club in Atlanta,
yet who'd just opened their second location in central
Miami-Dade County, on 77th Avenue. Lavender was a
former boxing champ who was known the world over,
and his new wife, Milan, was the daughter of a famous
jazz musician from the sixties. They were also raising
Lavender's son, Taj. Lavender's son's psycho mother was
serving time in jail for trying to kill Milan in a jealous
rage. But Milan and Lavender were now on the other
side of drama.

Rebe's young, hot lover, Armani, walked in with
Magnolia and Rebe on each arm like he owned the
place, as he was on the VIP guest list. He showed them
the ropes, so to speak, schooling them on the art of en-

gaging. He suggested they only watch the first time out until they felt more comfortable.

The club itself was two stories and looked like a giant warehouse, decorated in passionate colors like cherry red and grape, with intimate rooms lined with comfy sofas and chairs. Armani then walked off with Rebe, in her hot pants, sparkly, ocean blue bikini top, and high heels. Magnolia wore a black bustier with white embroidery, showing all of her upper anatomy, and a pair of tight cheetah jeans, showing her lower anatomy. She sat at the bar on a silver, retro-looking stool, sipping from a plastic cup of White Zinfandel that Armani brought for her and Rebe. It was always a BYOB-type party at Erotic City.

On the large dance floor, lit by turquoise flashing lights, the vibe and flavor of the sex club was a feast for horny sore eyes to see. The DJ's chosen sound was a mix of Latin favorites and pop. The totally uninhibited people got their grooves on, acting like they were at any other regular nightclub in the city, but these ready-to-rumble people were either scantily dressed or butt naked.

There was a huge overhead projection TV screen showing triple X-rated movies. The orgy scene was appropriate, with folks of every color and sex, size and shape, fucking on a row of six mattresses. Getting off. And right below the screen, sitting in a chair, was a man with his legs spread open, with a G-string-wearing woman giving him what looked to be first-class head right out in front of everyone, though only the newbies seemed shocked. Others watched without amazement just as voyeurs, and the man getting the blowjob watched those who looked on, just to satisfy the exhibitionist in him. It only added to his sex high.

"How are you?" a young woman asked Magnolia. But she'd walked past quickly before Magnolia could even answer. Magnolia looked back at her and the woman looked back too, winking.

Magnolia smiled back and turned around in a hurry. She wondered if she'd made the right decision by even being there.

Magnolia sat alone for another five minutes, just watching. She saw couples upstairs along the railing, others kissing, some bent over a chair, and some just looking down at the goings-on below. Magnolia tried not to be too affected by the kinky happenings and disclose that she was a true swinger virgin.

"Welcome to Erotic City," said the owner, curly headed, tall and fine Lavender Lewis.

"Thank you," Magnolia replied, noticing every bit of his attractiveness.

He replied, "I know the new ones when I see them."

She grinned, giving a sexy stare. "Oh really. I was trying my best to not let on. I see I failed."

"Maybe you didn't let on to others, but no one can fool me. I've been at this for too long. I'm Lavender, one of the owners." He extended his hand.

Magnolia looked impressed and offered her hand. "Hi. Nice to meet you. I'm Magnolia."

"Hello, Magnolia. Nice name. Can I show you around?"

"Sure." Without hesitation, Magnolia swiveled off the chair and picked up her cup of wine.

And Lavender walked Magnolia around the first

floor, showing her the private rooms, some with closed doors, some with open doors, and showing her one of the group rooms, very similar to the adult movie the club was showing, with two women doing each other, and about five men, lying around or squatted near them, dicks in hand, eyeing down the girl on girl.

He told her, "The upstairs is the S&M room and the girls-only bubble gum room." He took a step farther and pointed out beyond the window. "Outside, if you look through there, you'll see that the playground patio is covered and there are heating lamps. We have a few Jacuzzis, and a black-bottom swimming pool."

"Nice."

He asked, as they stood at the window to the patio for another moment, "You're here alone?"

"No." And then she looked out and saw Rebe and Armani, kissing in the Jacuzzi, totally naked, with three men and one woman watching them, crowded around as though if Rebe or Armani said even one inviting word or gave a join us glance, they'd be down for a fuckfest for real. "I came with them." She pointed.

"Oh, Armani."

"Yes."

"Oh okay. He told me about you and his girl, right?"

"Yes. Rebe."

"Right, right. Yeah. He's cool people."

Magnolia nodded as she took one last glance and looked away.

"Well, if you need anything, just let me know. My wife's name is Milan. We just want you to have a good time, and hope you come back if you like it here."

"I'm sure I will."

"Good. Nice to meet you."

"You, too." He stepped away.

She watched his swagger of a stroll, and said, "Now that is a man for your ass, there," walking back toward the dance floor, and past a mirrored room painted in dark blue, that was occupied by a couple. The woman was younger, naked, Asian, and the man was around fifty, thin, wearing only underwear.

As soon as the man saw Magnolia, he said fast, "Come on in. We'd love the company."

She stopped in her tracks, and took a step back to the doorway. She smiled and walked in very slow.

"Have a seat." He pointed to the chair near the wall. "I'm Tim. This is Shari. Do you want to play?" He cut right to the chase. "We call it a three-piece suit. You won't be disappointed."

Magnolia barely sat when she said, "It's my first time." In her mind she said, *sort of.*

"We'll be gentle."

His wife's smile said she agreed.

Magnolia set her wine on a small table and asked, "Can I watch? You know, help you out?"

The man stood, took off his briefs, and closed the door. "Sure. We won't touch you. And you don't have to touch us. Unless you want to."

"Okay," was Magnolia's reply, as though she was good at that.

The man lay on his back and motioned for Shari to come to him. She got ready to sit on his stiff dick, but he said, "Sit on my face." And Shari did.

Magnolia hesitated for only a quick second, and walked closer to the mattress. She couldn't see Tim's face, but she saw every inch of Shari's ass from behind and her mandarin tramp stamp along her lower back. Magnolia crawled onto the bed, fully dressed, and straddled Tim along his thighs, with his stand-up dick between her and Shari. Magnolia put one hand on Shari's slender back, and reached around, grabbing Shari's small, firm titties while Shari was eaten out. Shari's long black hair smelled like lemons.

Magnolia could feel every second of the stiffening of her own nipples in her bustier. She felt like she was about to have a hot flash, and looked through the side mirror and saw herself, on a bed of three, with her hand on a woman's breasts for the first time in her life. She felt a bit of panic and a bit of lust all in one.

Shari moaned the more Magnolia massaged her, flicking her nipple just as Magnolia knew how to do her own. Shari said to her husband, "Baby, look at her. She's rubbing my titties." She looked down at her breasts and noticed Magnolia's plum colored nails. "Look at her pretty fingers on my chest. Oh, baby, you're eating me out and she's rubbing my nipples. It feels so good. Ummh." She watched Magnolia in the mirror, too. "She's so pretty."

He said, "Uh-huh," from down under, and Shari reached back and stroked his dick from behind her back, gripping his shaft like her hand was her pussy.

Magnolia watched Shari's hand job before her, and said to Tim, like she was a sex kitten, "Eat that pussy."

It was obvious he shifted his tongue dance up a notch because Shari began to wail, shoving her pussy closer to his face, and squinting her eyes, doing funny things with her lips while pressing her orgasm onto his tongue. And then they were both silent.

And just as soon as Shari moved backward, crawling off his face, she then climbed onto his penis, with him still on his back, and jerked her pussy to take him in.

Magnolia scooted back to his calf area, and Shari sat straight up on it, raw and ready, and bounced on top of him with a professional precision. It was as though Magnolia was watching a porn movie live and in person. Shari flung her hair from side to side and worked her hips and legs, and ass, and stomach, and bent down to his face, sucking his tongue with a wild kiss, just as her pussy sucked his dick. Tim glanced at Magnolia, with her jeans unzipped, now rubbing the meat of her vagina, and then Tim made a deep, rolling, weeping moan while Shari kept up her fuck speed and he pressed his hips deeper into her and grumbled, sounding like the force of his semen racing from his ballsac to his tip was faster than he could handle. Shari sat up straight and took it all inside of her.

Magnolia said, "Yeah. Shoot that cum. Good boy." Her eyes were taking in the sight of a strange couple fucking, and she felt herself up some more, wanting to press her clit just enough to make it an equal opportunity orgasm encounter, but she came to a stance and zipped up her pants, while Shari climbed off of her man.

Magnolia took hold of her drink while the husband and wife couple lay side by side on their backs. Magnolia said simply, "Bye."

Tim said, "Anytime."

Shari winked, breathing heavily.

Magnolia walked out and closed the door, thinking

of the thrill of the kinky, and ran smack dab into a tall, tan, older white man with a bald head and salt and pepper goatee, and obvious lines of life on his face.

She said, while quickly lifting her cup just high enough to steady it. "Oh excuse me."

"Oh, no problem. It was my fault."

"No, it was mine. I wasn't looking where I was going."

She began to walk on, her head filled with thoughts of what she'd just seen and how her curiosity had been sated, and she asked herself, *Wonder if Rebe is still outside?*

"Would you mind sharing a drink with me? My name is Miller," the man she'd bumped into said.

Magnolia looked back. He was just a few steps behind her, awaiting her reply with a warm smile. "Hi, Miller. I'm looking for my friend, to be honest with you."

"I see. But I'm willing to bet she's having fun."

"Maybe so. She's here with someone. But I think I'm ready to go."

"It's early. Just one drink." He had on all black. His eyes were baby blue.

She stopped and turned back toward him. "Why yes. Yes, I will. That would be nice."

Miller led the way back to the bar area where Magnolia was earlier, and they shared his Malibu rum and pineapple for about an hour.

They laughed.

Soon it was one in the morning.

But Magnolia forgot about the time, and about Rebe.

They sat up talking, drinking, and shutting out the rest of the adult happenings, acting as though it were a Sunday afternoon at Denny's.

Their conversation was perfect.

Figuratively, communication-wise, they were two peas in a pod.

The next night they would go to the Grand Lux in Hollywood, Florida, and have dinner.

They would close the place down, talking, and then go to his place.

Literally, physically, they'd be two pieces that fit well together even better.

Nineteen

---❦---

"Voyeur"

Rebe

SAME PLACE—SAME TIME AS CHAPTER EIGHTEEN

While Magnolia continued to bond with Miller at the Erotic City bar, Rebe and Armani, who'd vowed to one another to only be with each other their first swinging time out, were outside, no longer in the Jacuzzi. They were lying on a king canopy bed that had sheer black curtains. The bed was on the enclosed patio, next to the swimming pool, right under the heat lamps. You could either leave the curtains open using the pullbacks, or close them completely. Closed meant do not disturb, open meant all aboard.

The curtains were open. And the heat lamps had some competition.

Rebe was on her back, mainly keeping her eyes closed, as if she really believed shutting her lids would block out some of the X factor of her first-time exhibitionist experience.

Block out the fact that she was getting her pussy sucked on while complete strangers watched.

Rebe tried to focus on her turn-on, to see if she could muster up an image in her own head, and satisfy herself that way, as opposed to going further with the voyeuristic swinger crowd around her. So in her head, she decided to be extra brave and imagined Armani fucking someone else. She wanted to know if the thought made her heart race like she was a girl gone wild. She wondered also if the way he ate her out would make other women come within seconds, too.

Wearing only her pink peep-toe heels, Rebe's braids rested to her left while she realized she couldn't stay in her head long enough to play with her thoughts, so she cheered herself on to snap out of it, and take in the real-life fantasy before her. To her it was different from dancing on a pole. It was time to play big girl freak now. After all, she'd gotten her own curious self into it.

She looked to her right, noticing about six people watching while Armani's head munched on the lips of her vagina. The feeling of being watched while having sex actually kept her two gears behind what she thought she'd feel. She needed to let go. She fought.

Rebe turned her head to the other side, trying to focus on the actual faces of those around her. She saw that the crowd was growing, now with four more sex-nosey onlookers, all looking like they were either hard or wet and/or ready.

Rebe looked down at Armani, who looked up at her with lustful eyes, and then she noticed a mocha-skinned younger woman getting closer to them both. The woman inched herself to Rebe's side, and within two seconds flat, began sucking Rebe's stiff nipple. Rebe's heart jumped and her open hand closed tight. She'd never been near a woman in a bed before, though she'd seen enough women at the strip club without their clothes on to stand in for three naked WNBA teams. She just had never had her nipple in a woman's soft mouth, or felt the sensation of a woman's hair draping along her skin.

She again eyed Armani.

While he still went to work in cunnilingus and anilingus paradise, his brown eyes begged her not to push away. They told her to let go. They told her to just relax.

Rebe forced herself to shut her eyes and simply go with the feeling.

The feeling of a woman's flicking tongue teasing her nipple, and a man's flicking tongue, fucking with her slit.

At the same time.

While she was in her head, there was a brief pause of action on her tittie and between her legs, and when she looked down, Armani and the nipple-flicking female swinger had traded places.

It was now the mocha colored girl between Rebe's legs, doing her thing just as good, almost better than Armani. Rebe tightened up and moved her hips back a bit as if she should shut her legs and say something. But by now, Armani was whispering up against her ear, saying "Did you see her ass? She's beautiful. Everybody here knows her. Her name is Trudy. They call her Big Booty Trudy. The infamous BBT. And she normally doesn't do this. She's usually the one who gets eaten out on the regular. People would pay to eat her out. I think she likes you, baby. I mean really likes you. Look at her."

Rebe eased her vision to Trudy, who pulled her long golden hair back out of the way, and looked up to give Rebe a giving smile, adjusting her hands to really get a grip on the good parts of what she needed to attack to please her newfound girl toy. Rebe remembered the words to the song "Poison," "*Never trust a big butt and a smile.*" *Oh hell* she said to her mind.

Trudy, like a pro, used her fingers to expose Rebe's engorged pink button, and positioned her gold-studded tongue against Rebe's gold-studded clit, closed her lips around the valuable jewel, and sucked.

Rebe's leg quivered.

Trudy stopped, moving her mouth down to Rebe's opening to lick like she was licking a chocolate ice cream cone, using a scooping motion and then again back up to her clit, closing her lips around it and sucking again.

Rebe's other leg quivered.

Trudy worked Rebe like a cat cleaning her fur, and inserted her tongue as deep as she could, making sure to leave room for her nose so she could breathe, tightening her eyes so she could further extend her tongue inside. From down under Trudy purred, "Sweet as Bazooka."

Rebe opened her legs even wider.

Armani watched, seeming to take mental note, and then he stood, took a condom from the clear bowl near the bed, pulled down his black boxers, and positioned himself strategically behind Trudy, who was world renowned for the donuts she had in her back seat, separating her heavy, rumpshaker ass cheeks to make room for the length of his ready-to-explore dick.

From between Rebe's legs, Trudy perched her asstac-ular booty in the air and asked before Armani entered, "Is that okay, sexy?"

Suddenly carefree, Rebe nodded and shut her lids, disappearing into almost climax land, in complete and total ecstasy, feeling as though she was floating. Trudy reached up and inserted her finger in Rebe's mouth and Rebe sucked without hesitation, sucking like Trudy's fin-ger was Armani's penis, all while Trudy got fucked by Armani while the three of them were being watched. Watched until they heard one screaming word. "Mommy!"

Rebe's eyes popped open. The familiarity of the voice caused her to stop her girl-girl finger sucking. She knew right away that she was the only mommy that belonged to that voice.

Her world that only a moment ago was swinging a virgin swinger's swing, came to an abrupt stop.

Armani said, "Trinity."

Trudy said, "Trinity."

And Rebe said, "Trinity."

Everybody knew Trinity.

Only the look on Trinity's face said she didn't know who her freaky mother really was. Trinity gave a stab-bing yell, standing in shock while wearing only a white thong, saying, "You are the biggest, most pathetic ex-cuse for a mother. You sex-craved, midlife crisis, girl loving, in the closet, pole dancing, crazy ass, cougar bitch."

Twenty

⚭

"You Sexy Thing"

Darla

INT.—MIAMI INTERNATIONAL MERCHANDISE
MART—LATE MORNING
March 28, 2009

G-strings. Bras. Corsets. Bustiers. Boy shorts. Nightgowns. Negligees. Camisoles. Baby dolls. Body stockings. On and on. Darla was in intimate apparel heaven.

Darla and Magnolia shopped and ordered and selected as they walked along the many aisles of the bustling Miami Garment District showroom. It was a massive complex with wholesale erotic distributors, and the intimate apparel section seemed to be one of the most crowded.

Newly smitten by her new man, Miller, Magnolia held up a pair of red-leather panties and put it in her canvas shopping bag. "I'm gonna need this for me."

"Looks like you may have gotten a boost of bravery since visiting that sex club you and Rebe went to. How was it anyway?"

"Wild."

"So does wild mean you did partake, or did not partake?"

"Oh, I partook. Sort of. If you could call it that. It was a threesome without the some."

"What the heck does that mean?" Darla asked, crinkling her nose.

"It means I helped out. Like a midwife. You're the visual. You talk to the couple."

"Couple. You were with a woman?"

"No. Not in that sense. But I did watch him go down on her. And I saw her ride him like she was a damn cowgirl. I've never done it like that before. No wonder men like the woman on top. Damn."

Darla looked at Magnolia like she was someone else. "Oh my goodness. And you didn't do anything to them, with them, did you?"

"No. I had my clothes on the entire time."

"See, you and Rebe, I need to watch out for you guys. What the heck did she get into?"

They continued to walk.

"Girl. That's what I wanted to talk to you about. Darla, you won't believe it. While we were there, you'll never guess who else was there. Who else is into swinging. Never."

"Who? Not Randall."

"No." Magnolia thought, *That's another story.* "It was Trinity."

"Are you kidding me?" she asked with shock.

"Not even."

Darla hurried her words. "What? Well, what happened? Tell me."

"What didn't happen? Trinity saw her mother getting eaten out by a woman."

Darla stopped, shook her head and said, "No. See. That is a straight-up tragedy. I feel sorry for that girl. And what in the hell was Rebe doing with a woman?"

Magnolia stopped. "She said the girl traded places with Armani when he went down on her, and before she knew it, she said she got caught up."

"See. I'm telling you. I'm glad I didn't go. No good could ever come out of a place like that. That is just pure evil."

"I don't know about evil. I'll just say it's a small world."

They walked again.

"So what happened? How will Rebe ever make up to her daughter after something like that?"

"Apparently, Trinity hasn't been home in a while. Rebe even had the nerve to be upset to know that Trinity is into swinging. She'd even played with the same girl Rebe was with. And get this. Armani, the young guy Rebe's been seeing? It turns out he was one of Trinity's good friends. Not like sleeping with, from what she told me, but they are very close. From what Rebe told me, all she and Trinity did was argue all night. It was bad."

"Oh no. Poor Trinity. If you ask me, Rebe asked for that, I'm sorry. Why didn't she get a private room? I mean dang. That's just sloppy."

"What would you know about all that?"

Darla looked at a vendor's selection of bras. "Please. Aaron and I went to one of those retreats when we were in Jamaica."

"You did not."

"Yes, we did. And we went to our room and did our

thing. He wanted to know what it was like. We went one time. Have no desire to go back."

Magnolia asked for clarification. "You and Aaron?"

"Yes, me and my husband. I think swinging or swapping or whatever you want to call it should only be for couples, not all these single people who get carried away and act like complete and total fools."

"I'm shocked." Magnolia looked like a nonbeliever.

"Don't be," Darla said, putting more items in her bag.

"I mean yeah, can't believe you would do it, but also, I'm talking more about square Aaron."

"Please. Aaron was no saint." Darla said it like she meant it.

"I see." Magnolia still seemed in shock.

"Anyway. So, Rebe got caught with her legs wide open. That's jacked up."

"Speaking of jacked up. Darla, there's something I've been wanting to tell you." Magnolia sighed.

"What?"

"It has to do with Rebe. A while back, I went to meet someone after going online to that site. And of all people, speaking of Randall, turns out it was Randall in the hotel room. And his wife."

Darla stopped and put her hand on her hip. "You went to a hotel room and met them. You didn't know it was them?"

"No. Actually, I thought it was Neal. Don't ask. But it was Randall and..."

"No, you didn't."

"I did the same thing with them that I did with this couple at Erotic City. Both were brief. With Randall, I was only there for about five minutes, and I was gone.

And Darla, it has been weighing on me so heavily. I can't believe I didn't just leave. Honestly, if I had it to do over again, I would've ran out of there. But I didn't. It was like my head said one thing and my feet said another."

"That's called curiosity killed the cat. What's up with that? What'd Rebe ever do to you?"

"Nothing. Rebe hasn't done a thing to me. I don't know what it is." Magnolia proceeded.

Darla followed. "That's bad. You've got to tell her before Randall does."

"I know. I've been worried about that since the moment I left the hotel room."

"Or before his wife does."

"Even worse."

"You know how she feels about Rebe anyway. I mean, it's not like it was just you and Randall, it was you, him, and her. If you don't tell Rebe, I just see it one day coming back to haunt you when he needs something to throw in her face."

"I know."

"And anyway, they say people who meet like that can have cameras set up before you even go in the room. They could've recorded you."

"Oh, Darla, please. Don't be silly. I was only there for a minute."

Darla flexed her hand. "Magnolia, if you can live with that, fine. I couldn't. It's one thing that you're doing this sex-with-strangers thing, but now you've got that guilt in the back of your head. Don't do that to yourself any longer. Man." Darla gave a head shake. "And here I am feeling guilty about buying sex toys at this erotica convention, and you and Rebe have all this drama going on, just from trying to cop a cheap thrill. I don't mean to sound judgmental. But damn, I guess I do, even though I'm no prude, as much as you might think I am. But honestly, you two need to slow down."

"I hear you."

"Anything else you wanna confess?" Darla looked to Magnolia as if braced for another surprise.

Magnolia's eyes gleamed. "Just that. The next confession will be to Rebe. And it's not going to be anywhere as easy as telling you." She looked around, changing her shoulder bag from her left to her right. "But, on a good note, I did meet someone. His name is Miller Lockhart. He's a retired finance guy. And speaking of slowing down, I've seen him every night since then." Magnolia's eyes were different. "I like him, Darla. And he really likes me. Likes me like he's ready to settle down, likes me." She batted her lashes.

"And you know that already?"

"I can't believe it either, but we've talked about everything. He said he's through looking, and he's shut down every woman he was talking to."

"Already? And you say you've seen him every night since when?"

"Since Erotic City. I met him at the club."

"He's a swinger?"

"No. He's not. No more than I am."

"But he was there, right?"

"He went to see if he wanted to do it, and decided he didn't. Actually, I saved him from this woman who invited him into a room with her." Magnolia giggled. "She was about six foot five and muscular. I saw her, or it, and agreed with him, it was a man."

"Wow."

"And Rebe, Miller is almost sixty."

"Magnolia. He's old enough to be your father."

"Oh, and one more thing. He's white. And you know I am down with the swirl, girl." Magnolia snapped her fingers.

"Now see. I'm gonna stop, because that's the best thing you've said so far. As far as that's concerned, I do think we should go beyond our normal boundaries. I told you guys before, I'd be open to any race myself. So, whether you met him at a swinger's club or not, congratulations."

"Well, thank you."

"Besides, you dated that guy back in college who married that porn actress. Who was it, Gabe, right?"

"Yep. Plus, Miller had a black girlfriend years ago before he got married. It's no biggie to us."

"Wow. Then I say go for it."

"We're in the honeymoon phase. It's all good. Very good, actually."

"I'm happy for you. I've been so busy trying to get this store opened in the next few months, and you and Rebe have all of this stuff going on. It's like watching a soap opera. But heck, at least you met someone. And once Rebe works through all this with Trinity, and you tell her about your little rendezvous with her ex-husband, we'll be cool. We're too close for secrets like that." She looked Magnolia up and down. "Dang, remind me to never leave you alone with my man if I ever get one."

Magnolia joked, "Maybe you need to go back to a swinger's event. You might find him there." She grabbed a black garter for herself.

"No thanks. Never again. I wouldn't go back even if I had a man. I'm too jealous for all that madness."

"I can understand that. Me, too." They walked down the last aisle. "Darla, aside from all this, honestly, I am proud of you. And I still can't believe you, getting that check in the mail. I mean, damn."

"I'm doing okay. With or without all the screwing you two are doing. All I know is, you need to talk to Rebe."

"I will. I have to." Magnolia thought hard. "You think if she knew already she would've called me on it by now?"

"Ahh, yes. Rebe Palo-Richardson wouldn't let that mess go."

"Shit. Let's just hope when I tell her she doesn't try to kill me."

"Knowing Rebe, that's just what she'd try to do. Our friend is a hothead from way back. Crazy Rebe comes from a long line of ass-kicking women."

"Literally. But, I'll find the right time to tell her. And soon."

"Good. Just make sure I'm nowhere around."

INT.—DARLA'S CAR—HIGHWAY I-195 EAST—LATE AFTERNOON

That same day

All the talk about the swinger's club and sex and lingerie and couples and cheating and going down and new men and freaking and watching took Darla on a walk down memory lane as she drove home from downtown Miami.

Even as she'd said the words, telling Magnolia she'd

been to a swinger's retreat, it felt odd to even speak it to anyone. She'd kept it to herself for ten years. It was her and Aaron's little secret. It was their one time to let their hair down and get buck wild while away on one of their annual vacations.

Thinking back to it seemed like a dream, like it wasn't even real. Aaron, who looked so conservative on the outside, had his fantasies like any other man. He'd been a bad boy without Darla before, and she knew it, it's just that once they agreed to freak, she'd told herself it was time for her to be bad with him. It was her time to push the limits as a married woman, but with her own husband. And she gave herself permission to do it, feeling certain she'd be okay if she just followed his lead.

It was August 1999, and Aaron and Darla had taken a three-day trip to Jamaica. It wasn't their first time, but it was their first actual Hedonism trip. Hedonism, an adults-only resort, was all about exploring, experiencing, and getting naughty, grown folks style. This trip was to a SuperClub, all inclusive meals, drinks, accommodations, activities, entertainment, all situated on the tip of Negril's seven-mile beach in Jamaica, which had two private sections. One of the sections was a nude beach. And that's the section they stayed at. It was an X-rated Fantasy Island.

The breathtaking sandy beach glistened sugary white, and the dazzling, calm water was so clear you could see down to the bottom of the ocean at the multicolored sea life. The night before, they soaked in the flavor, walking hand in hand along the shore in their white swimwear, but tonight, they were at a party wearing rainbow togas.

At exactly midnight, the togas were removed and every-one got nude.

Oh my God, how did I end up going for that? Darla asked herself as she reflected back.

Back then on that warm, still, anticipatory night, she was concerned about her shape since she'd just started to gain weight around that time. Aaron always con-vinced her she was beautiful so she shook it off, and took it off. The more she saw other people around, lying on the lounge chairs, and standing around talking, drink-ing, fully naked, the more she was able to shed her inhibitions and just relax. To her this was the easiest part she'd agreed to. The difficult part was yet to come. But, she sipped on a cherry piña colada and let go.

Aaron had a few whiskey sours and was feeling brand-new. He was six feet tall, a redbone, had a close fade with a little gray, a thin mustache, a buffed chest with a few gray hairs, a little bit of a beer belly, a tight, round ass, and he had strong, hard legs with big claves, from playing baseball in college. The ladies on the beach looked him up and down, but he stayed close to his wife, who was getting her share of head-to-toe looks herself.

A couple walked over and struck up a conversation with Aaron and Darla. It was really the young woman who flirted with Aaron with her eyes. The man seemed to be okay with whatever his wife was fine with. And she was more than fine with Darla's husband.

Under the twinkling stars and romantic moonlight normally made for two, the four of them talked about other vacations they'd been on and which locales were the best, about cruising and different types of drinks, but nothing personal. Not even exchanging names. They each knew the deal.

After lying out along the beach under the tiki torches, the four ended up putting the togas back on and heading over to the Breezes Grand Resort & Spa, to Aaron and Darla's third floor, one-bedroom junior suite.

As Darla drove farther on I-195, she thought back to the beautiful hotel ten years ago with the French doors and ocean-blue quartz foyer, crystal chandeliers, and panoramic view, bathrooms with multihead show-ers, and bedrooms with romantic spotlights that bounced off the natural fiber walls. Especially the mir-rored ceilings throughout. She recalled that the room smelled like Juicy Fruit gum.

There was a jade and ivory fitted bed, and the man, kind of square looking, who was in his early thirties, thin and tall and brown, bald head, just watched, stand-ing over by the balcony doors, facing the bed. He jerked off. Nothing else for the moment. He didn't talk much. He just jerked off. And that was fine with Darla because the rule was she couldn't and wouldn't be penetrated by another man. Aaron being with another woman, for that night, now, was a different story.

Darla tried not to stare at the man's long, dark penis, but it was very thin and curved and she'd never seen anything like it. What really helped to keep her from staring was the sight of her beloved husband, Aaron, getting his dick, which she couldn't stop referring to in her head as *her* dick, sucked by the light-skinned woman who sat in the octagon-shaped Jacuzzi next to the king bed while Aaron stood over the side of it, legs spread wide, hands on his hips like he was the man, getting deep throated by Linda Lovelace skills. She used lots of spit and gripped him with both hands, going deep without any sign of a gagging reflex. Aaron looked like he was fighting off a tidal wave that was about to hit big and hard.

The yellow woman was Cape Verdean and Welsh with an exotic look, leaning more toward her Portuguese blood. She had marshmallow crème nails, with long flowing, spirally hair, amber honey skin, and keen features. Big eyes. Medium-sized breasts. A small behind. She was half Darla's size. And Aaron, though when he first saw the woman on the beach told Darla she was way too thin to be his type, seemed to be enjoying the yellow woman's frame way beyond his own spoken words, watching her naked body from the reflection in the mirror overhead as she sucked him down. He seemed to have a newfound respect for the petite headed princess. He looked down to watch close-up. He even smiled.

Darla sat on the bed and kept an eye on Aaron's dick as it went in and out of the late-twenty-year-old yellow woman's mouth. His dick told Darla it felt stronger than ever.

The yellow woman backed away from his penis, but first scooped the rough side of her long tongue under his balls like a ladle and his upper head jerked back to the ceiling again, watching. She stood, water dipping off her skin like it was in slow motion. Her pussy was bare. She stepped out and Aaron helped her, extending his hand. She grabbed a large white towel and looked at Aaron as she made her way to the bed next to where Darla sat. Her eyes invited Aaron to play inside of her tenderoni body. She looked anxious to skip to the good part.

Aaron stood before Darla, his dick stuck out far enough to hang a coat on it. "Can I fuck her, baby? Or I can fuck you and she can do something to me."

The yellow woman nodded for either. Her man, still standing by the balcony with his hand on his walnut dick, nodded, too.

Darla only looked at the thin, beautiful lady who awaited Darla's very own husband with an intimate, anticipatory look. Willing.

Aaron lifted Darla's chin up toward him. "Which do you want, baby?"

Darla managed to say, after having gone this far, "I want you to do what you want."

Aaron looked anxious and reached into his gym bag, which was on the floor near the bed. "Can you put my condom on?" he asked his wife.

Darla sat up straight. "Yes."

Aaron handed it to her. He then said, as though he'd better, "Wait. Let me eat you first."

Darla put the condom on the bed and lay back, watching carefully as Aaron put his face *between* her familiar legs and licked her curly haired vagina. The *between* that only he knew so well. Darla looked up at the mirrored ceiling and saw the view from overhead, her redbone husband on his knees between her legs, munching with an audience. She looked over at the yellow woman and then at the brown man, watching them watch her. She felt the true meaning of three's a crowd, feeling that four was still two too many. On her own, she could enjoy Aaron's tongue loving, at least she could focus on the feelings the sensation brought to bring pleasure to each other. They'd have oral sex, and they'd have vaginal sex. That was good enough for her. This was so new, so different, that all she could do was think about the unknown, and anticipate.

Just that quick, the brown man laid his wife on her back and went down on her, too. The yellow woman began to moan, loud. To Darla it sounded like pain, not pleasure. The yellow woman was in a zone.

The yellow woman looked down at her man, and then at Aaron between Darla's legs, and then at her man, and then Aaron looked at the yellow woman while his tongue was inside of Darla, and he moaned, and the brown man watched Darla. Without looking, the yellow woman found Darla's right hand, took hold, and squeezed.

"You're beautiful," she said, eyeing down Darla's ample breasts that spread along her chest.

Darla started to moan and again glanced up at the ceiling. It was a sight for sore eyes. Two couples, two women getting eaten, two men doing the eating like they were devouring strawberry shortcake with whipped cream, legs spread, all in the same bed. She couldn't get past the sight of the freaks before her, including her, then wondering if she even qualified to be considered one, remembering that her good girl side was being overshadowed by her bad girl side, so she assumed yes. She looked down at Aaron, wondering how he could ever be in this situation, let alone bring her into it with him. He was her husband, and she was his wife. This was against all the rules. They were sinning.

The yellow woman looked over at Darla's face and

pumped her own pussy harder into her husband's face, and Aaron's tongue stuck deeper and stiffer into Darla's pussy and before she knew it, she realized that Aaron came inside of his hand at the same time the yellow woman creamed and screamed and stared at Aaron and raised her ass from the covers as high as she could. Her legs and feet were flexed straight out. Her husband stayed with her and kept it up and she came with a begging sound like she was being shot from a cannon, losing her X-rated mind. And the brown man stood up fast and stroked his penis, focused and precise, he held his breath and squinted, stopping his cum by squeezing his shaft and tip extra hard. He looked like he was about to bust.

Aaron stood up, went into the bathroom, and left Darla to watch an unknown brown man hold onto his dick, his yellow woman coming down from her orgasm caused by the sight of Darla's husband, eating his wife's pussy.

Whew, Darla said as she snapped back into reality, now turning onto Collins Avenue, but just for a second.

She remembered that right after Aaron came out of the bathroom after washing up, the yellow woman was on all fours, watching him. Her voyeuristic man sat in a flowered antique chair in the corner. Quiet.

Aaron was hard again and took the condom off the bed and brought his dick to Darla. She took her time opening the black foil package, looking up at him, but he only looked at the yellow woman, who squirmed in anticipation. His dick was again way stiff, way wide, and way long. Darla managed to fit the tight condom on his penis and he patted her on her shoulder, like "I'm going in," and walked over to the end of the bed and put his hand on the yellow woman's backside. She looked back at him with bedroom eyes, and Darla watched Aaron stick *her* dick into the strange yellow woman's body, and Aaron closed his eyes, pumping his ass muscles like he was digging for gold in a cave that only needed two more good grinds to drill into the goldmine that contained his fantasy fortune. He pumped and unzipped his eyes long enough to look at Darla.

She heard the brown man bust a nut, but didn't look at him. She didn't look at the yellow woman, either. She only watched Aaron, coming inside of the rubber, inside of the yellow woman, *her* dick coming from the feeling of another woman's pussy. A gorgeous, thin, young, yellow woman.

Darla lay on her back two feet away from them. Her nipples were hard but her hands were not on her body. They were under the pillow that was propped under her head, balled up from bridled jealousy.

Aaron was lost and the more he came, the more the yellow woman fucked him. Aaron completed his climax, and pulled out, and the brown man took his place in line, dick full grown again, penetrating his wife raw with his curved penis, riding her through her fuck, hitting some erotic spot that made her howl, and managing to flip her over and fuck her missionary. Two dicks in a row. Her pussy surrendered. Aaron lay close to Darla, condom full of his seed. He watched the couple fuck hard, and Darla again only watched him. The yellow woman came strong.

The four spent the night together, naked.

Hours later, at six-twenty in the morning, Darla's eyes popped open after hearing a lustful whisper, "Oh yeah.

Fuck me deep with that thick dick. Fuck me and make me come."

The mattress moved to their grinds as they fucked under the covers. A slight squeak could be heard. The room was dark. Darla was right next to them, and on the other side of them was the yellow woman's husband, sleeping.

This time, now sober, Aaron looked over at his wife, saw her face, pulled out, got up, and turned on the light. "Excuse us. It was nice, but we've gotta go pretty early, so we need to get ready if you don't mind."

The yellow woman shook her husband awake, leaned over and kissed Darla on the cheek, and in ten minutes, they were gone.

Aaron and Darla fell back asleep until the afternoon. They did nothing that day but lie out, eat, and sleep some more. She felt the need to pray.

Darla never said another word about it. Neither did Aaron. But that night, Aaron had the hardest orgasm Darla had ever witnessed him have in all their years. The yellow woman was in his head. And Darla was reaping the misdirected benefit.

The next day they were back in Miami, living life, working, planning their next vacation. Never again did they go to a Hedonism retreat. Darla never wanted to experience it again. Aaron knew, even without it being said, that it would never happen again.

As Darla arrived home after her flashback thoughts, she parked her car and prepared to turn off the ignition and go upstairs to her condo. But first she reached between her legs and felt the moisture. She'd soaked her panties from the swinger's rewind. She lifted the front of her black knit dress, slid her skimpy leopard print panties to the side, and stuck her finger inside of herself, right there in her car. Her middle finger was creamy wet, juices all under her fingernail. She had to admit, that vacation turned her the hell on back then, and even now. She'd never, ever forget it.

Twenty-One

—————— ⚭ ——————

"Suddenly"

Magnolia

INT.—MILLER LOCKHART'S HOME—KEY BISCAYNE,
FLORIDA—EVENING
April 6, 2009

Miller Lockhart lived on North Bay Road in the exclusive Key Biscayne area of South Florida in
Dade County. His custom, bone-colored, ornate
Victorian-style three-story home was built over ten
years ago and was over four thousand square feet. With a
spectacular pool area, it was the five-bedroom home he
and his wife bought before they divorced. When he retired from Bear Stearns last year, he paid it off. His ex-
wife, on the other hand, was living with their son. She
had a younger boyfriend she left Miller for, who took her
for the money she'd gotten from the divorce settlement.
She was getting a taste of the real world and was not
handling the reality too well. But from what Magnolia
could see, Miller, on the other hand, was.

Magnolia and Rebe had been playing phone tag. And
even when Rebe called her back, Magnolia took her
time returning her call. She convinced herself she

wanted Rebe to answer, needed Rebe to answer, but when she didn't, it was almost a relief to simply talk to Rebe's voice mail.

Just after work, all that was on Magnolia's mind was the peace and serenity of Miller's place. She entered his kitchen with her key that he'd given her the week before. Old-school Miller played a Lionel Richie CD, right now in the middle of "Three Times a Lady." Magnolia hummed along while dropping her overnight bag at the door, and set her purse and keys down on the soapstone kitchen counter. She approached Miller with a kiss on the lips, standing on her tiptoes. "Sounds good, looks good, and smells good in here. What are you cooking, sweetie?"

He stood before the stove in his shorts and black T-shirt, barefoot. "You said you liked Mexican food. I made enchiladas." He pulled back the foil paper from the baking dish. The steam and spicy aroma made themselves known. Extra cheese, black olives, and green onions decorated his baked masterpiece.

Magnolia inhaled and put her hand on his back. "Look at those. You are something else. You didn't have to cook for me."

"I wanted to."

She patted him on his backside. "Chef Miller, after those, I'd like to have you on a platter for dessert, please, sir?"

"I can make that happen, too." He stood tall.

Magnolia giggled and opened the cabinet to remove two ebony dinner plates. "You're so good to me. The other morning, breakfast in bed. Not to mention flowers. A girl could get used to this."

"You should. You deserve it, queen that you are."

"Thanks my king, that you are." She looked back at him and gave a wink. She couldn't believe the fairy tale words she was now hearing, and saying.

Miller took the liberty of placing two enchiladas on each plate as Magnolia held them still. She walked to the table where he'd already placed the utensils, white wine, and ice water as she sat. He was right behind her and then sat beside her. He said, as they joined hands and bowed their heads, "Bless us, O Lord, for these Thy gifts, which we are about to receive from Thy bounty through Christ our Lord. Amen."

"Amen."

He looked up at her and stared, releasing her hand.

Magnolia looked back at him, noticing his pause. "What?"

"Just thinking, which you'll find I do a lot. I mean, really. Who would've thought? Thought I would've looked all around while playing golf, taking cruises, and even to the point of walking around Walmart with one eye on the shelf and one eye checking out women in the aisles, as well as going on blind dates...and then I meet you, the woman of my dreams, at a swinger's club. Two virgin-curious swingers bumped into each other at Erotic City and, well, here we are. You, Magnolia, are something else, angel."

"Well thanks, but I don't know how much of an angel I am. I was coming out of a private room."

"Like I said, angel. Highly deserving of the very charm you wear around your neck."

"Thanks." She gave a sexy wink and a shy smile.

They picked up their forks and dug in.

He asked, "So, have you heard from Neal?"

She swallowed her bite. "This is excellent, sweetie. Very good."

"Thanks." He waited.

"No." She took a sip of water.

"Like you said, you see him at work though, right?"

"Yeah, but not as much as before. Maybe a few times a week. No biggie."

"And so even though he's been persistent, not willing to totally let go, you're sure there's no chance of you two ever getting back together?"

"No chance. Not on my end." She gave him full-on eyes. "Miller, there was no chance even before I met you."

"Good. 'Cause I've got plans for you." He took his first bite.

"Oh really?"

He paused to finish chewing, then swallowed. "Really. I'm telling you, if all goes well, this is it for me. I'm ready for this. I look at us in the long term, being together for the rest of our lives."

"Oh, is that right?"

"Oh, I'm claiming this. I've had a taste of being alone and I choose the alternative. I don't want to die alone. I want a companion. Life is no damn good alone."

"I agree." Magnolia heard his words, and kept eating. She took a few moments, and then asked, "And since we're asking, how about Beth? Your ex-wife. Nothing from her?"

"Beth will always be Beth. I did ask her not to call so late, like she did a couple of nights ago when you were here."

"But you didn't have to." Magnolia said, yet in her head wondered why his ex-wife still felt she could.

"I needed to. Her calls did wake me up at times."

"Okay, I just didn't want you to say it because I'm in your life now. I don't want to be the reason."

"Done deal." He leaned over and kissed Magnolia on the cheek.

She smiled and took another bite.

He asked, "So, are we going to your grandmother's house so I can meet her next week?"

"Yes. After church. You sure you're ready for that?"

"I am. I'm ready for whatever's in your life."

Magnolia put down her fork and rested her elbow along the table, her chin to her inside palm. She examined him closely. "Are you real? Wait, let me pinch your amazing ass to see." She grabbed the skin of his forearm and squeezed.

He laughed, moving himself away as though ticklish. "You're something else. And yes, I am real. And I was thinking about something. Angel, I want to help you find your father. I have a friend who can help out."

She leaned back in her chair and shook her head. "Honestly, after all these years, I don't want to know who he is, Miller. And besides, my grandmother knows. I've just never asked. Some things are better off left alone."

"Okay. Whatever you say." He ate another bite and sipped his wine. "Does your grandmother know my age?"

She nodded and leaned forward.

"Cool."

"Miller, I'm cool with you. You just keep showing me who you are by what you do. And from what I've seen

you doing, you've got my full attention. I told you before, you've also got my heart, and my trust. To lose it,
it's on you."

After a few minutes, he stood and took their plates to
the sink. He said, "Just remember what I said. My search
is over. Period."

"Okay now," Magnolia told him with a big grin that
seemed sure.

But it was her heart that felt like it was only half sure.
It braced itself for a usual replay of her past.

And just in case, for a moment, she imagined him not
being who he said he was. It was her usual mind-visitor
named Doubt.

Doubt had beaten her into shape for years, just from
relationships not lasting.

From saying I can't live without you, to managing to
live without you.

It was the doubt that made her a bit more reserved
than she wanted to be.

Reserved just enough to wonder at that very moment,
Why is Neal being so unusually quiet?

INT.—MILLER'S MASTER BEDROOM—LATE
EVENING

Magnolia spoke from the place where Miller explored
that was bringing her to a slow, lustful, dizzying place
that made her want to talk with her eyes closed. "I've
never been made love to. Like really made love to. Like
I want to stay close to you, like this. It's the best thing
I've ever felt." It was all brand-new to her.

"Yes." His precision grinds had soul.

They lay naked on his king bed. The headboard was dark leather. The bedding was blue and gray striped. His deluxe bedroom had vaulted ceilings with exposed beams. The amber light added a subtle glow, floor to high ceiling, and upon their bodies. Her gardenia scent was potent. The Hugo Boss cologne he'd sprayed added to the manly allure of man-to-woman bonding. His testosterone and her estrogen mixed well together. His strand and her strand of DNA were in the other's brain, making love. Dopamine at work.

She purred. "You're a great lover."

He growled. "So are you."

Another five minutes just as they were, and then she said with a sultry voice, "Baby, turn me around and let me stand at the end of the bed, and do what you did when I was in your swimming pool last weekend. Please."

He was on it without hesitation, pausing and easing himself off of her. She got up and stood at the foot of his bed. "Let's try it this way," he said, propping up a pillow along the mattress, under her knees as she got on all fours. "Now lower your head and poke out your rear end."

She did.

He kept one foot on the floor, and the other foot on the bed, he rose up as high as he could, pressing her down even lower so he could hit the top of her vagina at an angle, her light brown apple bottom was positioned before him, ready to submit, and he inserted himself, bare, just like they'd done ever since they'd gotten their negative blood test results just before the first time they had sex, the day after they met.

He grabbed the width of his dick and stuck himself inside of her soft opening. She gripped him with her anxious sugar walls, receiving him fully and pressing herself back toward him as he pressed in toward her.

And Magnolia began making that sound. The same sound she made when he had her in the pool. The sounds of a car that's been sitting out in the cold for too long, and now someone has finally turned the key that fits, the key that's trying to get it to start, trying to get it to kick over. It was a revving rumble, like a humming sound, a dick to pussy winding sound, almost as though in pain, yet with a tad bit of ecstasy. Magnolia's head was to the side, her eyes were closed, her mouth was open.

Her eyes welled up with tears, and she was going nuts.

His rear entry pussy fucking was fucking her up. As he thrust his hips, he aimed at an angle, downward, and then he switched up, aiming his angle toward his foot. He was at times very deep, and then at times shallow enough to add the right amount of pressure to Magnolia's soft yet rough spot, and he could tell when he hit it by her pleasure screams. He made sure he had a precise, direct hit, using his hands to grip her womanly curves that flowed from her waist to her hips. If he'd had neighbors close by, they would have known he was fucking, because all she said while sucking on her teeth was, "Shit. Shit. Shit," over, and over, and over again.

On her own, she brought her hand down between her legs to rub her fingers along her excited clit, and her orgasm approached fast. She suddenly stopped touching herself, as her new king conquered her by taking her to the greatest height while she ran around in the kingdom

of her spinning head, and again yelled, "Shit." She un-
raveled and froze.

In two minutes, Magnolia had Miller's dick in her
mouth as he stood and she lay across the bed on her
stomach, bobbing him into ecstasy with two hands serving a tight grip, standing in as her vagina, and a wet,
willing, sucking mouth, and even as quiet as he was
while he fucked, he did manage to say, "Will you marry
me?" And then he came.

Magnolia tensed up and took his release into her
mouth, swallowing twice to accept all of him the way
she'd done before. The way she'd done for no other
man. It was a real sexual resolution that she'd vowed to
try. And Miller was the lucky winner of her newfound
bravery. She backed away and could focus on nothing
but wondering if his out-of-the-blue question was out of
temporary orgasm insanity.

He looked down at her. His face was flushed, and his
hairy chest was, too.

She morphed into a sitting position. "What did you
just say?" easing her ear toward him.

"You heard me."

"Miller, you asked me to marry you?" She wiped her
lips with the back of her hand.

"I did." His breathing was unsteady.

"You asked me now?"

"I did." He looked no nonsense.

"You cannot be serious."

He had one hand on his hip and his other hand on his
flaccid penis. "I am. I don't have a ring, I know that's not
the best way to do it, but I'm ready to go get the ring you
want. Tomorrow if necessary. Hell, now, dammit."

"I'm just...I mean, this is what I wanted. I'm just a little surprised by your timing."

"I know." He sat beside her and then placed his elbows to his knees, looking down at the floor.

She placed her hand on his shoulder. "I mean, not even so much that you asked me while we're having sex, well, really, while I was giving you, well, while we're in bed. But since we just haven't known each other very long, Miller. It's so soon."

"At my age, what is soon? I know what I want."

His proposal still rumbled though her brain. "Oh my."

He scooted back and turned to her. "Listen. I'm also old enough to know one thing, and that is if the answer was yes, you'd have said it by now." He stood, stepped to the other side of the bed and got under the covers.

Magnolia turned to him and slipped under as well, snuggling close, hugging him, and kissing the side of his face. She rested her head on his chest and inhaled him. Bonding. "Can I answer later? Can I think about it?"

"You can. That's fine. You need to be certain."

She looked up at his face. "Thanks. And there's nothing wrong with waiting, right? I mean, if we're really for each other then, that's cool, right?"

"You want to get to know me better. I understand."

"I just want time to think. To be sure. I've waited this long, I can wait a little longer. It's just that I've never been married before."

"I know." He closed his eyes.

Magnolia shifted her body to lie on her back. She looked straight up. "Funny, I just heard on the radio that if you're over forty, and you find someone who loves your old ass, you'd better be glad."

"Uh-huh," was all he said.

Magnolia turned back toward him and tickled him alongside his waist.

He jumped, opened his eyes, and grabbed her hand. "I know one thing. If you keep hollering like that, my neighbors are going to think my name is Shit."

She laughed. "You're so silly. Whatever your name is, you're the man."

"I'm your man, angel." He hugged her.

She gave a little girl giggle. "You're *the* man who found my spot, you know?"

"Oh, okay, so I guess older men are good for something, huh?"

"Far from old, Miller. Far from old." She said it twice because she really, really meant it. She placed her head along his chest again and heard his heart, beating fast.

But so was hers.

He hugged her closer.

She snuggled in closer.

She closed her eyes and felt cherished. The word her grandmother told her about and tried to describe. But now she knew for herself, that it felt good.

Cherished.

She basked in the feeling.

His protection was her escape.

Twenty-Two

⸺⸱⸺

"*Give It to Me*"

Rebe

INT.—MAKE IT RAIN—EARLY MORNING
April 9, 2009

It was a busy Wednesday night at Rebe's place of, or what she called her *recreational* place of, employment, Make It Rain.

Rebe, no longer an amateur, in her olive thong and satin bra, gave an unfocused lap dance to a guy that her dancer friend told her was an up-and-coming rapper. His face didn't ring a bell, which Rebe swore looked like a cuss word, nor did his name ring a bell, MC Trick the Slick. His slick words weren't ringing Rebe's turn-on bells either. He smelled like he'd just come from playing a pickup game at the local rec center. And his breath told the world he'd been eating a large bag of Doritos in the car before he came in the club. Cool Ranch.

Over the past month or so, ever since the night Trinity caught Rebe at Erotic City, Rebe's patience for some of the patrons had been wearing thin, and she'd even called in sick a few nights. But tonight, part of her needed to get out of the house where the walls had been talking to her, get dressed, and distract herself just so she'd have something to do other than think.

Armani had been a no-show and no-call ever since that night. Not even a text. And he made a point to not come into the club anymore. Rebe realized he'd made a choice between Trinity's friendship and sexing Rebe up. And she understood.

Trinity had all but moved out, only coming home maybe twice a week. Each time she came in, she left with a few more of her things. And Rebe felt if either of them said something to each other, somebody would end up dead. So, rather than trying to explain things further, she left it alone.

She knew Trinity blamed her for everything, mainly for the freakfest at the swinger's club with Big Booty Trudy, and rightfully so, but also for being with a guy who Trinity knew, who was nearly half her mother's age. And if Trinity were to tell it, Rebe had to have been the reason Trinity's father left when she was a toddler. Trinity blurted out that night that if Rebe had helped him with his drug addiction, he wouldn't have overdosed that night. And also, Trinity told her she believed Rebe chased Randall into the arms of Kandi. Trinity seemed to hate her mother. But Rebe knew the feeling.

Rebe kept hearing her daughter say in her head, *If you'd only been . . . if you'd only been . . . if you'd only been . . . not so fucked up by your own mom.*

So, for the moment, Rebe stayed in the environment she'd convinced herself she belonged in. Right there at the strip club among all the other broken women, being the object of the affection of lustful men who based their hard-ons on the women's looks, not based on who they really were. To the men, all that mattered was the women's bodies, not their minds. And to Rebe, her body was in a lot better shape than her mind. She said in her head, focusing on her mind's eye, not on whom she was shaking her ass for, *Who I really am wouldn't garner much long-term attention anyway.* So she stayed a forty-year-old stripper for another night, until she'd muster up enough self-esteem to quit, grinding to "Pop, Lock and Drop It" by Huey.

The song said, *"Mami gon take it low if you can, then touch your toes."* Rebe did not.

"You ain't gonna give me no head?" the rapper asked, with chapped lips.

"No." She wouldn't look at his face.

"Why not?"

She was saved by the last note of the song. "Your dance is over." Rebe ceased her half-grind moves. She put on her powder blue boy shorts over her thong, and a sheer cover-up, finding herself trying to cover her body more, noticing herself gaining weight.

He spoke under his Cool Ranch breath. "Freak ass bitch."

This time she looked him straight on, squinting. "What'd you say?"

"Oh what's up? You surprised I knew your name?"

She put her hand out. "That's twenty."

He put two hundred dollars in her hand. "Keep the rest so you can take some dance lessons."

She said nothing, looking totally uninterested, like the only thing she had room in her mind for was an echo.

"You coulda had twice that if you'd have just put your head right here and sucked." He pointed at his crotch.

Now what suddenly popped into her was shared. "I would've bit down on your little peter. Guaranteed."

He flashed his gold teeth. "Just the way I like it."

Rebe cut her eyes and walked away, making sure her boy shorts were straight. She walked around for a few moments, not really working the floor, just passing by each small table without giving eye contact, without stopping, feeling like all she wanted to do was take a shower. And then she went to the back room and sat on the stool in front of the makeup mirror. She sat as long as she could and put her head down, praying the DJ didn't call her name, or that one of the girls didn't ask why she wasn't on the floor. And, she prayed that her life would turn around. Wishing she'd never made a sex promise. Wishing she'd never started out the year vowing to go beyond the limits. "I asked for it. I got it." Extra tired with a nagging headache, she pulled her phone out of her tiny purse in the drawer and sent a text to Magnolia.

Can I go to church with you this Sunday? Please. And then she put her phone back, and went back to work.

INT.—REBE'S HOME—EARLY MORNING

By three in the morning, after spending the rest of the evening acting like she was blind to the patrons, Rebe managed to finish her shift and head home. Her phone read, Sure. Absolutely. Love you. Magnolia.

Exhausted, both body and mind, Rebe stepped into

the kitchen after pulling into an empty garage. She went inside and disarmed the alarm. Again, she was home alone. No Trinity. Nowadays, Trinity would take the dog, Randi, back and forth with her when she'd come.

Rebe opened the mail she'd left on the island top earlier, and read the advance, save-the-date announcement of Darla's big, grand opening of her store that July. Brown Sugar would be a reality. She smiled in her friend's honor and secured the announcement on her refrigerator with a butterfly magnet.

Feeling all alone, she opened the fridge and stared between the bottle of Smartwater and a lone watermelon wine cooler Trinity had left, remembering that even Magnolia had a boyfriend now, who'd proposed, only Magnolia hadn't accepted yet. But Rebe felt Magnolia should go for it, even though she knew Magnolia was probably still playing what-if games in her head about Neal.

Her friends seemed to be doing well. They met their New Year's promises just fine. *Hell, I guess I met mine too. I became a freak. Mission accomplished.* She gave a laugh at her self-sarcasm.

Rebe took the wine cooler, first drink she'd have in years, and then her purse, and went up the winding stairs and down the hall to her solo bedroom suite that she and Randall once shared. She stood in the doorway before stepping inside and looked around, remembering when they'd bought the expensive, oversized maple furniture for the house that was now all hers, every single square foot of the place. But as she examined the space, to her it seemed empty.

Bang. Boom.

Rebe jumped out of her skin at the sound of a loud crack and a thud, and then heard footsteps, moving fast.

"Trinity," she belted out in a questionable panic, turning around to tiptoe down the hall, and then as she peeked over the banister she saw a blue skullcap, pulled down over the head of someone. She screamed with every ounce of her one-hundred-forty-pound body and ran back toward her room, hurrying to press the door shut and lock it. She sprinted to the bed and tossed her wine cooler and purse onto the mattress, dumping everything out of her purse, snatching her cell and dialing 911 in a panic, just as the sound of stomping made its way to her door and fists pounded in a furious cadence, assisting a male's words. "Open this fucking door. Freak ass bitch."

Before Rebe could even get an answer on the phone, all at once the male kicked in the door, ran and leapt to her, grabbed her phone, slammed it against the wall, used a back hand to scoop all that was on the bed onto the wood floor, even the cooler that shattered against the wall, and threw Rebe on the bed. The force made her bounce like a handball and she hollered like she had been shot.

The male spoke deep and demanded, "Shut the fuck up. You yell again and I'll stick this gun inside your funky monkey and pull the fucking trigger."

Rebe yelled in her head, mind racing a mile a minute, feeling like she was about to have a massive coronary. She felt her own vibration of her heart thump that bounced off the mattress, as though it received the message from her brain that this man had the sick mind of a killer. He slid off his knit facemask, and his manic, psychotic stare made her life flash before her eyes.

In his beady, cloudy eyes, Rebe saw a flashback of her mother, manic and psychotic as she was, lying on her, with a hammer in her hand, saying, "You're a damn ho." His eyes matched the eyes of her mother, who'd attacked her own seventeen-year-old daughter. And then killed her own twenty-year-old son. All because Rebe was promiscuous.

The male with the gun gave her a look of hate, and said into her ear, holding the gun to her chest, "Now suck my dick." His breath was again warm and stale, and this time reeked of tequila. His gold teeth gleamed. Her strip club rapper fan had followed her home, turned stalker.

The male backed up, unzipped his pants, and pulled out his ashy hardness. "Touch it," was his order.

She didn't. She turned her nose at it.

"Bitch, touch it. Fucking ho." He reached a higher notch of anger.

She did, though with fingertips only.

"You be slick and try to bite it, and I'll show you what head really feels like. Your head splattered all over this damn room. Now swallow it."

Rebe squeezed her eyes tight, and guided him into her mouth at the same time she felt her throat start to gag all on its own. She insisted that for the life of her, she'd better press her lips to his dry dick-skin.

She did.

"Deeper."

She went deeper, feeling the coldness of the pistol's barrel on her temple, his other hand on the back of her head, pressing her down farther to force her into a bob-bing motion.

She gagged harder at the taste of his salty, musty pe-nis, and felt a little throw up in the back of her mouth, and swallowed, and in that swallow she took a little of his sperm, and then she made a "Puh" sound, spitting onto the bed.

He still spilled the rest of his fluid with a despising look on his face, like there was no ecstasy in the act of his sick orgasm whatsoever. He didn't even grunt or groan. He just said, "I should slap you for spittin'."

She frowned deep, and wiped her lips.

"See, I knew you'd do it. All you had to do earlier was go down like I told you. But you had to have an attitude in the club because you thought you had some backup with the security folks, huh? Well, I will not be denied. You must not know who I am."

She looked away and wondered how quick she'd need to move to knock his pistol out of his hand and run.

"I'll have to show you some more, though. Now turn over on your stomach, bitch."

The words *turn over* rang in her head like someone had just rung her mind-chimes like a cymbal. *Turn over* were just the words her mother said before she hauled off and bashed the back of Rebe's head in with a large hammer, causing head trauma that would fuck up the rest of Rebe's entire life. She hated lying on her stom-ach. She never, ever slept on her stomach.

She halfway turned in slow motion.

He snarled and assisted by turning her the other half of the way with a yank.

Rebe held her breath, either waiting for the firing of

the gun, or the stabbing of his pitiful penis inside of her. He pulled up her skirt and snatched off her boy shorts and thong, jerking her lower body to prop it up high. She shut her eyes while her head traveled to the here and now, and she even thought she heard the sound of her old neighbor's German shepherd barking, just as it did back when her face was to the mattress when she was a child.

She felt the male shove his once-again hard dick in her vagina from the back. And something told her now was the time to turn around and elbow him in his Adam's apple, letting out every bit of anger she'd felt for the past twenty-eight years of her life on his crazy black ass, even if it meant getting shot.

"Mommy." Rebe swore she was dreaming, thinking back to Erotic City. She hadn't heard the word *mommy* since then. And the barking sounded louder. And louder.

Just when Rebe succeeded at aiming her sights behind her, as the pressure of the male's hand around the back of her neck eased, she heard him make a pained squeal sound, like an involuntary throat choking, and saw his beady eyes triple in size and then shut as he squinted.

He toppled back and his gun fell to the floor at the same time that a butcher's knife hit the floor, too. Deep red blood was on the bed, the floor, and underneath him. It was the blood that spewed from his lower back from the sharp, long knife that pierced his kidneys.

Standing at the foot of the bed was Trinity. Randi was beside her, barking the loudest, angriest, most vicious sounds she'd ever made. Randi hurried over to encircle the man, jumping back and snarling, hyper enough to send a signal that he'd dare not get up. Kneeling next to the motionless male, checking his pulse, was Armani.

Trinity, white as a ghost, grabbed Rebe as she turned over, and held her, her head on her mother's shoulder.

Rebe reached around her daughter and gave her a major hug, rocking back and forth.

Trinity cried.

Rebe cried.

And within twenty seconds, in response to the 911 call made from Rebe's cell phone that was connected the entire time, two police officers burst into the room and aimed their guns down at Armani, "Get up with your hands up."

"No. He's with us," Rebe yelled.

Armani stood and raised his hands anyway, stepping back, as the officers then aimed their weapons at the male. "He's still alive," Armani said fast.

One officer asked Rebe, "Are you ladies okay?"

"Yes," Rebe said for them both, sniffling, shaking, and hugging Trinity even tighter.

The officer saw the bloody butcher knife on the floor. "Who stabbed him?"

Trinity said with a shaky voice, "He was raping my mother."

"Is that true?" they asked Armani.

"Yes," he nodded, looking one hundred percent certain, keeping one eye on the male.

"Mommy. I'm sorry," Trinity said with tears streaming down her face so heavy she couldn't focus. "I'm so sorry."

They rocked each other side to side, not noticing the splatters of blood on Trinity.

"Trinity, you saved my life. I'm the one who's sorry."

Trinity spoke to the other cop. "He had a gun to the back of my mom's head. He was going to kill her. I had to."

Rebe said to her beautiful, traumatized daughter, "But instead, you stabbed him, and you saved my life just in time."

Twenty-Three

"In the Midst of It All"

Girlfriends

INT.—TRINITY CATHEDRAL CHURCH—CORAL
GABLES—MORNING
April 26, 2009

After thirty minutes of exuberant praise and wor-
ship, the choir gave a wound down, spiritual
rendition of Yolanda Adams's "Never Give Up," and
then the message for the Sunday morning service began.

The church was in Magnolia's neighborhood, so she
was usually the one to attend more than either of her
friends. Though as often as she went, she couldn't quite
get herself walking right.

It was a Sunday.

A day of mid-sun.

Hope was in the air, as the weeks of clouds seemed to
be lifting.

This day was brighter and warmer.

Much brighter than it had been in Rebe's bedroom in
the early morning hours of Friday, April 10.

The day the rapper, turned rapist, was stabbed in the

home of an ex-NFL player's ex-wife, by her daughter. Or at least that's what the headlines read.

And everyone seemed to know about it.

Seated in the very first row in their Sunday-going-to-church outfits, Trinity, who was named after the Trinity Cathedral back when Rebe would attend with Trent when they first met, sat next to her mother in an organza bubble skirt suit. Rebe, who wore a draped dress with a wide patent belt, was hand in hand with her daughter. On the other side of Rebe was Darla and Magnolia, both wearing all black. Darla's was a neutral twill pantsuit with a big straw hat and Magnolia's was a tailored trench dress. Next to Magnolia was clean-cut Miller in a dark suit and tie.

It was Pastor Kevin Broward's congregation, listening intently in the newly remodeled mega-sanctuary with marble columns and overhead projectors. It was filled to capacity as usual, and he had the place fired up as usual.

Right on time, the subject was the Retest. All ears were on the pastor, who had a way of breaking it down, whether reading from the Bible or preaching off the cuff, but he always managed to give life-survival battery charges.

He stood at the pulpit with his fellow pastors and wife backing him up, sitting in high back chairs just in front of the seventy member choir, who were all dressed in purple. The pastor was his usual sharp, in a tan suit with an orange tie and pocket scarf. He was tall and fortyish, energetic and animated.

"Crisis can mean change for the better. But you'll never change in your life what you're willing to tolerate. Don't curse the darkness. Light a candle."

The churchgoers raised their hands with a matching "Amen," as did Darla.

"You must reach beyond something you've already mastered. All change begins with a decision. When will you make the decision?"

"Now," a woman yelled, directly behind Rebe. Others said it as well.

"As suffering abounds, so does consolation. God is trying to teach us something. He's trying to train us."

A few shouts of hallelujah floated through the air.

He stepped from behind the podium, ready to dig deep. "The devil will distract you and break your focus. But you have to get back up. Falling is meant to happen. But failure is the result of quitting in life. Don't give up. Never give up, as the choir just sang. If something deep inside keeps inspiring you to try, don't stop. You've gotta keep the faith, to the light. The light. The light." He sounded like Dr. Martin Luther King, Jr.

"You don't get anointed unless you're bleeding. But some of you are hardheaded. See, you need a retest. You keep doing the same thing again and again, expecting a different result." He joked, "You know what the definition of crazy is, right? Keep doing the same old thing, warmed over." He stepped to the other side. "Well, see, God doesn't flunk you. God is patient. He'll just send you through it again until you get it right. It's called a retest. Same test, different set of circumstances, now what are you going to do? Same thing? Crazy." He shook his head.

Some of the members laughed, as did Magnolia and Miller.

He pointed among the churchgoers. "Ask some of

these older folks out here. They'll tell ya. The young are strong but the old know the way. How do you think they know the way? They've been tested. And it's you young, hardheaded, strong ones who keep messing up. Let me stop. Some of you old folks are serial repeat offenders, too. But hey. Pressure is a good thing. You'll get the lessons sooner or later. You've gotta boil to make things happen. It's gotta get to just the right temperature to boil. That's the valley. The peak is just around the bend. We are made bitter before we're made better. Some of you have your guard down, and that's when things happen to knock you down. You ever notice that just when things are good, something happens, right?"

Folks nodded and said, "Uh-huh."

"Well, that's when the devil starts messing, and when the devil starts messing, what?"

"God starts blessing," his members said out loud.

"Yes. God starts blessing. You've had some messing going on, huh? Accept the bitter with the sweet and find the purpose of the test. Make it your testimony.

"And know that you are not what's happened to you. Don't define yourself by your experience. Stop hating on yourself like that."

Rebe's face was flushed and she exhaled hard.

"But you must deal with the root of it all, and then move on. God is strengthening you for the journey. He has positioned you for a retest for a purpose. All things work together for your good. God is the lifter of your head. But you must get yourself over to the cross, one way or another. Maybe not today. But soon. Calm yourself."

"Yes, sir. Yes," Darla said aloud.

"You have to fail before you succeed. Champions are not those who never fail. Champions are those who never quit. There's nothing more powerful than a made-up mind. Question is, when will you make up yours?"

"Now," some of the members yelled out. "Right now."

"It's time to heal the hurting. Take away your shame. Don't let shame dictate your destiny."

And with that sentence, he looked directly at Rebe, who started to cry. Trinity held her hand tighter, and Darla patted her on her knee, squeezing as a sign of comfort to her friend.

Magnolia looked over at Rebe and her heart sped up. She started to cry, too.

"Believe that it's time for a new season. Watch what happens."

Twenty-Four

"Hot Stuff"

Magnolia

INT.—OCEAN BANK—MIAMI BEACH—LATE
AFTERNOON
May 1, 2009

Earlier in the day, Magnolia sent Rebe an email, telling her she wanted to come by and see her. She knew she'd needed to wait a while, considering what happened with the rape, but the stress of wondering if Randall beat her to the punch was too heavy to carry any longer. And so, they agreed. It would be the next Saturday afternoon at two o'clock. Just the two of them, no Darla, spending girlfriend time together.

Rebe seemed excited.

Magnolia seemed finally ready.

It was just after five o'clock and Magnolia was at work, telling herself if she was really a good employee, she'd stay a while longer to finish up the branch operations file she was working on. She'd sometimes head straight to Miller's house after work, or go straight home and talk to him on the phone. Every now and then she'd head to her grandmother's house and they'd have their own girl talk. Tonight would be a night to head home and chill, alone. But first, another hour or so of work.

Just as Magnolia clicked on her computer and focused on the spreadsheet, her office phone rang.

She grabbed the receiver from its base by touch, eyes focused on the document. "Hello."

"It's me."

"What?" Her face frowned but inside she smiled.

"I'm fine, thanks." Neal's sarcasm was accompanied by a brief laugh. "I left something in your car."

"Excuse me." She turned her chair from her computer to the view outside the window. "How'd you get in my car?"

"I still have a key and remote."

"Neal."

"Go to your car and get it."

"No. And what you need to do is get me those keys. You can even send them in an interoffice envelope."

"So you didn't know I still had them?" He sounded disbelieving.

"No. I didn't. And don't use them again."

"Okay. But when I opened the door and the smell from your car hit my nose, I'm telling you, that kind of bubble gum, vanilla, smell you always have hanging from that scented tree in your ride. And then I could smell your gardenia perfume, too. Mag, it made me wanna stick my dick in the vent." He gave another laugh.

She rubbed her temple and shook her head. "Neal. You are sick. Good-bye."

She hung up and just sat in amazement, flashing a very brief smile. She had to admit that curiosity had a grip on her mind. Magnolia fiddled with her orange enamel bangles and gave a "what the hell" look. She then shut down the computer and headed out.

When she got to her car, she had a single rose on her seat, with a note that read, *Tonight at six-thirty. Our spot. El Rancho Grande. Be there, please. Don't say no.*

Magnolia just sat in the driver seat and looked at the note, examining his writing, his distinctive way of printing every letter in all caps, at an angle, with the lazy way he'd fail to lift the pen, causing scribbled-looking words. Just one of the many things she noticed about Neal. She touched the dark red rose with her fingertips and started up her car, holding the rose as she backed up. She then pressed speed dial on her cell and put the call on speaker.

She asked her boyfriend on his cell, "Baby, where are you?

"Hey love. At home. Rudy's coming by in a minute with the kids. Can you stop by?"

"No. I don't think so. I'm bringing work home with me so I'll head straight to the house and get this done. Tell your son and the kids I said hello. I'll talk to you later."

"Okay. Don't work too hard. Call you later. Love you."

"Love you, too, Miller."

INT.—EL RANCHO GRANDE—SOUTH BEACH—EARLY THAT EVENING

It was seven-ten.

The weather was in the sixties.

Nighttime dark had not set in just yet.

The entire drive the short distance seemed not right.

She remembered the sermon by her pastor.

That God will give you a retest.

She knew exactly what it was.

And being where she was, was wrong.

But in a way it was important.

And besides, wrong had been knocking at Magnolia's door for a minute.

Even though she knew better, she just wasn't quite ready to shut it all the way. Not just yet.

The busy Mexican restaurant, the place where Magnolia and Neal first met, was busy with the after-work dinner crowd, as usual. The wait for a table was forty-five minutes.

Neal, dressed casual with a blue and white Yankees cap, checked Magnolia out up and down, like his eyes were deceiving him. He looked at her dark hair as it flowed straight behind her back, loose. "Why's your hair down?"

They sat at the oblong bar. Magnolia didn't want to wait for a table. There were two barstools to the left of her that were free, but all the rest were taken. They both sipped on the strong, ginger margaritas the restaurant was known for. Neal was already on his second.

She looked at his face, admiring his features, thick lashes, and white teeth. She always loved him in a fitted cap, but didn't let on. "I just wanted to wear it down. No biggie." Magnolia dipped a salty tortilla chip in the mild salsa and ate it.

Neal eased his eyes toward her hips as her backside spanned the width of the barstool. "Tight jeans?"

Her words were nonenergetic. She still chewed and said, "I went home and changed."

"Nice. You're looking really nice." He nodded.

"Thanks."

"Thanks for coming. I'm glad we're face to face."

"Yep. No one around like when we're at work and you're bugging me. No one at my house calling on my phone, cursing me out while you're there. And no one at your house, hiding in your bedroom like a sneaky little porno kitten."

He managed a smile as though amused. "That's true. Again, I apologize for that. No worries."

"You should be sorry. That was like a damn sneak attack, Neal. You cared more about that woman setting me up than how I'd feel. Really, how selfish was that?"

He raised his hand in surrender. "That was a mistake."

She picked up her margarita glass. Her heart spoke. "It'll never happen again because I won't let you do that to me again. I won't let you hurt me again, period." Magnolia licked the salt around the rim of the glass and gave a sip.

"You won't have to worry about that."

"Oh, okay. Just as long as you're sure she's not gonna pull up soon and come in here trying to jump me."

"No. Not gonna happen." He sipped his drink with a look like he was willing to submit to anything, just happy to have her to himself for a minute.

Magnolia said, "So, I see you've been trying to walk the straight and narrow for a minute. Been pretty quiet. Congratulations."

"Please, it hasn't been easy. You've been on my mind

the whole time. You told me not to bring drama into your life and I heard you. But I just couldn't take it anymore. I just needed to see you, other than passing each other at work."

Magnolia looked away from him, and to her left, up at the basketball game on the ESPN channel overhead. She asked, "You two still getting busy on GFF?"

"We're on there. But we don't do anything."

"So, you stopped because you're happy now?"

"I'm not really seeing her like that."

Even looking away, her eyes called him a liar. "Yeah, right. Not really? I don't know why not. You wanted someone dirty, and you got filthy."

"Maybe, but I would've preferred you."

Magnolia saw a Hispanic man looking straight at her. He smiled. She smiled. She looked to her right at Neal. "Yeah, anyway, you were the one complaining all the time that I wasn't this enough or that enough. That I wasn't open-minded enough. But it's funny, you never had a problem busting a nut."

Neal spoke energetically, "Don't get it wrong. The sex was good. Real good. I just wanted to explore more."

Magnolia took another sip and thought, looking to the TV screen again. "I see. Then maybe you should've been patient. You should have taught me and worked with me and talked to me and loved me through it." She turned to Neal, who also looked up at the TV. "You said I was the woman you wanted to marry." He then looked at her. "We picked out a ring together one day, and the next day, Keyonna was forwarding me the text messages you sent her. Funny, they say text messages are the new lipstick on the collar. The new evidence. You should've been more careful." She looked annoyed. "And then, to top it off, Neal, I had to look at her at work. I wanted to kick both of your dumb asses."

"We weren't even doing anything at that point."

"Yes, you were. You need to stop lying. I believe there was a text from you that read, 'I can't wait to watch you come on my dick again.'" She shook her head. "Why do you always deny? You know I saw the message. Damn." Magnolia now spoke with impatience and began to frown.

"Okay."

"No need for any more bullshit. You've got the freak. Mission accomplished."

"I'd leave her for you right now."

Magnolia darted her head back and eyed him down. "I thought you said you weren't really seeing her like that." She looked down at her glass, placing her fingers on the stem. "Neal, please. If you don't want Keyonna, you should leave her for yourself. Not for someone else. Besides, if she hadn't sent me those messages, you would've continued to make me look like a fool." She swallowed the last sip of her drink. "I guess I should be thanking her."

"I'm not done with you."

"Well, I am done with you."

He looked confused. "Mag, so you agreed to meet me here to tell me that? Uh-huh. Now I get it. You must be seeing someone."

"None of your business."

Neal took her chin into his hand and angled her face to his. "Magnolia. I'm sorry."

"You said that already before."

"I know, you always hurt the one you love. That's because they care so much. I blew the trust. I want you to forgive me." He looked serious.

"Neal, all I want is a monogamous man, and you're not it." She moved his hand and looked away.

"I can be."

"You've already proven you aren't. Not with me. And not with her, since you're here tonight." Magnolia thought that her own words could apply to herself, just for the fact that she was there as well, after lying to Miller. And that Neal's sentence about hurting the one you love reminded her of her guilt about betraying Rebe. But at the moment, her unresolved feelings of Neal abandoning her were first and foremost. She couldn't shake it. She knew she needed to take control. But her head and her heart were at odds.

"I'm telling you, she and I are..."

Magnolia interrupted, putting up her index finger. "Spare me, Neal."

He looked behind him as a couple of young women walked by.

"See, that's another thing. A woman's always gotta deal with your reckless eyeballing." She clicked her tongue. "Whatever."

He turned back around in a split second and simply went to another subject like he never even heard her. "Why did you get off of GFF?"

She looked surprised. "I didn't need it anymore."

"So you are seeing someone."

"Neal." Suddenly, Magnolia again looked to her left, and the Hispanic man sitting three barstools down who'd smiled slid a folded napkin over toward her and then turned his back, looking back up at the TV screen.

Neal asked immediately from behind her, "What the hell did he just do?"

Magnolia said, "Nothing." She took the napkin and moved it closer to her.

Neal stood up. "What'd he just do? What is that?" He pointed to the napkin. "Did he just pass you that?" He took it from Magnolia and opened it. It read, *Jose, 305-874-5564.*

Magnolia told Neal, "It's just a napkin."

Neal balled it up and spoke fast, walking behind Magnolia, standing to her left. "Man, she's with me, okay? What's your fuckin' problem anyway?" His voice was fully loaded. He tossed the napkin onto the bar.

"Oh man, I'm sorry. No problem. I, I, I . . . " The man stuttered and blinked fast.

"Dude. Your ass is trying to be slick. You slid that shit across the bar so I wouldn't see. Well I did see it. You were raggedy with it. We need to take this shit outside, muthafucka."

Magnolia leaned over closer to Neal, reaching for his bicep. "No, Neal. No."

He snatched his arm farther away and stepped closer to the guy.

The guy said, "Look, I'm sorry man. She looked over at me and I thought she smiled and I thought, maybe she was your friend, sister, I don't know. Obviously I was wrong. I didn't know what she was to you, but whatever. I'm sorry, man."

By now, Magnolia noticed all eyes on Neal. She gave a long breath and braced herself.

"Dude, if you thought she was just my friend you should've been man enough to ask me, instead of sneaking a damn note to her. But I don't buy that shit. I think you knew good and damn well what you were doing."

The bartender spoke as he stood on the other side of the bar, across from them. "Sir. You wanna keep it down." He looked dead serious.

Neal told him, "No, I don't." He pointed to the guy, speaking to the bartender. "You need to kick his ass out."

The guy continued, "Man, I'm telling you, with all due respect I'm sorry." The guy readjusted his expression. "Listen, let me buy you two a couple of drinks to apologize, and anything else you guys want is on me." He glanced behind Neal, at Magnolia. "And you lady. I'm sorry."

Magnolia frowned, staring him down.

Neal nodded, still frowning, too, but telling him, "Okay then, that's what I'm saying. You need to watch your ass." He took one step away. His tone downshifted. "A brotha can get shot over some shit like that." Neal headed back to his seat.

The guy said to the bartender, "Alonzo, man, whatever they want."

The bartender stepped to Magnolia and Neal, taking away both empty glasses, still looking concerned, "What can I get you?"

Neal asked Magnolia, "What do you want, Mag?"

Magnolia cut her eyes at him. "Nothing."

"You sure?"

"Yes."

He said to the bartender, "I'll have a Hennessy. Make it a double."

"Got it."

Neal looked the guy's way and then up at the TV screen. "Damn fool."

Magnolia scooted her body to face him with her hand on her hip. "If he's such a damn fool, then why are you willing to drink his liquor?"

"What?" Neal looked like he had to have been hearing things.

Magnolia asked with hot focus, "So you're telling me that being protective over a woman can be bought with a drink? Hell, I'll bet if I was Keyonna you wouldn't have backed off like that."

Neal looked amazed. "Oh, so what do you want me to do? You want me to kick his ass. You were just telling me to stop a minute ago, but now you're saying you want me to get in a fight with the man. And possibly go to jail?"

She looked self-assured and impatient. "What I didn't want was for any man I'm with to let an action like that be bought, exchanged for a glass of liquid. Is that what I'm worth to you? About eight to ten dollars? All this talk about us, and how you're not done with me, and you basically took a drink in exchange for my virtue. You'd have been better off just telling him 'fuck no. I don't want shit from you.' You should have told him what you wanted was some respect."

Neal looked through. He dug in his pocket while he spoke. "Oh hell no. Fuck it." He spoke to the bartender. "You know what, Alonzo, forget it man. I'm cool."

"You sure?" the bartender asked while holding the glass of cognac, prepared to set it down.

"Yeah, I'm good, dude." He said to Magnolia, "Good-bye. And here's my money for the bill." He slammed a fifty down on the bar and turned to walk away.

Magnolia said ultra-loud, as if she was way past insulted, "Where are you going?"

Neal was just as loud. "You haven't changed. You're still a trip."

"Oh, and you aren't? Don't you walk away from me. And hey, I still need my car keys from you."

He waved his hand back at her. "Good-bye."

"Dammit. Neal come back." Her voice shrilled.

Magnolia stood from the bar and ran after him. And just like old times, Magnolia and Neal were in the parking lot arguing. With vigor and with volume and with passion. Proving she hadn't learned to love him less and herself more. Or so it seemed.

INT.—NEAL'S CONDO—MIAMI BEACH—THAT EVENING

One hour later, Magnolia and Neal were at his place, fucking like triple-X stars on a mission to win an AVN porn award. Only this time, Magnolia was the director, and she called all the shots.

In the intimate dark, she demanded with the voice of an adult star lead. She straddled Neal's face while he grabbed her round ass cheeks with each hand. She held on to the slats of the walnut headboard, looking down at him. Her voice was scolding. "Look at me. See. Got my hairy pussy on your mouth, fucking your face like you'd always asked me to, but I wouldn't. So this is what you wanted all that time, huh? You wanted me to come in your mouth while you lie on your back and suck the sweet cum out of my pussy like this. Oh yeah, dammit. This mess feels so good, the way you pull on my clit like it's a damn sucker." She looked up. Her mental zone was on high. Beneath her turn-on, she remembered her experience at the swinger's club, and decided it was time to mimic the ride. "Yes. Neal. Shit. Umh, dammit." Her forehead sweaty, she tossed her hair back and grunted like she was either in the middle of a good come, or fighting one off. She then told him, still sounding mad, crawling off his face as she fussed, "Gimme a damn condom. I saw you fucking that whore without a condom. You made me stand there and watch you stick your naked dick inside of that bitch. Put that shit on. Now."

Neal looked extra turned on and hustled to reach over to the nightstand for the clear package. She snatched it from him, bit it with her teeth and ripped it open, yanking out the red Nigerian condom and securing it fast.

She scooted down and straddled his pubic area, reaching back to insert his straight-up, mushroom-tipped dick into her wet and ready vagina. She moved in a circle until it eased all the way in, and then rocked from side to side, working it. "Ooooo, I hate you, shit. Ummmmmm." She roared with eyes half closed, words half true, heart totally confused.

He started to follow her lead and pump back. "Oh yeah."

Her voice pointed in his face. "No. Don't move. Shit. And shut up."

He stopped.

"You just lay there, and don't say a damn thing. Be still just like when you'd complain I'd just lay there like, how did you say it, like a dead fish? Now you let me work it and see how long you can take this pussy fucking you." The sound of her bangle bracelets clinking matched her sex motions. Her juices were sloshing.

He licked his lips like LL Cool J, looking down at the sight of his dick swallowed by her hunger. "Damn, this pussy is tight. I forgot how tight this pussy is. Fuck it feels good. Wear it out. That's the way daddy likes it. Look at you riding that dick like you had lessons. What the hell?"

She bucked as she fucked and talked even more. "I told you to shut up. Yeah, look at me. Look at your ex-missionary woman, who you had the nerve to cheat on just so you could get a freak. There was a freak inside of me you never even took the time to get to know." She kept working it with precision. "Uh-huh. You had this. You threw it away with your horny, greedy, freaky, pussy loving, lying, serial cheating, big dick having, fine ass, curly headed, pretty faced, white teeth having, nice car driving, Mexican food eating, CÎROC drinking, clit sucking expert mother fucking ass. You like to fantasize about me with your woman when you fuck her, huh? Then imagine her licking your balls right now while I ride this long dick. You feel that shit? Huh? You feel her breath against your ass right now? You feel her tongue? You feel her hair along your legs? She's licking the shit outta you. I can hear her slurping while I'm bouncing. Yeah, you've got it all right there in your head, imagining all that. Your old freak and your new freak, freaking. Now come for us right now. Come right fucking now, dammit."

Neal's eyes were closed, and then he looked up at her doing her energetic dick ride and made an inaudible sound. "Uuuggghnhh."

"That's it. That's it. That's the sound you would make when you'd cream all inside this tight pussy when you had me all to yourself. But, since you wanted a freak, you got a freak. It just ain't me. Dammit. Fuck you." And Magnolia crawled off. "Punk ass."

Neal lay on his back, watching her get up, coming down from the depths of his expulsion, and also looking like she'd completely lost it. "Baby, wait. Baby. Mag."

"No. See, I don't want your woman to show up and catch me here and then I'll have to beat her crazy ass."

"No, wait. Please." He sat up, holding on to his condom-covered dick. His cell rang along the night-stand. He looked at the nightstand and then down at the floor and grabbed his pants, which he'd tossed in the throes of their feverish passion play.

Magnolia walked to his phone and read the display. "Awwww, your Keyonna's looking for you. Maybe I should answer it for you." Her face said, *Dare me.*

"No." He carefully pulled off the full condom and placed it in the trash can next to his dresser, keeping an eye on Magnolia.

Her hand was one inch away. "You sure you don't want me to?"

"I'm sure." He stepped into his pants fast.

"Oh, so you do care about her. Good." She leaned toward him. "Then don't you ever fucking call me or bother me again. Otherwise, I'm telling her about tonight. I'll show her your note about meeting you tonight, and tell her the exact time she called." His phone rang again. Same caller. "I'll be the one showing evidence this time. Try me."

"Mag."

She stepped to her pile of clothes and bent down. "Neal. Leave me the hell alone. It's time for me to get back to my life. Without you." Magnolia snatched her jeans and squeezed into them, then her blouse, buttoning it fast, and then grabbing her shoes and purse. She faced the bedroom door and walked as Neal had on only his pants, following her.

"Don't go yet. Wait."

She kept walking down the slick white stairs and he was right behind her.

"Mag, wait a minute." His words had warning and authority.

She jerked her body back toward him just after taking the last step. "What?"

He said, with a calm voice but his face looked alarmed, "You're bleeding." He pointed down near the back of her thighs. "A lot."

She looked down between her legs at the vivid red blood that had soaked her jeans just that fast. "Dammit."

He stood behind her. "Baby. It's just your period coming down. All that bed movement brought it on."

Magnolia looked as though she doubted it, intense fear in her eyes.

"Here, let me take you to the doctor. Let me finish getting dressed."

Magnolia's cell rang. A call from Miller. And before Neal could get back up the stairs to his room, Magnolia was gone.

A trail of blood led from his living room to his hallway, and beyond.

Evidence of Magnolia Butler's continued sins.

Twenty-Five

"Let's Talk about Sex"

Rebe

INT.—REBE'S HOME—AFTERNOON
May 9, 2009

The musical chime of Rebe's doorbell rang on a Saturday afternoon.

Extra hyper, Randi barked from a deep space, as though she thought she was a vicious Great Dane, twice her actual size.

Rebe had called Magnolia that morning to check on her, and Magnolia insisted she was well enough to keep their date. Also, Magnolia told her she had something for Trinity, who had now moved back home. But Rebe had something to tell Magnolia anyway.

The sound of the alarm keypad deactivation was loud.

"Just a minute," Rebe yelled at the door before opening it.

More barking.

Rebe calmed Randi by shushing her, grabbing her by the collar and moving her to the side while Rebe opened the front door.

Magnolia held a gift bag and her purse, and said as soon as she saw her buddy Rebe, "You look good. Look at you, all boobalicious, filling out in all the right places."

Rebe wore a black, low-cut baggy shirt and spandex pants. "Thanks. Believe it or not, I feel good." Randi made a whining sound and Rebe let her go. She jumped all around Magnolia.

Magnolia leaned over to pet Randi's dark brown, shiny coat. "Hey Randi. What's up? Pretty baby. Hey." Magnolia walked into Rebe's home and Randi ran ahead of her, anticipating her next move as though she might be able to get more affection. "I see she's a house dog now, huh?"

Rebe again pressed the buttons to reset the alarm. "She is. She earned her stripes." Rebe said to Randi in a baby voice, "No more backyard for my Randi, right baby?" She then pointed. "Go lay down, baby. Go." Randi tucked her tail and headed over toward her large doggie bed in the kitchen. "Good girl."

Magnolia sat on one end of the sectional in the family room.

Rebe sat on the other. "This is nice. Just the two of us."

"It is. Very nice."

Rebe said, pointing toward the kitchen, "I've got sparkling apple cider and some chip and dip if you want some."

"Oh, that's sweet. I'm fine. I had an early lunch already."

Rebe crossed her legs and glanced at Magnolia's midsection. "So, you're pregnant. Still can't believe it. Expecting suits you well."

Magnolia adjusted the waistband of her palazzo pants. "Crazy, huh? Who would've thought I'd end up being a mother, especially at the age of forty. Not to mention Miller a father. I would've sworn every one of my nine-thousand eggs we talked about would have been fried by now, and that Miller was shooting blanks anyway."

Rebe gave a mild chuckle. "True. It's just plain old meant to be, I guess. And so the bleeding was normal?"

"The doctor said it's common in the first trimester. Especially at my age, and especially after intercourse."

"Oh, you'd just had sex?"

"Yeah." Magnolia blinked fast.

"How far along are you?"

"Just about five weeks."

"Nice."

Magnolia took a moment, and then looked distracted by her thoughts, shifting back to what she was saying. "My doctor said thirty percent of women have bleeding like that after sex since the cervix is so tender. Just making sure I take it slow. Making sure I don't have any cramping."

"You won't. Let's just hope you're better at the mom thing than I am."

Magnolia gave an easy laugh. "You're fine. Where is Trinity anyway? Is she home?"

"Out with friends. She's been a doll."

"Good." Magnolia reached over for the bag she'd placed on the floor. "Here. I brought this for her. It's just a black angel charm like I wear. She's always liked it. And I admit, I haven't been the best godmother."

Rebe took it and placed it on the side table. "Pretty pink bag. You know what? Honestly, you've been just fine. That's sweet."

"Well, either way, I should've been closer."

"Anyway. So, what's the due date? Has the doctor given you one yet?"

"Yes. December 19. Can you believe it?"

"Wow. A blessing."

"It is." Magnolia's nerve was as high as it was going to get. "Rebe. I just want you to know, I didn't bring it up at church, but I'm really sorry about what happened, with the guy who broke in here."

"Yeah, well, the girls at the club warned me to always watch out, you know, make sure to literally look in my rearview on the way home. I didn't. But, he plead guilty. No trial to go through. Having to testify against my mother was enough court for me. For now, we're going to victims' counseling together, me and Trinity. It's been tough."

Magnolia looked around. "I still can't believe that happened in here. I was wondering. Don't you think you should move?"

"I've thought about it."

"I mean, I don't want to scare you, but his people know where you live and, for Trinity's sake, too, I think you need to start looking for a new house."

"I will. You know, I haven't slept in that room ever since. I sleep in the guest room next to Trinity's. For now, I've got my 9 millimeter, fully loaded, and we keep the alarm set, even if we head out to dump the trash, we reset it again."

"Good. Still, you know, just the energy."

Rebe looked sure of herself. "We're working through it."

"Good. I'm proud of you both. And I'm glad you're

getting counseling." Magnolia uncrossed her legs and crossed them again. "No word from Randall? After all that happened, I would think he would've been supportive."

Rebe's face was nonchalant. "They sent a card. Trinity tells me he sends his best. He talks to her a lot more now. Took her out to dinner. They're cool."

"Good." Magnolia nodded long after her one word. Then she said, "Listen, I know a lot's been going on, and I'm glad you're better. But there is something I've wanted to talk to you about. It's been weighing heavily on me, and I just can't keep pretending it didn't happen. I have to tell you."

"What is it?"

"I want you to know I did something that was totally fucked up. But, I also want you to know I'm telling you because I love you. I want your forgiveness."

"What the hell is it? All this preliminary set up shit is scaring me to death."

Magnolia had an expression like she was trying to carefully decipher her words. She managed to say, "Rebe. You know I was online doing the dating site stuff, well, no it wasn't a dating site, but you know what I mean."

"It was a booty call site. So?"

"Right. For sex. Well, one night I went to meet a couple."

"You did?"

"Yes. When I got there, I didn't stay long. I just kind of stood there while they played."

"Damn, Magnolia. That's brave. Okay. But what the hell does that have to do with me?"

Magnolia just spit it out. "Rebe, it was Randall."

"It was who?"

"Randall. The guy was Randall. It was Randall, and Kandi."

Rebe spoke each word with a slow, distinct, flow. "You have got to be kidding me." She uncrossed her legs.

"No. I'm not. I wish I was."

"And you got with them?"

"I watched them."

"Magnolia, please tell me you're kidding."

"I'm not."

Rebe's nostrils flared. She scooted to the end of the sofa cushion. "Hold up. So you were blindfolded, right? No. Don't tell me. You had to be drugged, right?"

"No." Magnolia looked ashamed.

Rebe stood up fast. "Then what the fuck was it?"

"Rebe, I just got caught up."

Rebe walked away from Magnolia and then turned toward her to speak. Loud. "Caught up? That sounds like a man's excuse when his dick ends up in some woman's pussy. Caught up? Like to the point of no return? Oh you could have returned all right. You just didn't want to? And you end up in a hotel room with Randall's ass, knowing the way that man fucked me over. You know he's my ex. He's your best friend's ex, Magnolia. And you played with him and that bitch, Kandi? Is that what you're telling me?"

"I didn't know it was them until I got there."

"Oh, but once you got there, you saw his big goofy ass, right? Like I said, you weren't blindfolded. And you still stayed?"

"Yes."

"And he still wanted to once he saw it was you?"

"Yes."

Rebe heard her heart speed up. She swallowed hard. "Dumb ass question." The visual in her head was stabbing. "Why don't you just tell me what the hell happened? I'm asking the questions here and you're just giving me these short ass answers. What fucking happened?"

Magnolia gave a nervous-sounding ramble. "I was online and kept getting all these instant messages from someone named Lean and Jean, and I thought Lean was Neal's name backward. See, I checked Neal's banking account and found out he'd been paying for a GFF membership, too, so when I kept getting the messages over and over, I just thought it was him and Keyonna. But when I got there, it wasn't. It was Randall."

Rebe walked toward Magnolia, flailing her hands. "Magnolia, you sound crazy. That is some real fucked up shit. With all the shit going on in my life and you... You know what? I'm about to snap. Fuck! You need to get, you need to step away from me for a minute. Please. 'Cause I'm trying my best to not beat your ass. I mean, I am so damn mad right now. This is way fucked up. When in the hell was this?"

Magnolia looked up at her. "Back in late February."

"That long ago and you're just now telling me?"

"I know. I'm sorry."

Rebe turned again and took a few steps. "Oh hell no. You can be as sorry as you wanna be. Your sorry isn't important. My pissed is what's important, and I'm hella pissed." She turned back to Magnolia. "That's what matters. Me. Your 'friend.'" She made quotation marks in the air. "And I'm fucking embarrassed that Randall would even think you'd betray me like that. Damn. I mean, he probably thinks you believe I'm a piece of shit like he does. Not even worthy of your trust because of some dick and pussy in a hotel room. Does Darla know?"

"Yes. I told her the other day. She warned me to go ahead and tell you."

"See, I look like a dumb ass fool, still letting him and her pull shit on me. Damn, girl. You're a trip, you know that? A real trip. We're forty now. We're not back in college."

"Rebe, I'm so sorry. Truly sorry."

Rebe rubbed her hands together and took a few more steps away from Magnolia. "My fucked up mind sometimes dares me to take the low road. It has for a long time now. I've got my mother's gene, you know, her sick-ass temper. I take pills to keep me from doing all the shit that a bashed-in head does. You know all the hell I've been through, and you know how I've been trying to get past all my shit, Magnolia. You know. I've been trying to listen to what we heard in church. Trying to not let the shame of my past dictate my destiny." She was now just below a shout.

"Yes, I do know."

"To go through all this when I'm at an age where my life should be getting calmer, not crazier, is so hard. My daughter caught me with my legs wide open. She saw her mother two seconds away from an orgasm served by a woman's mouth, at a damn swinger's club that my ass had no business being in. But my daughter forgave me. I got raped by a man who's locked up for life, who I'm working to forgive in my own head. And here you are, my best friend, telling me she did the same thing to me, that I did almost twenty years ago."

"What?"

"I guess payback is a dog, huh? I crossed the line and got with my best friend's guy and I even got pregnant. You're not pregnant by Randall, are you?"

"No. What are you talking about?"

"My senior year, I was out at a bar, depressed about my life, and about raising Trinity alone, about her dad's drug problem, and I saw Aaron, Darla's husband there. An hour later, we were in a motel, having sex, unprotected. Two months later I had an abortion. So, I guess all this is my turnaround, huh? You and Randall. You saw Randall's dick. Me and Aaron. I saw Aaron's dick. I fucked up. You fucked up. Who knows what the hell Darla's hiding from us. Some best friends, huh? If that's the best I'd hate to see the worst."

"Rebe. You've kept that to yourself all these years?"

"I have. Funny how Aaron picked the most broken one to creep with. But he was no saint, either. He was deep into the freak closet. "

"Darla knows that."

"Well, she doesn't know this."

"And you're not going to tell her?"

"No."

"Rebe. Darla's the one who's always been so protective of you."

"Oh please. Don't shift to righteous woman now. Just because you did your shit and needed to get it off your chest, doesn't mean I'm the same way. I come from the school of not every damn thing needs to be told. That was part of the way I lived when I was young. What happened in our house stayed in our house. Besides, it was too long ago for all that talk about the shit that went on in college. I'm dealing with today and that's enough. And today, in spite of what you think of me, I think you, Magnolia Butler, are a stank ass bitch." Rebe pointed at Magnolia's very being. Her eyes were red. No tears. Just heated emotion with a tiny hint of sisterly love.

Magnolia nodded, knowing she deserved it, and looking like she was waiting for Rebe to say she was kidding, or to kick her.

Rebe continued. "The only reason I'm not jumping on you right now, and knocking the hell out of you, is, for one, I'm almost not surprised. When I was with Randall, I'd see how he'd look at you. I'm no fool. Or maybe I was a fool, because apparently I missed the way you looked at him, too."

"Rebe. I never ever thought of him like that."

"Whatever. The second reason is, I refuse to hit you because I'm pregnant, too. I haven't had a period since last December. I'm due September 23, so I'm further along than you. I've been wearing these oversized tops. Don't have to worry about dancing since I quit after my rapist, who was their patron, was captured. Actually, they offered me one thousand dollars to go. That's a joke. Told them to shove their money. They even acted stupid when they found out I was Randall's ex-wife. Hell, Randall ain't nobody." She blinked a long blink. "But the real trip is, I'm pregnant by a man who doesn't even exist. I fucked that guy DeMarius on the first day of the new year and got knocked up. Hell, I guess a six-condom night of screwing increases your chances of getting pregnant. Plus, I wasn't on the pill."

"Rebe, you're kidding me? How far along are you?"

"More than four months."

"Oh my God. Rebe. We're both having kids at our age."

"Well, for some reason, maybe God wanted me to have another chance at motherhood, even after all the crap I've pulled in my life."

"These are disguised blessings."

"Yeah, well, those are some serious disguises. But today, for once, I'm gonna take the advice of my victim's counselor and look at the bright side. Look for the light, as the pastor said." Rebe stepped to the sofa and took a seat, crossing her arms and legs.

"You have every right to be mad at me."

"Maybe, but just like what I did back in 1991 with Darla's man, life has a way of remembering, so you watch out."

"I understand." Magnolia nodded, knowing darn well what her friend was saying. "As far as DeMarius, we'll need to find out who he is. What do you know about him?"

Rebe looked like she didn't want to discuss it, but she did. "All I know is he said his last name was Collins. I can't find a DeMarius Collins anywhere. I thought he said he was interviewing for job as a track coach at Miami-Dade. I called and the coaches there said they've never heard of him. And I checked to find out the name the room was under, and it was under the name of a woman. Googled him up and down, too."

"Wow. We'll keep trying. We'll find him. Doesn't he know your name?"

"Just my maiden name, if he even remembers."

"I see."

"Bottom line is, I've got to do this parenting thing by myself. And I will."

"How long have you known?"

"My ass thought I was just gaining weight. I kept throwing up and skipped my periods, but I thought it was perimenopause. I just found out not long ago myself."

Magnolia sat back. "My Lord. Two old broads being moms."

"Yep." Rebe looked tired of it all.

"Rebe, I didn't play it safe. I risked our friendship. And for that, I'm sorry."

"Apology accepted," she replied without eye contact.

Magnolia placed her hand over Rebe's. "Thanks. I made a misstep. I'm far from perfect." She breathed in slow and out slower.

"Yes you are. And why in the hell were you checking Neal's bank account? Cut that shit out. I hope you're not doing that with Miller."

"I'm not. I trust him."

"Good." Rebe could not believe her own calm.

The new her was a complete and total flip.

Even as angry as she'd gotten over Magnolia's confession.

It was a retest.

And this one she had to pass.

Pass so that her walk on the bright side would be her normal.

Rebe looked over at the end table as a text message sounded on her cell.

She picked it up.

It was Armani. It's not mine, is it?

She picked it up. No, was all she typed.

Twenty-Six

———— ❧ ————

"You Got It All"

Magnolia

INT.—MILLER'S HOME—EARLY EVENING
May 11, 2009

I t was a warm, still, quiet Monday evening.
The sun was barely on duty.

The champagne sunset was a sight for sore eyes.

Magnolia sat on the deck that extended from Miller's kitchen, three floors above his beautifully landscaped backyard. The view of the rectangular pool with shimmering blue water was outlined by a ninety foot tamarind tree with green feather-like leaves with purple veins.

Magnolia looked around at the exotic, tropical scenery, eyeing the peacock flowers with brilliant flame-red clusters. She inhaled the scent and the ambiance, and surrendered her body on the silver lounge chair.

She'd kicked off her two-inch kitten heels, still wearing her crème work skirt and blouse.

Miller approached with a glass of Chardonnay for

him and a cold glass of cranberry juice for his future baby's mom, and sat next to her in the cushioned chair. "So how do you feel?"

"Good, sweetie. Very relaxed." Her sentences agreed with her look of calm. She took the glass. "Thanks," she said, and then took a sip.

"You sure?"

"Yes." Her nod added an exclamation point.

"I'm glad to see that. Dr. Hayes said you need to slow down. Your fibroids could mean a hostile uterus. I think it'd be good if you put in for some vacation time."

"Sweetie, I can't right now. Too much going on." She set the glass down on the tabletop.

"Well, when you're ready to get away, just say the word."

Magnolia closed her eyes. "Thanks." Her voice was soft.

"How'd your visit with Rebe go?"

"It was good." Magnolia looked over at him. "Baby, Rebe is pregnant, too."

"Rebe? Pregnant?"

"Yes, I know. I felt the same way you look."

"By whom?"

"There was this guy she got with on New Year's Eve. Long story."

"Okay. What does he have to say about it?"

"He doesn't know. It was a one-night stand. Rebe doesn't know who he is or how to reach him."

"Oh, man. That's gotta be tough on her." Miller took a sip of wine.

"She's tough. She'll be fine."

"Is she keeping it? The baby."

Magnolia nodded with certainty. "Oh yes. And she's obviously further along than I am so it'd be a little late for that anyway. She seems happy about it, actually."

"So both of you, pregnant at the same time. Kids the same age. That is something."

"Yes, it is."

"You know, I was thinking. I'll be seventy when our baby is in the fifth grade."

"And? You look good baby." She gave him flirty eyes. He winked.

She asked, eyes now excited, "Hey. Do you like the name Paisley, sweetie? I've always loved that name."

"I like it. It's different. But what if it's a boy?"

"If it's a boy, you pick."

"Okay. Deal." They both looked out along the beautiful tree-lined view of his backyard. "So, I told the kids today, especially now that you feel you're far enough along and everything's okay as far as the bleeding. You know, I told them about us being parents. And I told my ex-wife."

"You did? What'd they say?"

"The first thing the kids asked was if we're getting married. That is, after they teased me about our child being an aunt or uncle to my grandchildren." He smiled hard.

"Really." Magnolia gave a laugh. "I didn't even think about that. But they're right. And your ex?"

"She was a little amazed. Amazed I'd want to do it all again. At my age."

"And you said to her?"

"I told her I'm happier than I've been since I can remember. That this was meant to be. That I'm excited."

"I see." Magnolia took a small sip of her juice. "Then did she stop being opinionated?" She looked like she wasn't joking.

"She stopped."

"I think she needs to move on." She held her glass with both hands. "I don't see why she needed to be told directly anyway, really."

"She didn't need to be. She was with Rudy when I called him."

"I see."

He saw her expression. "Are you okay?"

"Yes. Just don't want her to be such a part of all this. I'm not used to this. The ex-wife and my man being so tight. I mean, the kids are grown."

"Magnolia. My ex-wife and I are friends. I've set new boundaries for her and she's following them. I don't want her. She doesn't want me. She has a boyfriend. She's going through some hard times, which she knows are not my concern. She's simply my kids' mom."

"Miller, I admit I have trust issues. As much as I don't want to bring that to you, it is a part of who I am. I need someone I can really trust."

"You can. And thanks for admitting that, baby. Like I said, she just happened to be there when I told my son. She wished us well."

"Okay," Magnolia said, sounding like it was a warning. "I'll give you the benefit of the doubt. This is new for both of us, but I'm willing." She shifted. "So, your kids wanted to know when we were getting married, huh?"

"Yeah."

"Did you tell them right away?" She looked directly at Miller. "Because I want to get married right away."

His expression showed surprise. "You do?"

She nodded. "Miller, you can propose again when you're ready."

"Oh really?"

"Yes."

Miller's lightbulb went off. "Well damn. Hold on." He put his wine glass down and got up. He went into the house and moments later, came back out and stood over Magnolia. His question was simple. "Magnolia Denise Butler, will you marry me?"

Magnolia wanted to giggle because he remembered her middle name, but her heart was louder than her head. She looked up, deep into his blue eyes, her mouth open, and then she looked at his hands, seeing the black leather ring box, and she replied just as simply, "Yes, Miller Thomas Lockhart, I will. I will marry you."

"Then this is for you." He handed her the box, and she scooted her chair back and came to a stance next to him, taking it into her right hand. She flipped open the top, and there was a four-carat, emerald-cut solitaire with four heart-cut diamonds along each side, set in platinum. It sparkled brilliantly.

Magnolia brought her hand to her mouth and froze. She gave a quick blink.

Miller removed the ring from its place inside of the satin-lined slot, and took her left hand in his. He gradually placed it on her ring finger, kissing her cheek as she still stared at her new engagement ring.

She spoke with a weak voice. "Miller. It's beautiful. Oh my God. I love it."

"Good, because you are beautiful. You are amazing. And I love you."

"I love you, too."

"Thanks for saying yes."

She panted. "Oh my. Even though I asked you to go ahead and ask again, you still got this for me?"

"Even though. After the first time, I didn't blame you for wanting to wait. But I got the ring anyway. Let's do it." Miller looked serious as a heart attack.

Magnolia still looked in shock. "Oh my God." She remembered her evening with Neal, when she lied to Miller, like so many men had lied to her along the way. Would it be better to let her left hand know what her right hand had done? She looked up at him. Or should she lie by omission? "Miller."

"Yes." He looked down at her, fully attentive.

"I've gotta call Gigi. I've gotta call the girls," she said in a childlike voice and then whisked off in her stocking feet, headed from the outside deck, making a beeline into the kitchen like Santa had left her a bike under the tree on Christmas morning.

Before she could get close to the kitchen table to pull open her purse and grab her phone, it rang. She grabbed it and placed it to her ear, with a voice straight from Happyland. "Hello."

"Mag. It's me." The voice was deep and slow.

Her face still stayed thrilled. Her voice only shifted a bit. "I can't talk to you. I'm busy."

"I just need to tell you."

"Tell me what?" Her question was rushed.

Before Neal could answer, Miller could be heard right behind Magnolia, asking, "Who is that?"

Immediately, Neal asked, too, "Who is that?"

Magnolia turned back toward her brand-new fiancé,

and said to him first, "It's my ex-boyfriend I told you about. Neal."

"Why is he calling?"

Her shoulders shrugged. "I don't know."

Miller's face was serious. "Put it on speaker."

Magnolia didn't hesitate. She pressed the speaker button and handed Miller her cell, taking a step back, all eyes and all ears. She glanced down at her ring for a split second, and then looked at Miller.

He held the phone down under his chin, and asked in a sarcastic tone, "What can I do for you?"

"Who is this?"

"This is Magnolia's fiancé. But honestly, you have no right to be asking any questions. But I do. So answer mine."

"Look, I didn't call you. This isn't your phone. This is Mag's phone."

Miller looked amused. "Mag, huh? Well, Mag is busy, like she told you. And not only that, Mag is no longer accepting your calls. I know for a fact that you know this already, but I'll say it anyway. Mag is not available to you. Mag and I are telling you not to call again. Do you get that, ex-boyfriend?"

"Let me talk to her."

"I'm speaking for her."

"Then that means you're saying what you want her to say, not what she really feels. I'm just making sure she's okay. Funny how she told you about me, because she sure didn't tell me about you. From what I can see, sounds like you're insecure and controlling."

"I'm a man, is what I am. And rest assured, she's okay. She's more than okay. And her well-being is no longer your concern, ex-boyfriend. I've got her. She's fine. But you won't be if you call her again."

"Oh? Sounds like a threat to me. See, that's sad. You've got to speak for your 'fiancée' and the two of you aren't even married yet. Wow. Controlling her already. Bad sign."

Miller looked as if he'd bitten his tongue hard.

Magnolia didn't blink. She kept focused on the conversation between her past and her future. Miller looked at her. Her eyebrows gave a nervous lift.

He asked, "Magnolia, baby, is there anything I just said that you don't agree with?"

She spoke close to the phone. "No, sweetie. I agree with everything you just said. One hundred percent."

"Got it, ex? One hundred percent," Miller said, as though he felt a hint of pleasure from her acquiescent reply.

"Oh wow. Okay. Got it. I'll talk to her later. Or at work. This is cool for now."

"And things will be cool later. Tomorrow, her cell number will change. And if you harass her at work, we will file a formal complaint with your employment department."

"I'll see her. I have something to tell her but also, I need to give her something. She knows what it is."

"What?"

Neal dismissed his question, only asking one himself. "Hey anyway, how long have you two been together? Because . . ."

Magnolia held her breath. "Good-bye, Neal. And don't contact me again," she said, further solidifying her future husband's efforts.

"Good-bye. I feel sorry for you." And with that, Neal hung up.

Miller handed Magnolia her cell, and she made sure it was disconnected, looking down at the screen.

Miller asked, "What does he want to give you?"

She took a moment and then said, "Oh. I'm sure it's my car keys. I'll send him a text, telling him to mail them."

"No more contact." He took the phone back and scrolled, pressing the call button, and then speaker. He told her, "Except this one call."

The phone picked up but Neal said nothing.

"Hey, ex-boyfriend." It almost sounded as if he was calling Neal a punk, but it was semi-vanilla. "We're re-keying her car immediately. So keep the other one as a memento."

"Oh wow."

"Wow is right."

"Mag. Sounds to me like you've got yourself a case of jungle fever. That's really funny. I thought you liked chocolate." Neal chuckled.

"Bye, Ex," Miller said, not amused.

"Hey. Can't say that I blame you, Billy Bob. She *is* a good fuck, man." Neal emphasized *is*. His words were antagonistic and cynical. And then he said, "Mag, Key-onna and I eloped."

While Magnolia gasped at both sentences, looking like someone had punched her in the back, Miller hung up.

He shook his head and gave half a "Ha," placing the phone on the table next to her purse, folding his arms along his stomach. He spoke with calm, looking unfazed. "What matters is, you're a great woman. Let's wish them well. Now weren't you going to tell Gigi and the girls?"

Magnolia watched him, as though expecting some evidence that maybe his button had been pushed. Nothing. Though she was sure her face told that her button was being pushed, she aimed her glance downward toward her ring again, and sighed. "I will. Thank you. I love you."

Miller took her by her left hand as she looked into his eyes, standing face to face. "You're my last love. No mess. No drama. No rough times. My job is to protect you. If you're happy, I'm happy."

Magnolia said, "I'm happy," and her face seemed to agree. She didn't want to ruin it. Not at this point in her life. Not at the age of forty. Happiness was too hard earned.

Too difficult to come by.

Too very necessary.

"Good. Then that, your happiness, is all that matters."

INT.—GIGI'S HOUSE—THE NEXT EVENING

Magnolia spoke close to her grandmother's ear. "Gigi, I heard the birds singing this morning. I mean they really sang. And I really listened. It was beautiful. And I remembered what you told me on my birthday. To stay positive and get ready. That God would bring me the right man when the time is right. You were right. Again."

Gigi's eyes looked pleased. "See, not saying I told you

so, but it's that ordained mate I was telling you about."
Gigi spoke close to Magnolia's ear as well, sitting next
to her after Magnolia and Miller arrived at Gigi's home
that Tuesday after work.

"Yes. That and more."

"More singing. More love. Well deserved."

Today, Magnolia had driven Miller's gunmetal metallic Jaguar to work, and he took her SUV. He had the
locks and the alarm system changed himself. They'd
driven her car to Gigi's house. And Magnolia had a new
iPhone, with a new phone number.

Miller returned from Gigi's bathroom and sat on the
other side of the sofa, next to his new fiancée, his hand
on her leg. Her hand on his.

Gigi stared and said, "You two look good together.
Very good."

"Well, thanks, Mrs. Grace."

"Oh no, please call me Gigi. I'm Magnolia's Gigi.
And as happy as she looks, glowing like she's been
plugged back in, I'm your Gigi, too."

Magnolia gave a snicker and watched him as he and
Gigi smiled.

"Thanks, Gigi." He confirmed her name with a re-
spectful nod.

"Speaking of glowing, so, I'm going to be a great-
grandmother, huh?" Gigi put her hand on Magnolia's
tummy.

"You are. And less than two weeks before my birthday."

Miller said, "You see we didn't waste any time."

"God didn't waste any time. It's all God. He knows
what He does, and why." She slowly leaned forward,

picking up the pitcher of lemonade, pouring more into Miller's empty glass. Magnolia's was nearly full.

"Thanks," Miller said.

"Sure. So, how'd you two meet?" Gigi set it back down and seemed anxious to hear.

Magnolia looked at Miller and then told her, "We met out. We were at a club and sat at the bar for hours. Just talking. I mean, it was just like we were old friends who hadn't seen each other in years. Gigi, the things he said were so similar to the things I thought. It was crazy. And since then, I don't think there's been a day we haven't seen each other, right, sweetie?" She looked at her fiancé.

"Right." He squeezed her leg.

Gigi grinned. "See, that's how it's supposed to be. I miss that. I remember when me and your grandfather Norm met, it was just like that. It was just comfortable, not forced. When it's time, it's time."

"I agree," said Miller.

Magnolia gave a major smile. "Gigi, it was kind of funny, but yesterday, Neal called, and Miller answered my phone."

Gigi looked surprised. "What? No."

"Yes." Magnolia bumped Miller with her arm. "I'm sorry, Miller."

"No. Not at all. I took the phone because I wanted to. He wasn't respecting you. Maybe he'll respect me."

Magnolia added, "Let's just say, I doubt he'll be calling back. He tried to get ugly, but Miller didn't give him any room for that. Besides, Gigi, he said he and Keyonna eloped."

"Good. Very good." Gigi said smiling. "Glad to hear it."

"Me, too," Magnolia said, giving her grandmother a matching look.

Miller noticed their bond. "It's good to see Magnolia so close to you. My parents passed away, and I sure miss them. It's just nice to have a family connection like this. I'm glad to be part of it."

"We're glad to have you. I'm sure Magnolia told you, I'm like her mom. And I'm so excited about this baby coming. What a way to end the year."

"Yes, it is," Magnolia said, and then she frowned and gave an exhale, hand on her stomach.

"Magnolia, what's wrong?" Miller asked.

"I just feel a little dizzy. A little nauseous." She scooted back and bounced her leg.

Gigi asked, "Do you need anything? Maybe all the sugar from that lemonade doesn't agree with you."

"That's probably what it is." Miller asked, "Do you want some water, baby?"

"Yes, please. I'll just go to the bathroom real fast. My stomach is acting up. I didn't eat much today." Magnolia prepared to stand.

"She barely finished her food. Here, I'll help you." Miller stood and reached down to take Magnolia by the hand.

She stood at a snail's pace, bent over, and then squinted. "Ouch. Awww, ouch. Oh, it hurts, Miller."

"Your stomach?"

"Yes." Her face was pained.

"We need to get you to the hospital." Miller eased Magnolia along, prompting her to take careful steps toward the front door.

"I'll go with you. I'll just grab my pocketbook."

Miller said as Gigi stood, "Hurry, Gigi. Get her purse. I'll get Magnolia to the car."

Gigi looked in shock. "Okay. I'm right there, two seconds."

Magnolia walked slow, assisted by Miller, thinking in her head what Gigi had said moments earlier, *He knows what He does. And why.*

Magnolia said to herself, heart skipping a beat, *I just pray God's will agrees with mine. Would that be too much to ask?*

Twenty-Seven

—— ✃ ——

"Try It on My Own"

Darla

July 12, 2009

It was a Thursday, the day of the grand opening of Darla's baby, Brown Sugar.

The glittery shimmer from the speckled caramel walls, pewter and glass gas fireplace, and gilded crystal chandelier were twinkling in a celebratory sparkle. The soft silver sectionals faced each other, each with oval leopard pillows, and leopard club chairs at each side. There were sheer taupe curtains with animal-print drapes with gauzy brown tiebacks. The bar area had leather stools and birch cabinetry. And hot pink, shapely mannequins were garbed in colorful corsets and thongs and stockings and spiked heels.

The look and feel was cozy and fancy and sexy.

Darla served banana penis cupcakes, pussy jellybeans, and lolly cocks. Virgin pink pantie cocktails flowed from the champagne fountain.

The proud owner strutted around in a pink bustier

with a tight white leather skirt and leopard stilettos. She held the rhinestone-studded microphone, smiling hard.

Rebe, now seven months pregnant, wore a baggy T-shirt dress with white mules, and Magnolia, no longer pregnant, wore a short black dress and animal print flats. They stood in the front of the crowd of over one hundred people. Miller stood beside his woman, Magnolia, holding her hand while sipping his drink.

Darla spoke. "Wow. This store, my store, all came together in only a short amount of time. I really can't believe that not long ago, me and my girls, right here, Rebe and Magnolia," she aimed her hand toward her friends, "all dared each other to try and break out of our boxes and try something new. Well, here it is, evidence of beyond my box, my store, Brown Sugar."

Rebe and Magnolia led the applause and everyone joined in.

Darla looked humble. Her face was aglow. "I want to thank all of you for being here tonight. I've got something naughty and special for each of you in the gift bags we'll be passing out later."

Darla's father sat in a chair watching and listening. He was dressed up as though going to church, in his Sunday best black suit, white shirt, and black tie.

Darla smiled at him, convincing herself not to go full-out-kinky.

He smiled back, as though giving thanks.

"This is a dream come true. You are all witnessing something happening to me that I never thought I'd do. It's more than the thrill of opening my own retail store. It's the thrill of coming out of a place where

I was, as some of you know, after my husband died years ago. At times I thought I wasn't going to be able to make it through. Last New Year's Eve, my friends and I vowed to take a braver shot at life, even though in the back of my mind I still doubted myself. It was comfortable being in that box. But God had other plans."

The crowd again began to clap.

As they ceased she said, "I prayed and believed and took the steps. A couple of miracles happened along the way that pointed to the fact that maybe, just maybe, this could become a reality. And as it turns out, it is.

"So, I won't take up any more of your time with my words. I'll let you look around and enjoy what Brown Sugar has to offer. Also, we have plenty of pink drinks flowing, bottles of wine, champagne, and some desserts and appetizers all around. And if any of the intimate merchandise strikes your fancy, I would appreciate your business. I want Brown Sugar to be your one-stop intimate boutique, kind of a brown Victoria's Secret and your local adult video store all rolled into one. In my videos, it's ladies first, though. Okay?"

She giggled and her audience laughed, nodding in approval.

"Again, I thank you, and ask you to remember to live your sexy dreams. Enjoy the sweetness."

Again her patrons and friends applauded and one by one stepped up to her to give her their individual best wishes.

Magnolia hugged Darla close and placed one of the same sterling silver, engraved BFF key chains she'd given Rebe in Darla's hand. Darla's initial was first. Magnolia winked and walked on with Miller, looking over the intimate apparel with a sparkle in her eye. Miller pulled out his credit card.

Rebe already had her keys in her hand, and after giving a congratulatory hug, walking slowly, she left.

INT.—DARLA'S CONDO—LATE THAT EVENING

After all the excitement and glamour of her opening, Darla wore a silk royal blue and white polka-dot baby-doll with the stringiest of matching G-string undies, lying on her back in her own bed, alone as usual, in bed early with the lights out.

Her head was filled with the thrill of her new business, the possibility of future sales projections, and the continued restoration of her once bottomed-out bank account.

Life was great.

She was on a high.

All except fulfilling her sexual bucket list of allowing a man inside her body again for the first time in years, and hopefully one who could satisfy her, taking her to the brink of satisfaction. She got up, slipped off her wedding ring, and got dressed.

Within forty-five minutes, Darla, alone, stepped inside of the Red Bar at the Catalina Hotel & Beach Club on Collins Avenue, a contemporary two-level lounge just a few miles away from her condo. She'd seen the advertisements for the live weekend performances when she'd walk by on the way to and from work.

Tonight, the soulful swaying jazz music was loud, and

the room was cozy dark, with only bright gold shining neon lights here and there, other than the bright lights on stage.

Darla was still wearing her fitted, polka-dot baby-doll. But she'd slipped on her perfect fit CJ jeans by Cookie Johnson, and a black bolero jacket, with steel gray sling-backs. Silver hoops. Silver beaded bag.

She headed straight for a seat at one end of the trian-gular bar, sat down and straightened her back, stuck her butt out against the back of the barstool, and adjusted the sheer fabric of her negligee along her waist, making herself comfortable, then placing her purse on her lap, looking down and then to her left to see an older bald gentleman with a gray moustache nodding at her. She nodded back.

To her right, a younger man with dreadlocks and dim-ples eyed her down and smiled. She smiled and reached into her purse nervously as if she may have heard her cell ring, grabbing it, eyeing the display, which indicated nothing was missed, not a text, not a call, nothing. She scrolled through the All Calls menu and carefully pe-rused the entries as though she was really checking for some unknown information that needed her attention. But she was simply looking busy enough to not look the men in the eyes a second time.

It made her feel as though her intentions were obvious.

She felt on display.

And being there was bad enough.

The butter-blonde, female bartender approached. "Good evening, lovely. May I suggest one of our de-signer cocktails? An espresso margarita maybe?"

Darla stuck her phone back in her purse and tapped

her turquoise fingernails along the walnut bar top. Her mascara-glazed eyes glanced toward the ceiling in thought and then met the woman's gaze. "Well, I'll have a red berry CÎROC with Sprite, please."

"You got it," she said, winking while placing a napkin before her.

Darla rotated her body one-half turn to see the live quartet that played, led by a tall, dark, Afro-wearing saxophone player with a rust and orange jacket and brown pants, as he blew into his horn, playing Smokey Robinson's "Cruisin'." His medium-brown eyes met Darla's and she grinned, and then looked down again. She was sure her face said she was new at going out to a bar alone. And her jittery heart cosigned.

She looked to the bartender, who set her slender drink on the napkin, placing two black straws inside. "Here you go. Anything else? An appetizer maybe? Our lemon-pepper wings are pretty popular. Not as pretty or popular as you, I see."

Darla's face flushed. "Oh really? Thanks. No. Not for now."

"Okay." The bartender put her receipt near her drink and stepped away.

Darla wondered why it seemed she was getting so much attention being alone, as opposed to with her friends, even from the ladies. She always said when she was with Magnolia or Rebe, she was usually the last to be flirted with. They said it was just her imagination. Perhaps it was.

She used the straws to stir her drink clockwise and then in reverse, then sexily sipped while finding herself bobbing her head to the jazzy beats. She turned to look around the small room, noticing a few couples sprinkled here and there at the bar tables, but for the most part, she was only one of a few unescorted women in the place. As she took another sip, a man walked by and licked her from head to toe with his eyes. Just as she thought he'd completely passed her by, she heard a deep voice in her ear. "Pretty lady. When this set is done, would you mind coming over to the table with me and my friend for a drink?"

She looked to her left and saw the same man standing just behind her, his arm next to her back. He took a small step before her. He was average height, very slender, and had straight hair and dark features, as though he were Indian. His breath smelled like he'd just had an orange Tic Tac. His eyes were big and sexy, and his lashes were long and thick. She liked what she saw, even though he was shorter and thinner than what she usually preferred. She gulped and then replied. "Well, I suppose so."

"I'm David. My friend's name is Bill." He pointed to an area near the wall.

"Okay. Hi, David. I'm Darla." She playfully brushed aside her wispy bangs.

He focused on speaking to the side of her face. "Nice to meet you. I know the music is loud, but I'd love to talk to you when they break, so please feel free to come over. I'll buy you your next drink. We're at that table near the window."

She aimed her sight to where his eyes pointed and said, "I see," and then focused on his dark brown skin as he leaned his head closer to hear her. "I will. Thanks. That's nice of you to offer."

"My pleasure."

Ten seconds after he walked away, the sax player stepped to Darla, still playing his sax, and stood to her left, serenading her with a rendition of "God Bless the Child." He played his instrument with an alluring glance, tilting his horn and grooving his head to the flow. Darla looked around to see who was noticing her being the center of attention and blinked fast, feeling flushed, readjusting herself on the padded barstool.

He continued to blow his specially designed musical breaths into his sexy brass sax, and she continued to bat her eyes while he proceeded past her and winked, heading toward another woman who sat with a gentleman.

As the song ended, the sax man announced their fifteen-minute break at the same time Darla looked at her bar tab and took a bill from her purse. Then the sax man said, "Don't worry. I've got that," just as she stood up to go back near the window to sit with her admirer and his friend. The sax player nodded to the bartender, who nodded back, and then he took Darla by her hand and began to walk toward the VIP area near the stage. Darla followed, trying her best to not look over at the table where she knew the two gentlemen waited.

The sax man spoke with a deep, slow voice. "Baby, let me just say, you are by far the most beautiful woman to walk into this place since I've been playing here. I saw you and it was like my mind and eyes froze. You are my kind of woman. I mean the kind of woman I've imagined for years. Truly. If I'd drawn you myself, the image would look just like you. I'm Grainger. Grainger Brown."

In her head, his name sounded familiar. She thought

back and only said, "I'm Darla." He was known in Miami as a rising musician on the brink of stardom.

His fans nodded to him, one tapped him on the shoulder, and he nodded back and waved along the way with one hand, holding Darla's hand with the other. "Hi Darla. You are a darling, now, I will say that. I hope you don't think I'm being too forward, or that you think I say this often. I promise you, I've never said this before. But, I just had to meet you. I couldn't let you walk out of here tonight and miss my chance to see if maybe this is just what I've been looking for in my life. You are a bombshell. Lady, I'm telling you. I hear the song 'Brick House' when you walk." He looked her up and down. "You are something else."

Darla's ears spun. She blushed. "Well, I thank you for your compliments, but I'm sure there've been a lot of pretty women in here, Grainger."

He brought her over to a private section that had been reserved for him. There was a sofa and a table, and on the table was an empty ice bucket and a plate of fruit. "I guarantee you, not like you. And you are wearing those jeans." He motioned for her to sit and then he sat beside her.

"Well, thanks."

He asked, "Do you want to take off your jacket?"

"Oh no," Darla replied. She shook her head to say no for extra measure. Darla told herself her sexy lingerie would make too much of a first impression, and probably the wrong one. And that wouldn't be right.

He leaned his elbows to his knees, looking toward her to give her his full attention. "So, what do you do? What's your line of work?"

"I was a dental technician, but I quit my job back in March. I own a store. A boutique in Midtown."

"I see. A businesswoman. Nice. I like that. We're off to a good start already. You are single, right?" He looked hopeful, checking out her left hand.

"I'm a widow."

His eyes expanded and he rubbed his trimmed goatee with his thumb and index finger. "I'm a widower. My wife died in a plane crash ten years ago."

Darla patted her hand along his upper arm for one second. "Oh my God. I'm so sorry."

He moved closer. "Thanks. I'm sorry for your loss, too. It takes time to move on. It's not about replacing. You just want to be the best you can inside so you don't bring your hurt, or baggage, into someone else's life, you know?"

Darla put her purse on the wooden table. "I agree. Have you been successful at that?"

"I think so. I always say time will tell."

"I see." Darla rubbed the back of her tapered neck and checked out his white teeth, wondering if he'd had work done, they looked so perfect. She was turned on. She swallowed hard. Her inquiring mind wanted to know. "So, no relationship since then?"

He watched her mouth and then spoke. "I had a brief one about a year ago for a few months. Someone I met while I was on the road in DC. She couldn't handle the long distance part of it. Plus with my busy tour sched-ule, I mean I'm always on the road and she didn't come along with me. She didn't like to fly, of all things. Can't say that I blame her. She wanted someone local. I live here in Miami."

"I'm local, too. So you have no trouble flying?"

"Flying was part of my recovery. I had to get on a plane just to get past all that. I can't limit myself. But, like I said, I understand the fear. I just couldn't make it mine." He shifted his thoughts. "Listen, I know you had one before, but can I get you a drink?" He looked at his watch. "I've got one more real quick set and then I'm done for the night."

"Okay, sure. Thanks."

"Would you mind waiting here for me? My way of keeping you away from the wolves," he joked.

She grinned. "That'd be nice."

"I'll make sure you're well taken care of. Anything you want, I've got it. If you're hungry or whatever, just say the word. And I can understand if you're not hungry this late, but I promise you, they have the best chocolate chip pancakes. They're known for them, day or night."

"Oh, no thanks. But, I'm sure they're good."

He stood. "They are. My favorite. So what can I have them bring you? What were you drinking before?"

"Vodka."

"Okay."

She spoke up. "No. I guess I'll try something different. I'll try the espresso margarita, if you wouldn't mind."

"Great choice. I'll have one with you." He got ready to step away, and turned back to her. "So, Darla, what's your favorite song?"

"Oh, I don't know." Her face showed shy.

"Just think of one. Anything that comes to mind. I'll play it just for you."

She looked up at him as though impressed. "You can play anything?"

"I can. Rap. Old School. Whatever. All on the sax."

"Okay. How about 'A House Is Not a Home.'"

He flashed a big smile. "I'm gonna like you. Keep an ear out. I'll make sure your drink is sent over and then I'll be back in about thirty. Okay?"

"Okay." Darla sat back along the sofa cushions, crossing her legs, getting comfortable. So comfortable that she leaned forward and pulled off her jacket, placing it next to her on the sofa. She began rubbing her arms as though she was cold.

Her mind spoke loud. *I'm sitting here with "the sky's the limit" thoughts in my head, about to share a drink with this man I just met, wondering if it would really be so bad to take a chance and just do something crazy like ask him over. But no. I can't. Not me. That would be a move for someone else to make, not Darla. One thing I know is, that's just not me.*

Later, Darla heard the melody of the Luther song that had been her mantra, "I am not meant to live alone, turn this house into a home," that he, Grainger the sax man, sang close to her skin. But it wasn't the skin of her earlobe, it was the skin of her right thigh, as Darla looked down and watched Grainger sing his lyrics close to her vagina, teasing her lower lips with his song, while his gifted sax-playing hands grabbed her wide hips.

He looked like he was in the womb of heaven.

She was bare.

Her polka-dot baby-doll was intermingled among his clothes, across the white settee at the foot of the bed.

The room smelled like the scented lemongrass candle.

It wasn't her place.

It wasn't his place.

It was a neutral zone, perfect for sexploration.

Or even saxploration for that matter.

Two floors up from the club, in the Catalina Hotel.

In a hotel with a strange man like Rebe had done the first morning of the year.

Darla did her best to yield, and the espresso margaritas were just the right amount of liquid courage needed as she squirmed like a snake, feeling his warm breath against the crevice that resided where her pubic area and leg adjoined.

The candle flickered in the pure darkness of the swanky red and white hotel room. She lay on her back with her legs wide open, giving permission for her new lover to please her with his mouth. Her nipples were hard and big and long, like a stack of pennies.

Grainger ceased his singing and began to kiss her middle split and then inserted his long tongue with precision, wiggling it inside of her like it was now a snake charmer. It moved from side to side with a soulful rhythm like a wave, and she shook. Her left leg began to involuntarily quiver. She couldn't stop it from acting out on its own, couldn't stop it from telling on her wild sensation. She felt uneasy that her own extremity was doing its own dance, but she gave a surrendering sigh, resting her head back on the feather-down pillow, looking up toward the tray ceiling.

She felt dizzy and focused her mind on Grainger's serious mouth work. It was like he was blowing the mouthpiece of his saxophone, playing her pussy as though seeking a melodic reaction to his mouth magic. She moaned and he flicked her sugar lips harder, even licking the chocolate mole on her labia, and she felt like she could really, actually, maybe, let go inside of his mouth if he could just do—something. Something more perhaps. Something that would top off the feeling of him licking the turned-on meat of her insides over and over while he looked up at her anticipating her cum. She fought it, and then told herself not to, and felt her breaths quicken from the nervous anticipation, and from the fact that what he was doing was not working.

I'll fake it, she told herself. "That's so good. I like that. Yes. That feels nice."

"Uh-huh," he moaned from between her legs like he was the man. He readjusted himself and again licked her inside like a lollipop, up and down. But something was still missing.

She squirmed downward to get his tongue to meet her clit and when it did, she jumped and felt her vagina clench. The heat inside of her turned up a notch and she wanted more. Darla thought back to what Magnolia had told her about speaking up and telling a man what pleases her, and that she should simply ask for it. And so, she said, "Can you suck it please? My clit I mean. Can you suck it?" The tone of her request was extra polite.

And without another word from her, or a word from him, he centered his mouth over her clitoris and brought his tongue to the underside of it, and quickly flicked while he sucked it in and out of his mouth, moving his head up and down, with a force. Her ass muscles tightened, and she squeezed the sheets and scooted back, saying as though in a panic, "Wait." She seemed out of breath. Her blood raced. She wondered if she should be a little more careful in what she asked for.

"Uh-uh," he said, denying her request to wait and

coming back to get it just right. Again he centered himself and sucked. Fast. Flicking. Fury. Her clit was getting a suck-fuck.

The voice in Darla's head told her not to enjoy. That it would be betrayal. That she would be a bad girl if she went ahead. That this was a sin. A sin to be in bed with another man when after all, her husband died in bed with her. And it was her fault.

As the voices reminded her of what they'd taught for five long years, instantly Darla felt like she was going to lose it and scream for dear life if he kept it up, so she scooted again.

Again, he found her and sucked, flicked and held tight to her ass, placing his hand under her plump cheeks to keep her in place. "Take this," he said into her opening.

The voices still spoke and she felt again like she wanted to scream and realized maybe the screaming would be the only way to silence the unwelcomed guilt that had her so stuck in abstinence. She knew about unsaintly Aaron, who suddenly became so saintly once he passed away, like most. Her mind dismissed him and said it was her turn to be unsaintly, and she tightened her jaw. And even though another voice that sounded maternal grew even louder, reminding her that she didn't even know this man who had her vagina in his mouth, Darla said aloud without even being able to catch herself, "That's all part of the turn-on. Oh hell."

Grainger said nothing in reply to her nonsensical sentence as she groaned loudly, and began bucking, grinding back at his face like she was the one screwing his mouth, and in an instant, Darla pressed a feeling forward, forcing all of the negativity from her very being in a liquid rush like she was going to pee on herself, and then, her slit throbbed like it was being squeezed by a ghost. She rode through the dizzying feeling and pressed her orgasm from her opening. Her blood rushed and her muscles tightened and her voice went off in a curdling scream like she was being hurt and pleased at the same time. She rode it. "Oh. Oh. No. Yes. Oh. No. Yes. Oh, Grainger. Help me please. Yes. Yes. Yes." And Darla busted a slow, freshman nut that curled her hair, toes, fingers, and crossed her eyes, bringing her to tears as Grainger simply took it all, waiting until her clit ceased its powerful throbbing and she ceased her high-pitched yelling.

And then, while she breathed as though she'd run a marathon, and cried as though she'd been reborn, he licked her secretions from her insides, kissed her clit as he backed away, and within fifteen seconds, he had on a rubber and inserted the full length and girth of his instrument into Darla's tight, wet, abandoned vagina, inch by inch.

Darla kept her eyes shut and could hear the juices from her cum that escorted his penetration. Each and every millimeter of her insides that met his hard dick gave off a feeling that she'd never known. She lay back, sniffing the scent of his blue rain cologne, and Darla found the strength to just let it all happen, letting this big man, just the way she liked them, knock the back out of her deepest nooks and crannies, pressing himself in and out at a slow pace, while he lay his long and muscular body on her curves, kissing her earlobe, saying, "You are amazing. I want you. I want you to be mine. I want this to be all mine. I want you Darla. Say you want me, too."

"I do." Her hips accentuated her voice.

"Open your eyes. Tell me you want me."

She inched them open. Her eyes looked wet from her tears.

Their eyes locked.

She said as though in a trance, "I want you."

"Kiss me," he said like it was an order, just as he hit a spot that made Darla tighten up.

The order was followed. She kissed his dark brown lips and sucked his tongue as he ground inside of her and she ground back in exact response. The headboard was pressing against the wall with pounding sounds, and just as quickly as the X-rated sound sped up, it stopped and Grainger ceased his kissing and threw his head back and grunted, "Uuuggh, I'm coming. Ahh, damn, I'm coming. Damn. Tight ass hot pussy got me coming hard. Dammit."

Darla felt his pulsating dick shoot his hot fluid into his condom as the fatness of his dick was wall-to-wall. She was full.

He didn't die while inside of her like the last time she had sex. His head fell upon her shoulder and he lay on her, and she kept track of his breathing. It was fast and deep.

She said softly, looking up at the ceiling again, "Oh, my God."

"Oh, God, is right." Grainger lifted his head to look at her face. His nose and forehead were sweaty. His breathing was fast. "Darla. Darling Darla. You came so good, baby. I know men in your life love watching you get off like that. You sure know your body."

"You'd think so, huh?" She didn't tell him he was the first to make her come. And she wouldn't.

Before she knew it, Grainger was up, in the bathroom, and then stepping back toward her, placing his
excited hands on her baby-making hips, and adjusting
his face between her curvaceous legs again for a tongue-
ride. "Yep, I knew you had a killer body," he said, eyeing
her down as he again spoke from the giver position.

She looked down at him as he kissed her anatomy.
Her stare was different. Sexy. Liking. Her pheromone
rush had caused her to see him in a new, adoring light.
Out of the blue she asked, "Chocolate chip pancakes in
the morning?"

He gave her a sexy, liking look back. "My second favorite thing." And again, he went to work, licking her
pussy, moving up slightly to focus his attention on her
awaiting clit. He sucked.

Darla exhaled and squeezed her eyes shut again.

No voices.

No sight of Aaron in her runaway mind.

No sight of anything.

Just the feeling of being satisfied sexually.

And the thought of one day enjoying her own house
as a home, with someone, maybe Grainger. Maybe not.

But the orgasms tonight would do.

Later, they slept.

She didn't wake at 4:44 in the morning.

Grainger by her side, spooning the shape of her thickness, head to toe.

And then it was breakfast at nine a.m.

Darla Clark was finally replete.

Finally orgasmic.

Having finally lost control of being in control.

Twenty-Eight

"Back When"

Rebe

INT.—REBE'S HOME—MIAMI BEACH—LATE
EVENING
July 17, 2009

The sale of Rebe's house would close within three
weeks, and she'd take the cash and finalize the purchase of her new home next month. She'd spent two
months looking at houses and finally found the one. It
was in Broward County, in Hollywood, Florida, in a
gated community called West Lake Village. She felt the
four-bedroom, pale-yellow stucco, a mile from the
ocean, close to schools and shopping, was far enough
away from her current place to help her shake off some
of the bad memories of the house she'd won in a divorce
settlement, the same house she was raped in, nearly
killed in, the house where her daughter stabbed her own
mom's attacker.

The move would be just in time to get settled in
before the birth of her second child, decades after the
first.

A little after midnight, Rebe was home wearing an

extra-large-tall T-shirt, cuddled up in charcoal satin sheets, still sleeping in the guest room.

The electric fireplace glimmered an artistic, tie-dye-like glow on the pale blue walls.

It was a Friday night.

She was forty years old and nearly seven months pregnant.

She was manless.

Her baby would be fatherless.

She hadn't yet wrapped her brain around that fact. There was no room for such thoughts yet.

She was suddenly jerked from her mental ramblings by the ringing of her home phone. Looking at the clock, seeing that time had slipped into the next day, she wondered who it could be as she reached over, saw the caller ID, and picked up the receiver. "Hello." She sounded like she'd been fast asleep, but she wasn't. Her tone was tainted more with a self-warning about the caller than that of being tired.

"Sorry to wake you."

"I'm still up." Her heart insisted she should have an attitude. Her head was too crowded and too exhausted to comply.

"Good." The voice was familiar and deep, slow and reserved. "How are you?"

"Fine, Randall. How are you?" Her words were insincere.

"Good." His word was elongated. He paused. His inhale-exhale could be heard. "Listen, I've wanted to have a talk with you for a while now. Is this a good time?"

"Yes. What?" She said both as fast as one word.

"Rebe, I'm sorry. I'm sorry for everything. For cheating. For lying. For leaving without taking the time to talk about giving us another try. For getting someone pregnant before you had a chance to even file divorce papers. For hurting Trinity. And for the fact of what happened to you with the guy who broke in. It's bothered me for a while. I want you to know I'm glad you survived."

"Really?" Rebe wondered why his speech was so slow. She sensed a slur. Knowing him as she did, she was willing to bet he'd been drinking. It brought back memories. Memories of how the only time he'd talk was when eighty-proof something chased away the fear of communication.

"Yes. You've been through enough with your mom as it is. Really, I'm sorry that happened. I should've told you this before now, but when I heard, all I felt was anger over what he did to my ex-wife. I'm sorry Trinity had to see what she saw, and that she has to live with the fact that she stabbed someone. And in our house. It's bothered me. All of it. I just didn't know how to say it. Until now." His breathing was heavy.

Him saying *our* house had her on guard. She said what she thought would be best. "I got the card you two sent." Rebe behaved but couldn't say his wife's name. "Trinity told me you guys sent your thoughts and prayers. All that."

"Well, we did. But this is from me. I want us to find a way to be okay with all this, good and bad. I want Trinity to see us getting along. I want Chyna to see that. I want her to know you. And, I want your new child to see it, too. By the way, congratulations."

"Thanks." Rebe shook her head a bit to make sure her ears weren't failing.

He sighed. "Well, I guess that's what I wanted to say."

She shifted the phone to her other ear. "My goodness." She just had to ask. "What's gotten into you?"

"Life. Tired. Trying to find a way to say I'm sorry. To forgive. Hell, to live. Plus, I'm fuckin' drunk." He gave a laugh along with his admission.

Rebe offered a laugh in return, not surprised one bit.

"I fucked up a lot, Rebe. The life I led in the NFL opened doors that weren't always the best for me, but still I indulged. Even after, it was just hard to stop pushing the envelope. But, I'm tired of hurting people. Bad decisions hurt people. And hurt me."

"I see. Well, I'm fine. But obviously, I've been pissed off for a long time. You both know that. Trinity knows that."

"I know."

She couldn't *not* say it. She turned to her side and went there. "And by the way, Magnolia told me."

"I figured she would." He didn't miss a beat

"But why didn't you?"

"I never would've."

"Why did you do it?"

"Believe it or not, I did it because I could. I didn't do it to hurt you. Telling you would have been hurting you. I took the small chance that she wouldn't tell you. At the moment it happened, I went for it. But, I knew when I went to bed that night, doing that only made things worse. Though that was my mentality. I wanted it all. I just can't do that anymore. At least I know I need to try and do better. And Rebe, Magnolia fought it. She left fast."

"Whatever. That was messed up on both your parts."

"It was. And to be honest, I was surprised you didn't call me and go completely off."

"Me, too."

"I'm just sorry. Don't know what else to say."

"Wow. Those two words, *I'm sorry*. I think if it's true that love means never having to say you're sorry, then I guess I've never experienced love before, because I've received and owed more *I'm sorrys* than anyone should ever have to."

"You're strong. You're a survivor. And I want you to know I'm glad you took this call. Thank you." He sounded extra drained.

"Good-bye, Randall."

"Good-bye, Rebe. If you need anything, I'm here."

"I'm fine."

"Good. Oh, and by the way, good luck with the new house. I got a notice about the sale, verifying the quit-claim."

"I know."

"Good luck. Maybe we can stay in touch. Call me on my cell."

"Bye." And Rebe hung up.

She turned to her back and rubbed her forehead with one hand, having never expected that conversation, and placed the other hand on her belly. Randall's voice was still in her head. "Did he just say he's sorry?" she asked out loud. "My God."

She looked over at the two photos of Trinity beside her bed. One from when Trinity was a toddler. Barely two years old. Trinity was in her white and pink Easter dress with a real, live bunny rabbit on her lap, looking half thrilled and half scared to death. The other was a recent photo of Trinity that was taken while she was in Las Vegas. She stood in front of a roman statue at Caesars Palace with a drink in her hand, looking happy, and carefree.

Carefree was all that Rebe wanted for her offspring. Not bringing a baby into her confused life was her goal. She wanted that feeling for both her adult child, and her expected baby. A life different from the one she'd lived thus far. She wanted her children to have a life free from pain, free from anger, and free from tragedy. If she could. Or at least, she wondered if Trinity, unlike her, could be normal? And could her new baby be happy with a mother like her?

Rebe could have sworn she felt a kick. And then another. She said, "If that was a yes, I'm smiling. If that was a no... well, I'll just believe that two kicks means yes."

She felt the new life inside of her in the form of a tiny fetus, and in the form of her own newness, awaiting her own new life, ready to no longer be a product of her childhood, but a shining example for her children of what life can be like, especially when given a second chance.

She fell asleep. Mother and daughter. Alive.

INT.—OFFICE OF VICTIMS' SERVICES—PINECREST, FLORIDA—LATE MORNING
The next day

It was a new counselor. One who Rebe was meeting for the first time. The neuropsychologist she had before transferred during the couple of months Rebe stopped going, but Rebe felt it was time to again try to get her mind right.

Trinity had been attending her sessions, but for the moment was out of town in New York trying to get a modeling agent. She'd dropped out of school and Rebe didn't push it. Rebe was learning to let go and cut the cord. She gave in to the fact that Trinity was a grown woman, and had been through more than enough to earn her independence stripes.

The counselor was a bleached blonde, conservative, middle-aged woman, plain Jane type in a tight top and knee-length skirt, oddly bordering on pinup-girl curvy. With her legs crossed, she sat in her small, sparsely fur-nished office in a tweed desk chair facing Rebe.

Rebe sat on the tan sectional, with her hands cupped in her lap, wearing a purple top that showed the full shape of her expectant belly, a pair of gray drawstring cotton pants, and gym shoes. She'd taken out her braids and her dark brown hair was flat ironed past her shoul-ders. No makeup, no expression, just words.

Ten minutes into the allotted hour, Rebe looked at the woman at times, and at times out the window to-ward the tropical, butterfly-like palm trees, spanning into the beauty of the heavens above.

"Dr. Love, my mom's in jail. She'll spend the rest of her life in prison. I'm ashamed and I totally reject the blood ties that bind me to her. Violet Palo. I don't like to say her name, but, Violet Palo is a child killer. Violet Palo is a mother, a woman, and she's convicted of child murder, and attempted child murder. She'll spend the rest of her life in prison. Double life. My mother. Violet. Is a convicted killer."

Pain was spelled out on her dark face. "I really, truly
don't want her in my soul. I pray every night that she's
not. I've been determined to break the like-mother,
like-daughter curse. I keep telling myself I'm not the
seed of a monster. But I am. My mother is just like her
mother. My grandmother, named Opal, committed sui-
cide after beating her own children for simply forgetting
to brush their teeth. Her own mother threw boiling water on her husband while he was sleeping, because he
was snoring."

Rebe waited a minute.

Dr. Love let her wait.

"My story was in the headlines back in 1982, you
know? Not sure if you heard of it." Rebe's big, dark eyes
lifted Dr. Love's way and flashed a question mark.

"No," Dr. Love said, showing focus and patience,
shaking her head.

"Ocala, Florida, where I grew up, was on the map.
The headlines read that when the prosecuting attorney
asked me who hit me on the back of the head with a
hammer, I said, 'My mom.' Sad.

"Some of it I remember, some of it I don't. All I know
is my brother Maestro had gotten in trouble the night
before and got a beating before he went to bed, as usual.
That happened every night. He was fifteen and six foot
three, and still got whippings. Every night.

"By then my father had left my mother and was out
there, chasing women, usually the younger women, fed
up with my mother's temper tantrums and her 'ugly
ways' as he called it. In his absence, my brother found
males to bond with. In the streets."

Her eyes sort of lit up.

"He was good at basketball, having played in the neighborhood when he could get out of the house, which was rare. He wasn't allowed to play sports in school. We weren't allowed to go anywhere after we got home from school. A lot of rules. I liked to dance, so I'd just dance in my room, to silence. No music allowed in the house either. Another rule.

"By then, my mother had actually found a way to start preaching at a nearby church. It was the epitome of a holy, sacrilegious, hypocritical, Bible-toting, false prophet, Christian claiming mess. She was the last person who should have been preaching the word of God. If anyone needed to be literally born again, rebirthed, it was her. Violet Palo.

"I do remember some of that night when the devil took my joy. And I know it went something like:

"Rebe come here." Her loud, raspy voice always sounded like she had phlegm stuck somewhere between her tonsils and her esophagus, like she was about to choke. I wish. She wasn't a smoker. Not even a drinker. Not on drugs. Just naturally evil. The sound of her words stung from the living room and seeped past my bedroom door, which I was never allowed to close, and right into my ears. My lobes sweat upon hearing and feeling the sound.

It was about six-thirty and it wasn't dark yet outside, but the house was dark. Blackout curtains throughout, you'd need a light on to see anything, any time of day. I ran straight from the tiny room I shared with Maestro. He wasn't home yet. I knew that woman, called my mom, would be in a bad mood just because of that.

"Yes, Ma'am." I stood before her, my feet on the tattered throw rug. My toes flexed. My knobby knees shook. Skinny as a rail, I wore yellow shorts and a pinafore blouse. I'd just finished cornrowing my own hair. She never did my hair. Never called her mom, you know. Never did.

"Barefoot, she was reading the Bible, with only the light of the floor lamp behind her, reclining all the way back in her beat-up black leather chair, and though the Bible was opened to a certain page, her bloodshot eyes were zeroed in on me. The closer I got I smelled the usual calamine lotion on her scaly, itchy forearms and elbows. I still don't know what caused it. It was nauseating.

"So. How was your day?" Her gray hair seemed grayer, hanging loose but stiff and broken off, barely touching her shoulders.

My puberty-ridden stomach turned. "Good," I told her almost sounding like I was asking instead of answering.

"Really?" She always had a look about her that made me feel like she had the ability to see my every move, every second of every day, even when I was shitting, like she knew the color and smell, but asked about it anyway.

"Yes."

"You do anything after school?"

"No." My armpits were dripping already.

"You do anything after school?"

"No, Ma'am."

"You do anything after school?" This time her look changed.

I knew better. "Yes."

Silence. Frown.

I spoke on. "I went to my friend Alicia's house."

Silence. Deeper frown.

"That's it," I said, sounding like a mouse.

"Alicia's mother called." She closed the Bible, placed it on the end table, and adjusted the handle on the side of her recliner to sit straight up. Her scent was even stronger.

"Yes, Ma'am."

"Caught you hiding in the closet. With Alicia's older brother."

"Yes, Ma'am."

"Why didn't you tell me that part?"

"Ma'am?" Oh God, I felt like, what more does she know.

Silence.

"Because it was nothing. Alicia wasn't supposed to have company and I didn't want her to get in trouble." I felt like Pinocchio. My nose grew like a weed.

"Naked, Rebe? You and her brother were in the closet naked?"

I felt a little pee leak from between my legs. "Yes, Ma'am."

"Go to your room." She reached to the other side of the chair.

"Yes, Ma'am."

"Get naked."

Physically, I did what my mental begged to reject. I moved slowly, and then looked back to see her, two steps behind me, her hands behind her back, the impatient, wild look in her eyes. One eye was bigger, angrier than the other. I sped up.

"Lay down."

My room had only the light from a low-wattage lamp, aglow on my bed like a mini-spotlight. I lay on my back on my twin bed, plaid covers, and she hopped on top of me in her leggings and baggy brown smock, and right away, slapped my left cheek and then my right, left, right, left, right, over and over while I kicked my feet and blocked my face with my hands.

"Move your hands."

She socked my hands and arms, and punched me in the head.

"You're a tramp. You're twelve and you're a tramp already. Mark my word, you're gonna end up pregnant."

"No. I'm not." I screamed bloody murder.

"Shut up. You're a whore. Did you have sex with him?"

"No."

"Yes, you did. Turn over."

"No. Please." I closed my eyes and started swinging.

She jerked back and yelled, "Did you just hit me? Turn the hell over."

I heard the neighbor's German shepherd, named Queenie, barking and whining like he'd heard an ear-piercing siren.

She shouted, "You're a damn ho!"

I opened my eyes as she stood and held my breath, turning over, and then as soon as my belly and face touched the bumpy mattress, I heard, "Mom. No." And in an instant, it was like someone shot me in the back of the head. I tried not to scream but my voice failed. I tried to talk but my words slurred in my head. I went black.

When I awoke, I was in the hospital. My brother was dead. And my mother was in jail for first-degree murder, and attempted murder. Funny thing was, even though my mother said my brother hit me over the head and that she was the one who saved me after managing to fight him off, hitting him on his forehead in self-defense . . . that night, it was her, Violet Palo, who called 911. The ambulance was there in five minutes. That call saved my life. Otherwise, I would have been dead.

I was in the hospital on the day of my own brother's funeral. I testified against Violet Palo six months later.

Rebe scooted back and massaged her shoulder, just at the point where her brother's name, Maestro, was tattooed on her skin.

Dr. Love said, "My goodness. Are you going to be okay, Rebe?" She checked Rebe's face, expecting an oncoming barrage of tears to match her cracking voice, and offered a box of tissues.

"Yes. Thank you." Rebe took one and balled it up in her hand. She went right back into speaking again. "I lived with my father here in Florida while I healed the first year. I missed that year of school. I was recov-

ering from a depressed skull fracture. It was the blunt
force trauma that dented my skull bone, causing a hem-
orrhage in my brain. The dent was one-half inch deep.
They operated to get rid of the bony pieces in my head,
and when they inspected my brain for injury, they re-
lieved the bleeding that had begun between my brain
and skull. It was from the rupture of a vessel. I had a
brain injury caused by Violet, well, caused by my own
mother.

"My father couldn't keep his fast self home often
enough to raise me. He said he was depressed about
losing his son. So he kept chasing women like he'd
been doing when he left us in the first place. I kind of
raised myself. In high school I met my friends Darla and
Magnolia, two girls who were more like sisters than anything. The other kids in school who heard about my
mother and what happened said I was weird, some said
fast, some said crazy. Oh well.

"So, that's when I met my daughter's dad, Trent. I
got pregnant, didn't even tell my dad, and moved in
with Trent in his small bachelor apartment while we
were still in high school. Dad moved back to Maui. It
was no big deal to me. I thought I'd be better off under
the same roof as Trent, but he had as many problems
as I did. He was an addict, broken like me. I thought
we were the perfect pair. But like he said, I had a temper. And people didn't believe it but, as fast as everyone
thought I was, I hated sex. He loved it. He left, and
later died of an overdose.

"So anyway, I've been on these hormone pills all my
life, and then on these new hormone therapy pills that I
think finally kicked my sex drive into fifth gear, and on

Zoloft still, even now. But no matter how much I started craving sex, or how much my depression lifted, I still haven't felt lovable. Just unhappy.

"Doctor, I'm sure you know from reading my file, but the same thing that happened to me when I was twelve happened to me at forty. To have my own daughter save me while being attacked is more than I can bear. It's more than I want her to bear. Our demons are not something I want my unborn child to have to inherit.

"As a mother, I now realize that she didn't have babies so she could love them. She had babies so they could love her. She was a narcissist. A sociopath who didn't feel empathy. She was hard on us from day one. So hard that we couldn't love her. And now I know she couldn't love us either. She couldn't identify with another person's feelings. It's like we were a burden to her.

"By the way, just like her, I got pregnant at seventeen. But now, the legacy of this anger gene can't be mine. I don't want to screw up this chance at having another child. At times, I'm this doting mother, and then I flip into a distant mom, unavailable, unable to empathize, like my mother. That's not normal. And with all the money I have, it won't buy my happiness. Please. Help me." She sniffled and tried to hold it. But this time a tear did flow, and then another, and Rebe sniffled and wiped her eyes and nose. "I miss my brother." Rebe's slow tears turned into a full-out cry. She covered her face with her hands, and just let it out.

Dr. Love's face saddened, and she again offered more tissues, but Rebe didn't look up. The counselor pulled out four tissues and leaned forward, rubbing Rebe's arm and putting the tissues on her lap. Rebe took them and wiped under her eyes with mascara running, and fanned her face with her hand, blowing her exhale past her lips.

"I'm sorry," Rebe told her, looking embarrassed.

"Oh, no. Please don't apologize. You've been through a lot. Your brother tried to protect you. That was a tragic death. Surely it's hard to take still."

"You know, my mother never cried. Ever." Rebe sniffled more and fought to make herself calm down.

"It's good that you can cry, Rebe. Very good. It kind of cleanses, like rain. This is major stuff that's happened to you. Would you like to take a break and get some water or coffee?"

Rebe looked down at her hands that maneuvered the tissues. Her nose was red, her eye makeup was smudged, her foundation was all but wiped off. "No. No thanks. Really. I'm okay. It's just that I really miss my brother. We were all each other had. I'm surprised I haven't had a total breakdown by now. There was so much evil back then. So much that went wrong. Even though I was born on the day of love, Valentine's Day, it still didn't make a difference. "

Dr. Love reached over and touched Rebe's arm.

Rebe looked up.

The doctor sat back. "Rebe, yes, a lot of evil. Though one thing I can tell you is, I don't believe you have some 'evil gene.' Psychopathy can be an inherited trait, but I know for a fact there's nothing wrong with your moral compass. It works. If it didn't, you wouldn't have raised Trinity the way you did, being there for her, making sure she made it through school, and providing for her like you have. I think at some point in your life, there was enough nurturing, probably from your father, as distant as he was, or from your older brother, to overcome the traits of your mom. From what you tell me about Trinity, you broke the curse. Yes, Trinity and this new baby are your bloodlines, but they don't have to suffer. Trinity needs to keep coming in and she needs to continue her victim's advocacy counseling. She nearly killed a man. That's extremely traumatic. She needs consistent psychotherapy. You're smart, Rebe. You're a college grad. You can even help other kids, just like you can help your own children. Victims of heinous crimes are the best advocates for victims' rights."

Dr. Love picked up a clipboard and pen and started writing. "I want you to continue coming. I won't prescribe meds for you. Based on your history of brain injury, you need to consult with your neurologist, and also with your gynecologist if you still need pituitary stimulants for your brain injury, like hormone therapy, but only after the birth. I think still being on Zoloft, which is a category B drug, is fine, just don't breastfeed while taking it. But in my opinion, taking it outweighs the risks of not taking it." She picked up a paperback book from her glass desktop. "But I will ask you to read this book called *Trauma and Recovery* by Dr. Judith Herman. I suggest Trinity reads it, too. It covers the aftermath of violence for those who might experience posttraumatic stress disorders. It's a good source of finding a way to feel good based on our thoughts, and not buying into our negative thinking."

Rebe's face was still flushed. Her eyes glassy. She took the book and looked over the cover. "Thanks."

"But most important, enjoy the rest of your pregnancy. Live in the present. And I'll see you next week.

Okay?" Dr. Love's voice sounded as though she was prompting Rebe's agreement.

"Okay." Rebe reached for her suede purse that was on the coffee table in front of her.

"And Rebe."

"Yes, Ma'am," Rebe said while placing the book inside the middle compartment of her bag.

"First of all, no need to call me Ma'am."

"I'm sorry. I know better. I hate that, too."

Dr. Love caught Rebe's eyes and they both smiled. "What I want to tell you is, you need to forgive your mother, forgive yourself, and heal by bringing closure to the past. Enjoy the rest of your life. Your brother lost his life so you could live. So live."

Rebe blinked on hearing the doctor's last word, and another tear fell. "Thank you, Dr. Love. I will. In his honor, I absolutely will."

Her hand on her belly as she stood, she felt the life in her kick.

And Rebe's lips spread into an enormous smile.

Twenty-Nine

"Love and Happiness"

Girlfriends

INT.—TRINITY CATHEDRAL CHURCH—CORAL
GABLES—EARLY AFTERNOON
December 19, 2009

That day, the birds sang even in the afternoon.
The sky above was the color of love.

Paisley.

And though they'd lost their child due to the miscarriage, on the day the baby was due, December 19, the vows had been exchanged and the *I Dos* had been sealed with a forever kiss. Sealed to cement the union between two people who'd met, of all places, at a swinger's club.

The long walk down the aisle by a brand-new husband and wife had been taken, and all the family members and guests had caravanned behind the couple's black stretch limousine, the short distance from the church, across the causeway from Miami to the private tropical island oasis of the Mandarin Oriental Miami hotel for the elegant reception. The Asian serenity was the perfect paradise of private beaches and prestigious bay views. Eighteen-foot ceilings, silk and velvet wall coverings, crystal chandeliers, and glistening skylines framed the spectacular room that was totally decorated in only black and white.

Guests finished up their meals, laughing, joking, smiling, and enjoying the celebration of true love found. The happy couple sat at the wedding party table for two, ready for their reception, him in his black tux and tails with a cream tie, her in her cream satin strapless gown with a black sash and jeweled bridal shoes. Her hair was swept away from her face, curled loosely down her back. Diamond and pearl drop earrings accented her classic beauty. Her wedding bouquet was made of exotic white magnolias and White Naomi roses. They'd spend their wedding night in the Asian serenity of the five-star hotel's Dynasty Suite on the ninth floor, and head off on an eight-day South Caribbean cruise to Aruba the next morning.

Miller's son and his wife and child, and Miller's daughter and her child, were all seated at a table with Magnolia's grandmother, Gigi, who sat next to Miller's ex-wife, Beth.

Rebe and Darla, the maids of honor in all black, sat with two of Miller's friends who were the best men, named Rich and Juan. While Rich was extra friendly with new mother Rebe, Darla was busy enjoying talking to her lover, Grainger. And on the other side of Darla was her father, who for the life of him, couldn't take his eyes off of Gigi at the other table. And Gigi noticed him notice her. It looked to be her pleasure.

Darla had a look of amazement on her face while taking a moment to nudge her father. She asked, speaking only loud enough for the two of them, "Daddy. Are you staring at Magnolia's grandmother?"

He didn't lick his lips but he looked like that was the next step. "Darlin', it's been years since I've seen her. She's sure held up nicely," he said, giving a "Mac Daddy" grin, peeking at her beyond the lavender chrysanthemum centerpieces.

Darla seemed as though her ears had deceived her. She'd never seen her father like that about anyone but her mom. She looked away, trying not to make too big a deal, but made a point to honestly tell herself it really was long overdue. She distracted herself from her father's visual-admiration party, and turned toward Rebe, asking, "Are you enjoying living in the new house?"

"I am." Rebe told the others, "I bought a new place in West Lake Village. Just really getting settled in."

"Nice. In Hollywood?" Rich asked.

"Uh-huh."

"Cool area," he said. "I work in that county. As a sheriff."

"Really?" Rebe watched his full, brown lips as he spoke. "Small world."

"Indeed." He looked at her lips, chest, and all that he could get his eyes on from where she sat.

And sitting to the left of Rebe was Trinity, holding her three-month-old, off-the-charts long, baby brother. She handed the baby boy, who had a cleft chin, over to his mother.

"Cute baby," Rich said to Rebe, admiring her big brown boy with the full head of hair.

Rebe said, "Thanks. Actually, these are my two children. My baby son, Tristan, and this is my daughter, Trinity." She put her hand on Trinity's back.

"Oh. Wow. Nice-looking family," Rich said. He

turned toward his friend Juan and they began talking.

Rebe moved her focus from him to Darla. "Are you ready?"

"Yes." Darla came to a stance.

Trinity took back her baby brother. Rebe planted a kiss on Tristan's lips, and then as Rebe stood, she kissed Trinity's forehead. Trinity, dressed in ivory chiffon with teal and lime gemstone dangle earrings, wore the angel charm Magnolia had given her. Trinity closed her eyes briefly and smiled.

Darla joked in Rebe's ear as they walked, "Surprised you didn't have twins like you joked, considering the way you described the night you got pregnant. Tristan is a doll, sis."

"Thanks," Rebe said, with a chuckle. She held Darla's hand, still very aware after all the years that had gone by since she had betrayed her friend. But she just couldn't bring herself to come clean.

Rebe and Darla approached Magnolia and her new husband, standing right in front of them at the bride and groom table, and raised their glasses high, as did Magnolia, Miller, and everyone else.

Rebe said, "Today is your wedding day. When 2009 started out, we had no idea a wedding would even be happening for you, Magnolia. Miller, yes, she was the one out of the three of us who always joked about being the bridesmaid, never the bride. Well, today, Magnolia, you are the bride."

"Yes she is," Miller said, platinum band on his finger, holding his new bride close.

"When we started out the year, we had no idea that some of the things that happened so far would've happened at all. But God had other plans than ours. If it wasn't for our New Year's promises, Darla probably wouldn't have her new store, I wouldn't have my new child, and Magnolia, you wouldn't have a new husband. Miller, thank you for coming into Magnolia's life and loving her the way she needed to be loved. For cherishing her and making her laugh. She's changed in a way I can't explain, but it's a beautiful thing to see. I guess that's what real happiness will do for you."

Darla took over, raising her glass even higher. "May you both enjoy the sanctity of marriage in a way that is the ultimate love for the world to see. What God has put together, let no man put asunder. Here's to you, Mr. and Mrs. Miller Lockhart. We wish you all the happiness in the world and pray that the love of your hearts reaches beyond your God-given years, into eternity. May you never be farther than the arms of your hearts can reach. Magnolia, you found your soul mate. Cheers."

The bride and groom and everyone else said, "Cheers," and took sips to seal Rebe and Darla's words. Magnolia had a tear rolling down her cheek, and Miller kissed her right where it flowed.

The song "Spend My Life with You" by Eric Benet began, and Miller removed his tux jacket, took his bride by the hand, and led her to the dance floor. When Magnolia heard the words, *"Never knew such a day could come,"* she fanned her flushed face with her hand. She faced her new husband in her vintage dress as their family and friends watched, and placed her head on his chest, left ear to his heart, and the words continued, *"I was incomplete till the day you walked into my life."* And then,

the record scratched, and Magnolia and Miller looked
at each other with a question mark, looking over toward
the DJ, who began to play Heavy D & the Boyz, "We've
Got Our Own Thang."

Miller suddenly sang along like he was okay with it,
getting the feeling, "*Everybody shake your body, we don't
ill we chill at a party*," and he broke out into his own
corny version of poplocking, attempting to moon-walk
to the beat, encircling Magnolia as she watched him
like she was shocked, but by the next chorus, Magnolia
raised the fabric of her petticoat, exposing the baby blue
garter Darla had given her, and turned around to him,
backing it up and working her hips. He put his hands up
in the air, waving them around like he just didn't care.
"*Started with a pow and I'm going to end it with a bang,
we've got our own thang.*"

Everyone started clapping, and singing along, while
Magnolia and Miller did their prerehearsed routine,
skipping and jumping, doing some youngster moves, and
then heading over to those standing around to bring
them into the mix, even Trinity who had stood up with
the baby, and Magnolia's Grandma Grace took Darla's
father by the hand, bringing him onto the floor, hugging
him while they did a funky slow dance version.

Miller's son and daughter and their families jammed
too, even his ex-wife, and Darla and Rebe danced together, with Rebe making a point to head right on over
to Miller, bringing her backside around to his front side,
and she shook her moneymaker around in a circle, while
he first looked at Magnolia for approval, but before he
got it, he focused down at what Rebe was working with,
pretending he was rummaging through his pockets to

look for dollar bills, throwing fake bills up into the air to make it rain. Rebe pretended to catch each one and stepped back to Darla after passing by Magnolia who gave her a look of warning and pointed her finger. "Okay now. Don't let me tell Darla on you," Magnolia whispered. She then held her hand up. The silver heart friendship bracelet from Rebe dangled. She gave Rebe a high five, and said, "Our sixty-nine days are over, girl."

"Agreed," said Rebe, without a word of disagreement.

Rich, Miller's best friend, took Rebe by the hand and they danced, doing what Rebe loved to do most. They did a version of the whop, holding hands the entire time. She smiled continually, finally a real true wide, continuous grin. Like maybe if she kept dancing, the curse would be broken.

Darla danced back over to Grainger and sat down, staying close while he whispered what he was going to do to her when they got back to his place. Darla swatted his arm and then hugged him closer, whispering back to him to bring it on.

And Magnolia looked in the eyes of her new husband, her arms draped around his neck, feeling as though she could really truly exhale, her large rock and his diamond band on their ring fingers shining bright as symbols of their life together.

The next song was theirs alone.

The floor cleared and Etta James resounded from the speakers. "At Last."

Magnolia's gaze was triumphant. Her life was like a song. Her love had come along just when he was supposed to. They moved in slow dance, swaying to the tune, Magnolia humming the song to him, Miller humming the song to her. The song later wound down with all eyes still on them.

As the song "Perfect Combination" by Stacy Lattisaw began, another selection of Magnolia's, Gigi appeared behind Magnolia, though shorter than her, on her tiptoes, touching her on her back and making an effort to whisper in her ear as Magnolia leaned back to get closer.

Magnolia could smell her peppermint breath as she spoke in a low tone. "Excuse me, baby girl, this is your new husband's ex-wife. Her name is Beth. And she is the most beautiful spirit. She asked me to introduce you." Gigi looked at Beth. "Beth, this is my granddaughter, Magnolia."

Magnolia ceased her dance and turned toward them, keeping one hand clasped in Miller's.

Gigi stepped away, headed back toward Darla's grandfather, whose eyes expected her return.

Beth stepped forward, giving a quick smile and head nod to Miller, who looked frozen, and then she took Magnolia's other hand into both of her hands. "You are a beautiful bride." She smelled like roses.

"Thank you, Beth. It's nice to meet you."

Beth was short and slightly plump, in her sixties, but looked hip in black caged Louboutins, in a black tulle dress with pearls, and auburn hair cut into a classic bob. She wore three-inch red nails and bright red lips. "And I want you to know, you are my children's stepmother. We welcome you. I honor you for allowing me to come today and see my children's father get married. A lot of women wouldn't have been able to do that, but you did. I got your invitation and was thrilled. That's all I wanted to say. Thank you."

They gave cheek-to-cheek kisses.

Magnolia told her, "Thank you for coming. That's so nice of you to take the time to be here, and to introduce yourself. Believe me, if my mom says you're okay, you're okay."

Beth patted Magnolia's hand and then let go. "I'll let you two finish your dance.

Magnolia took Beth's hand into hers. "No. Here. You dance with Miller." She placed Beth's hand in Miller's hand.

Beth looked surprised. "Are you sure?"

Magnolia looked certain. "I am."

"Miller?" Beth asked, seeming cautious.

Miller gave a bow, as in, *May I have this dance.* "My wife knows me, Beth. It's my pleasure." He pulled Beth close, and they danced together, chatting while he led the way.

And Magnolia walked away in her designer wedding dress, feeling nothing but happy. Nothing but secure. Nothing but free. Free, now knowing what the feeling of being cherished can do.

Having learned to trust and experience life from the other side. Magnolia Lockhart, just like her best friends, was changed.

And changed for the better by trying something just a little bit...different.

Epilogue

"Better Days"

Girlfriends

INT.—MAGNOLIA AND MILLER'S HOME—MIAMI—
AFTERNOON
January 1, 2011

By that next New Year, it was a new way of celebrating hot new lives on a chilly first day of 2011. There was no longer a girls' night out on New Year's Eve. It was a new and different day for Magnolia, Rebe, and Darla.

Miller and Magnolia had everyone over to their new waterfront, Mediterranean home in Indian Creek Village to bring in the year, and to celebrate Magnolia and Darla's birthday.

Rebe was there with fifteen-month-old Tristan. And she was also allowed to bring Randall's daughter, Chyna, who was three and a half. Chyna called Rebe T-mom, meaning she was Trinity's mom. Rebe and Kandi were actually on speaking terms.

Trinity, who did not graduate from college, but promised to go back, got her own place in New York and was finally working as a runway model. She was making a lot of money, even without a degree. Rebe knew she probably would not return to school. She was just happy that Trinity was happy. Also modeling in New York with Trinity was Armani.

And Darla had ended her first year in the black. She was up to date on her condo payments and had cleaned up her credit.

She sat on Grainger's lap in the sunflower leather chair in Magnolia and Miller's family room, watching little Chyna try her best to dance to the song "Billie Jean" by Michael Jackson. They laughed and clapped their hands to the beat. On the ring finger of her right hand, Darla wore her tiny black diamond ring in yellow gold. She and Grainger were simply promised. But this time, the subject of sex before marriage was not an issue for her.

And in the backyard on the deck, along the edge of the narrow creek, surrounded by a menagerie of towering trees, minding the grill, in the sixty-degree weather, was Darla's father, grilling the chicken and ribs for their feast, working the barbeque pit like he was thirty years younger.

"Do you need anything? Are you okay?" Gigi asked, coming outside in her sundress from the kitchen after making her signature cabbage and turkey wings, stepping up behind him to wipe the sweat off his brow with her hand. She still wore her same old wedding ring. She handed him a bottle of Dos Equis.

"Yes, dear." He still wore his same old wedding band.

They kissed on the lips.

"Watch it now, Mister," Magnolia warned Darla's father as she stepped outside to check on him.

"I'm good," he said, sipping on the cold bottle. "Very

good. Excellent," he told Magnolia, eyeing his new
woman down. They'd spent nearly every day together at
one or the other's place the entire year of 2010.

Miller came outside and joked, "Okay now, don't
burn those. I spent a lot of money on that meat."

"Oh he's got it just fine. My spousal equivalent knows
how to grill, all right," Gigi said, chomping on a piece of
hard candy. Her light brown eyes devoured his image.

Darla's father said, "Yeah. If I burn one, it'll have
your name on it, Miller." He laughed and Gigi laughed
louder. She sat down at the patio table and continued to
watch him do his thing.

Magnolia said, looking protective, "Spousal equivalent. How cute." She spoke directly at Miller. "My
grandma is happy."

"Looks like they both are." Miller took Magnolia by
the hand and led her back into the kitchen and then
into the family room. "Happy birthday, love." He leaned
into her.

"Thanks." Magnolia held on to his arm and kept her
shoulder to his.

As the Michael Jackson CD ended, Grainger picked
up the TV remote and turned up the volume, switching
to ESPN. That's when Rebe heard a familiar voice.

"I will continue my contract as the WNBA head
coach of the San Antonio Silver Stars. These allega-
tions are untrue. I have not been involved in a sex
ring, as I've been falsely accused of. I am innocent until
proven guilty." He had a cleft in his chin, big man, perfect goatee.

Magnolia and Rebe watched as well, seeing the familiar face, all ears.

The sportscaster said, "That was Marcus Cotton, former track coach at New York University, who left his position to coach the WNBA team recently, who's under fire for alleged charges of promoting prostitution. We'll have more tomorrow after the team's press conference. Back to you in the studio."

Rebe looked as though she'd seen a ghost. She was in sheer shock. Her eyes were the size of ice cubes.

Two years after she met him, she found out her baby's father's name was not DeMarius Collins. It was Marcus Cotton. She now, at least, knew who he was.

"Ain't life a flip," Rebe said to her BFFs, and then looked over at her and Marcus's young son, Tristan, who was curiously toddling near Chyna. Tiny dimple in his chin.

"Yes it is. A real flip," said Darla, looking stunned.

"It surely is," said Magnolia, still holding on to Miller. "In an instant."

The best part of life is when your family become your friends, and your friends become your family. Unconditional commitments to imperfect people.

LINKS TO FACTS AND ISSUES FROM

SIXTY-NINE

- Every two minutes, someone in the United States is sexually assaulted. For further information, you can visit the Rape, Abuse & Incest National Network website at www.rainn.org.
- Depression is not something you can just snap out of. Take charge. For further information, you can visit GlaxoSmithKline's website at www.depression.com.
- For further information on enhancing fertility after the age of forty, you can visit the Mothers Over 40 website at www.mothersover40.com.
- For further information regarding issues of sexual health, you can visit Dr. Laura Berman's website at www.drlauraberman.com.
- For resources and connections for women entrepreneurs, you can visit the Ladies Who Launch website at www.ladieswholaunch.com.
- For a dating site on interracial love, you can check out the Salt and Pepper Singles website at www.saltandpeppersingles.com.

- For information about pole dance workout classes, you can visit the S Factor website, www.sfactor.com.
- You can log on to www.scarleteen.com to learn about your pink anatomy.

BEING SEX-SEE

From the Undersexed to Paying for Sex

The theme of *Sixty-Nine* is sexual freedom, and also showing the shame, disgrace, and consequences of reckless lust with the undersexed, just as I did with the oversexed in *Sexaholics*. It's a thin line.

Each character had a goal, and some sort of conflict that kept each woman from that goal. I wanted to challenge these women to go beyond their comfort zones. Sometimes it's safer to experience what we know, and not challenge our self-built boundaries. These boundaries often come from our upbringing and society's standards, etc. But when inner happiness and self-satisfaction and faith come first, we are better able to go beyond the norm, within reason, and just be free to be. I hope you enjoyed Magnolia, Rebe, and Darla as they lived out their nonmissionary risks and discoveries, as much as I enjoyed creating them.

And my next Pynk book, preview chapter ahead, is called *Politics. Escorts. Blackmail.*

I'm intrigued by the many stories in the news about

how men of power and privilege, in sports and politics
especially, feel such self-empowerment, as though they
feel they can get away with anything. Funny how we
don't hear about female politicians getting caught—
some say because maybe we women are better at cheating. Maybe so, but I think sometimes these men of
privilege are the guys who didn't get laid in school and
now they have the power and money to get attention.
Men romanticize the women they cheat with or pay
to sleep with, and the more innocent the woman, the
more desirable she is to the man, and the more he feels
like a man.

It's about entitlement. Some well-known men in
prestigious or public positions often feel they can't be
touched. Can't be punished. They love the prostitute
with the heart of gold who doesn't give them any grief,
and start to trust her, sometimes even falling in love
with her. But all things in time must come to a head.
And what happens in the dark must come to light. Even
the most passive of women can reach their breaking
point, prostitutes or not.

In *Politics Escorts Blackmail*, you might even see an
appearance by Trinity and Armani, from *Sixty-Nine*, or
even Marcus Cotton, the escort who is the father of
Rebe's son.

Some say bread eaten in secret is more filling. I guess
so. Because in this story, Money Watts's world of call
girls and guys, escorts and mistresses, is being served up
on an undercover Pynk platter. Enjoy!

PREVIEW CHAPTER

POLITICS. ESCORTS.
BLACKMAIL.

⤸

by PYNK

Notice from PYNK:
If you are erotica squeamish, be
prepared to squirm.
Consider yourself warned!

Prologue

---∽---

March 2012

In a City of 8.4 Million People

Hey there, Mr. Big.

I'll bet you think this book is about you, now that it's all said and done, right? Wrong. It's not. It's about me. Money Watts. And how the world of politics, escorts, and blackmail came to a head, all in one day in 2011. It's about my side of the escort coin. The side of making a business out of sex for money.

This is my own version of *Sex and the City*. Sex in the Big Apple. Sex with big names. Sex for big money. Sex that made big news. You were my Mr. Big. But now...well, like I said, this story is not about you.

I had the baddest high-end call girls and call guy in New York City. My agency, called Lip Service, was comprised of just the four of us. We kept it small, we kept it exclusive, and we kept it high-class. And I kept all the juicy names in my little pink e-book.

I was the provider, or organizer. And they, the clients,

were called hobbyists. We did it all over the Internet on an adult website, or sometimes over the phone. Sometimes the hobbyists would even rate each of us and give reviews. They'd rate us on price, cleanliness, honesty, and attractiveness. And we always received ten out of ten. This was no street corner operation. These were not escorts of ill repute. This was not a brothel. This was about meeting a classy man or woman to "escort" you to dinner, and then going somewhere after for an intimate evening together. That's it. No different than a first date with someone who doesn't call the next day. Only there's a booker who gets ten percent. I split the rest fifty-fifty with my escorts. And at two thousand dollars per hour, sometimes even thirty thousand per weekend, we did very, very well. We were providing a very necessary service. And we were very, very good at it.

The Politics

In private, he patronizes escorts. In public, Democrat **Darrell Ellington** is a New York senator for the 21st District in Brooklyn, married to Ursula Leah Ellington, a former Republican who came from a long line of politicians. They met while working together at Paine Webber years ago, and married in 1995. Darrell worked in government affairs and Ursula was a senior consultant. He was elected to his senate seat in 2002, and if Ursula had it her way, she would one day be the next African American First Lady to the second African American U.S. President in history. And her son from a previous marriage, Micah Daye, knew that all too well. His mother had dotted the *i*'s and crossed the *t*'s, willing to do whatever it took to keep their noses clean so that she could make it to the White House before her competitive ex-best-friend, Kendra Graves, married to the New York senator from the 60th District, made it there first.

Republican **Kalin Graves** was a New York senator for the 60th District. His wife, Kendra, was a marketing executive at Saks Fifth Avenue corporate. Just when Ursula's husband, Darrell, made it known he was interested in politics, Kendra sought out a politician of her own and married Kalin Graves the next year. The beef between Kendra and Ursula stemmed from the fact that they were once secret lovers.

The Escorts

Like I said, I'm **Money Watts**. My home in Cobble Hill West outside of Manhattan was where I ran my business. In 2005, I was married to a well-known sports anchor who brought me to New York after he was hired for a big announcer job with the NBA, co-anchoring with Ahmad Rashad, but he left it, and me, all behind when he went back to Los Angeles to be with a local weather-girl whom he met during a National Black Journalists Conference the year before. We'd only been married six months. I'd signed a prenup. I had nothing, so I made a way. I had sex for money. The money was good. I was good. I still take on clients if it involves my expertise, which is role-playing and dominating—my dom name is Brooklyn. I personally service Tyler Copeland, the NYPD police chief, who is a certified cross-dressing sissy.

As a runaway teen and aspiring actress, strolling through the lights and wonder of Times Square at the age of seventeen, **Midori Moody** saved a pimp's business card for a rainy day. She left home because she said her big sister was the perfect child, and she was the misfit. Two days after she called the pimp named Romeo, she became a good girl gone wild who drank and partied, and screwed for money. She found out that feeling love through those transgressions was easier than dealing with her own abandonment. She'd later break away and buy herself a condo on the Upper East Side of Manhattan, but by the time she met Micah Daye, her new boyfriend, that's when she started to get sloppy. Bailey Brenner, her regular "hobbyist" who was on the city council, started getting crazy jealous.

Malaka Sutton's three-story townhouse is in Crown Heights, Brooklyn. Malaka's own mother was an escort when Malaka was a child in Denver. Her mother would even take her along to see clients. Malaka learned firsthand how to make sexy ends meet. And in New York, they were meeting like a muthafucka. Malaka was my highest paid escort. She satisfied the cream of the crop. She was my number one lady.

Tall and fine and in demand, **Kemba Price**, Italian and Sudanese, from Staten Island, was my one and only call guy. He lived in Harlem on 128th Street, and when he wasn't on "dates" for Lip Service, he was at the gym, chiseling his six-foot-five, model-type body. And that's where he first met Ursula Leah Ellington, the wife of Darrell Ellington. And he also met a new friend, Romeo, the pimp.

The Blackmail

March 2010

So tell me what happened." I sat in the lobby of the historic Algonquin Hotel on Club Row. Midori made me frown.

"Bailey's just jealous. He's making up stories."

"What's he jealous of?"

"He knows about Micah."

"And how does he know anything about your private life, Midori?"

"I guess he followed me. I guess he's been watching me."

"You guess? Midori. Listen to me. This is a problem. I send you to meet Bailey at the St. Regis, and you take money from him on the side?"

"I didn't."

"Then what happened to that hotel room? Why was it damaged like that?"

"It wasn't damaged when I left. I left him there."

"So, you didn't tear up the room and threaten to accuse him of roughing you up?"

"No. He said that?"

"I said that."

"I make enough money. I wouldn't do that just to get some cash from a client. He's the problem, not me.

What I didn't tell you is that Bailey did the escort bonding. He said he loves me."

"See, that's something you should've told me. Then I wouldn't have assigned you to him. He's good money, but he won't be requesting you again, I guarantee you that. I smell messy."

"Okay."

"So what's up with you and Micah? You two are still serious?"

"It's coming along."

"And he still doesn't know what you do?"

"No. Still thinks I'm a realtor."

"It's too close for comfort, Midori. He's Senator Ellington's stepson."

"Yes. And that's something I wanted to talk to you about. See, the other night, Micah was talking about playing around on the computer. He's doing this tech job, and with his IT schooling, he knows how to hack into email. He's talking, well joking, like a prank, about hacking into Senator Graves's personal email account."

"Midori, that mama's boy is looking for something on Senator Graves that would embarrass him. Cause his political career damage. That's called blackmail, not a prank. And he'd do it just to please his mother. But he could go to jail for the rest of his life. He really thinks he'd be able to get away with something like that?"

"He won't really do it. He was just talking. Sometimes he acts like he's young Microsoft or something."

She had the nerve to giggle, but it sounded nervous, which it should have been. I kept a very straight face. "I see nothing funny. What do you see in a nerd like that?"

"He's nice."

"Still looking for the knight in shining armor. Still looking for love to take you away, like in the movie *Pretty Woman*, huh?"

"No."

"See, it's sad that your little boyfriend has no idea that the dirt he'll uncover could be his own. If he did that, he'd not only uncover evidence linking Senator Graves to prostitution, but that would open a whole ugly can of worms that would expose his own stepfather's kinky other life, and expose Lip Service. Now there are three ways to solve this. One would be for you to tell him what you do and what his stepfather is into. But that's a no-no. Do you understand?"

"Yes."

"Another would be, you keep an eye on your little beau, and talk him out of that madness. You'd need to keep him close. You understand that?"

"Yes."

"Micah had better watch himself. Kemba said Micah's own mother all but propositioned him while he was coming out of the gym the other day."

"She did?"

"Yes. She did. Your boyfriend Micah is so busy trying to blackmail the enemy, he'd end up destroying his own political family."

"I've got him."

"Yeah, well, you'd better."

"How'd you know about the hotel room being torn up?"

"Back to your boyfriend. The third way would be that I could have someone handle him. I've been at this for years and I have a lot to lose. My clients have a lot to lose. I'm not going to let anyone ruin this. If you don't talk him out of his little brainstorm, I can fix it myself with one phone call."

"You wouldn't do anything to Senator Ellington's son."

I just looked right through her.

She blinked fast. "Like I said, I've got him." She swallowed hard. "And actually, I'm ready to quit."

"Not just yet. I need you near him. Trust me, this is not a joke. Handle this."

"Or else what?"

"Midori, even if you are my sister, I won't let you fuck this up. We're in the world of politics and sex in New York City, and right now, there's porn and kinky sex on tons of government computers as we speak. It's the perfect place to be to make money for the service I provide. And before I let some amateur, sorry-ass blackmail scheme happen, I'll do what I have to do. I'm not going to jail. I'll stop anyone." I gave her a look serious enough to let her know I'm a madam first, and a sister second.

Midori angled her stare like a puppy.

I imitated her angle. "You could learn a thing or two from Malaka. Clean and easy." I handed her an envelope. "Now, I'm flying you to the Florida Keys for a late dinner, and then a full day with a Long Island physician. Meet him at the Little Palm Island hotel tonight at nine. Your flight is at noon."

"Got it." She took it.

"And tell your little nerdy boyfriend you're going to look at property. Keep him in check." I did not blink. "And, Midori, this conversation never happened."

She did blink, fast as usual, and nodded yes.

That would have all been well and good, if Midori's sneaky ass hadn't been wired the entire time.

PYNK DARES YOU TO BE SEX-SEE

Twenty-one and over please!

1. Walk around the house naked all evening, whether alone or with your mate.
2. If you have the privacy, plan a weekend to have sex in every room of the house.
3. Compliment your mate on what he/she does that pleases you, and then tell him/her what else turns you on, in and out of bed. Then try it together.
4. Check into a hotel by yourself for a night with a bag of toys and treat yourself to strawberries, chocolate, shrimp, and champagne, whatever— don't forget candles and incense—and then spend the evening finding your G-spot, and focus on bringing yourself to the highest level of orgasm ever. Learn your body. Find your spots. Make love to you.
5. Send a sex text to your lover during the day and promise him/her (1) a chocolate tongue bath, (2) a butt massage, or (3) oral sex, without a word being said, as soon as he/she walks in the door. Let him/her pick one.
6. Do a topless lap dance for your man while wearing boy shorts (these flatter the booty) and heels.

7. Try out a nude beach together or with willing friends while on vacation.

8. Play board games or cards together and the loser has to perform fellatio or cunnilingus for ten minutes (or less, depending on how talented he/she is).

9. Meet (hotel or at home) for lunch-hour sex.

10. Put on some Johnny Gill or baby-making music equivalent and have a pillow talk evening where you speak sexy to each other the entire time you're having sex, especially cheering the other on while they climax.

11. Have phone sex with your lover while you're each in different rooms, and then meet up in the shower together.

12. Ladies, ride your mate reverse cowgirl until he...well, until he yells "Yippie yi yo yippie yo yippie yay." Or you yell it.

13. Go to a sex shop together and pick out a pocket pussy that he likes. Use it on him while giving him a hand job, you gripping it around his penis. Make sure to use lubrication.

14. Have him pick out a dildo or vibrating clit stimulator for him to use on you while in the 69 position, while he gives you oral sex from the 6 position. It'll be hard for you to concentrate well enough to reciprocate from your 9 position, but try your best.

15. Play sexy chef and prepare breakfast in an apron and high heels.

16. Have your mate penetrate you with a frozen penis, a Popsicle, also known as an iced lolly. The phallic-shaped, single ones. Green is good, but any flavor. Have him/her lick it as it melts. If you're hot like

an oven, it should melt in your walls pretty quickly. (Be warned: the sugar can lead to a yeast imbalance—there are homemade frozen versions you can make using only water.) Or ladies, let him watch you suck the Popsicle erotically until it's gone.

17. Listen to your lover's moans and reply physically by doing more of that.

18. Learn a few sexy sentences in another language and break them out in bed.

19. Try oral sex on the woman while she stands up.

20. Have a morning quickie every day for one week.

21. Please him, mouth only, with your hands tied behind your back with a silk scarf.

22. Please her, mouth only, with your hands tied behind your back with a silk scarf.

23. Give oral sex after a sip of warm coffee. Coffee head, it's called. Or, give oral sex with ice chips in your mouth.

24. Make mental love by sharing each other's day, cooking together, enjoying a movie while cuddling, and going to bed simply spooning. No sex, oral or otherwise.

25. Talk, laugh, get in a silly mood, and yell, "Race you to the bedroom," and make love. Kiss. Look into each other's eyes. Caress. Compliment. Afterward, hug and talk some more.

26. Masturbate while fantasizing about the best lover you've ever had in your entire life. Say their name, say their name!

27. Wash your hands thoroughly, take a hand mirror, and lie back in private. Place the mirror between your legs and get familiar with your vulva, which

means your entire outer and inner genital areas: (a) the mons (the top, under your belly where the pubic hair starts); (b) discover what your urethra looks like; (c) examine your clitoral glans/shaft (pull back the fold of skin called the hood to take a closer look—the clitoris is the only organ on the entire body solely for sexual arousal); (d) notice your outer labia; and (e) your inner labia; (f) as well as the vaginal opening, which leads to the vagina (the vagina is not the outer genital; it is the inner organ); insert your finger and squeeze, using your PC, or Kegel, muscles—notice your own unique shade of pink; (g) look at your hymen (the membrane just barely inside at the top). Be gentle and take your time. Know your pink anatomy. Remember, no one should know your vulva better than you do.

28. Select a few chapters from your favorite erotic novel, hopefully a Pynk book, *wink*, and read the scenes aloud to your guy. Test the sexiness of the steamy scenes based upon his hard-on, or hard-off. Just reach over and rub it to see if it's hard. Say, "Oh, you like that, don't you?" He'll thank you for it later.

Be safe and sane. ☺

READING GROUP GUIDE

1. Who was your favorite character in *Sixty-Nine*, Magnolia, Rebe, or Darla, and why?
2. Do you know of anyone who had a drug-addicted and/or mentally unstable parent, similar to Magnolia's mother and Rebe's mother?
3. Did you think Magnolia, Rebe, and Darla were true, unconditional friends?
4. Would you have forgiven Magnolia for her indiscretion with your ex-husband? Has a friend of yours ever crossed the line and gone behind your back to have sex with someone you were with, either during or after your relationship? Is it okay if your friend dates your ex-boyfriend?
5. Would you have told your friend that a mutual friend slept with his/her husband back in college? Why or why not?
6. Would you consider taking pole-dancing classes as a form of exercise? Have you ever had a secret fantasy of being a stripper, or other type of job that would be considered taboo?
7. Do you or would you date outside of your race, "down with the swirl," as it's called? What race other

than your own do you find sexy? Name a celebrity of another race who is your type. Pynk says Brad Pitt can get it!

8. Would you have enough trust and understanding to invite your fiancé's ex-wife to the wedding?

9. My stripper name would be Chiquita Coliseum, the name of my pet and the street I lived on when I was young. What would your stripper name be?

10. Did you learn anything sexually from reading *Sixty-Nine*? Are you willing to try it out?

11. Magnolia, Rebe, and Darla all ended up leaving a little bit about their lives unsaid. Is it true that some things are better left untold? Would you confess your infidelities to a friend if it involved their ex? Would you tell your fiancé about an indiscretion to clear the air before saying I do?

12. Is there an issue in your sex life that you'd be willing to improve? Do you ask for what you want in bed?

13. Do you consider yourself closer to oversexed or undersexed? Please explain.

14. Would you allow a sexual cheerleader into your bedroom?

15. Do you need any sexual healing? If so, what would your New Year's sexual resolution be?

16. Would you consider having or adopting a child if you were/are over the age of forty?

17. Which guy in *Sixty-Nine* do you think was the best man in bed? The best out of bed?

18. Do you prefer missionary or sixty-nine? Why? What is your favorite position?